# SEVEN JAPANESE TALES

BOOKS BY JUNICHIRO TANIZAKI

*Some Prefer Nettles* (1955)*
*The Makioka Sisters* (1957)*
*The Key* (1961)*
*Diary of a Mad Old Man* (1965)*

*AVAILABLE IN PERIGEE BOOKS EDITIONS

# SEVEN JAPANESE TALES

BY

JUNICHIRO TANIZAKI

TRANSLATED FROM THE JAPANESE BY
HOWARD HIBBETT

PERIGEE BOOK

Perigee Books
are published by
**The Putnam Publishing Group**
200 Madison Avenue
New York, N.Y. 10016

This is an authorized reprint of a hardcover edition
originally published by Alfred A. Knopf, Inc.
*The Tattooer* appeared originally in *Show*
and *Aguri* in *Cosmopolitan*

Library of Congress Cataloging in Publication Data

Tanizaki, Jun'ichirō, 1886–1965.
Seven Japanese tales.

Originally published by Knopf, New York.
1. Tanizaki, Jun'ichirō, 1866–1965—Translations,
English. I. Title.
PL839.A7A26    1981        895.6'34        80-39965
ISBN 0-399-50523-7

First Perigee Printing, 1981
*Cover illustration by* KIMMERLE MILNAZIK
*Hand lettering by* DAVID GATTI
PRINTED IN THE UNITED STATES OF AMERICA
20 19 18 17 16 15 14 13 12 11 10

# INTRODUCTION

The seven tales collected in this volume span half a century in the extraordinary literary career of Junichiro Tanizaki, a career which has outlasted more than one edition of his "Complete Works." Among his many distinctions have been an Imperial Award for Cultural Merit in 1949, after he had published the whole of his great novel *The Makioka Sisters*, and, in 1943, the suppression of that work as a menace to the national war effort.

Tanizaki continues to alarm or delight the Japanese reading public with the audacious vigor of his recent novels. One of these is *The Bridge of Dreams* (first published in October 1959), the confessional narrative of a young man who has grown up in the shadow of a guilt-laden obsession with the memory of his mother, and with the beauty of the girl who took her place. Here the exploration of erotic mysteries leads into a tangle of relationships as bizarre and unhealthy as those of Tanizaki's earlier novel *The Key*, in which a middle-aged professor attempts, with gratifying success, to corrupt his demure wife. *The Bridge of Dreams*, in the form of a memoir rather than a pair of diaries as in *The Key*, has a similarly tantalizing blend of candor and deviousness.

Again the reticences of an old-fashioned Kyoto household provide a hushed setting for scandal.

But there is also a subtle nostalgic flavor to *The Bridge of Dreams* and a hint of thematic reference to Lady Murasaki's eleventh-century *Tale of Genji*, that towering masterpiece which few were able to scale (except in the lucid English version by Arthur Waley) until Tanizaki made his long, loving translation of it into modern Japanese. The moving coda of *Genji* describes a young man's frustrated pursuit of a girl whom he identifies with the obsessive memory of her dead sister; and its last chapter is entitled "The Bridge of Dreams"—an image symbolizing the insubstantial beauty of life itself, once poetically alluded to by Prince Genji as "a bridge linking dream to dream."

Dreams, daydreams, elaborate fantasies—often dramatizing the secret affinity of love and cruelty—have had a significant place in Tanizaki's fiction ever since he began writing short stories in his twenties. The first and most famous of these is *The Tattooer* (1910), an elegant little sadomasochistic fable of an artist who fulfills his wish to tattoo the skin of the Perfect Woman. The time is late Tokugawa (around the 1840's), the place Edo, and the style lush *fin de siècle*. Aside from being "representative," in the Japanese sense of being an obligatory anthology piece, *The Tattooer* illustrates at once Tanizaki's fascination with the Japanese past and with the seductively evil blossoms of exotic decadence. *Terror* (1913), a highly colored fragment of the case history of a man with "morbidly excitable nerves," is set in a modern urban milieu of streetcars and jostling crowds, as disturbing in their way as the phantoms of the past. It is another of the early stories which depict abnormal psychological states in a prose of great sensuous beauty.

*The Thief* (1921) is in a plainer style and exposes a different sort of aberration, one which is confessed ("I have not written a single dishonest word here") in the equivocal manner of the narrator of *The Bridge of Dreams*. But the predominant tone is rational. In *Aguri* (1922), however, Tanizaki indulges in a vein of almost surrealist fantasy: Okada, drained of health by a vampirish young mistress, is a prey to terrifying hallucinations. Aguri herself is merely a pleasure-loving, acquisitive young waitress or bar girl, a mannequin requiring adornment in order to become the idolized fatal woman who appears in so many guises in Tanizaki's fiction. Her metamorphosis is to be accomplished, not by actual tattooing, but by dressing her in those alluring Western garments which seem to give the female body a fresh, vividly tattooed skin, and yet which, unlike the constricting trousers, coat, and tie (with stickpin) of fashionable Western-style gentlemen, release its vital powers.

Another of Tanizaki's cruel beauties is the gifted blind heroine of *A Portrait of Shunkin* (1933), perhaps the finest in a series of short novels which reflect both in style and in subject his deepening appreciation of the traditional culture of Japan. This time the narrator is a scholarly man with antiquarian tastes who has come into the possession of a curious biography of Shunkin, a few anecdotes and reminiscences about her, and a single faded photograph—apparently the only one ever taken—of her bland, lovely face. Shunkin grew up in the still-feudal merchant society of the late Tokugawa period and lost her sight before the arrival of Perry and the upheaval of the Meiji Restoration, events which (though unmentioned) doubtless would not have made such a strong impression on her as the death of one of her prized larks or nightingales. Indeed, as her servants remark, she has more affection for her birds than for any human companions, even her long-suffering guide and pupil, the devoted Sasuke.

The theme of blindness—so often associated with love in Tanizaki's world—occurs also in a slightly earlier novel centered on a servant and his mistress: *A Blind Man's Tale* (1931). But here the setting is one of the most confused and violent ages of Japanese history: the century of civil war which ended with the decisive victory of Tokugawa Ieyasu at the Battle of Sekigahara in 1600. Among Tanizaki's characters are two conquering generals—the ruthless, vindictive Oda Nobunaga and his cleverer and even more ambitious successor, Hideyoshi—who imposed a harsh order on the chaotic pattern of relations among the warlords of sixteenth-century Japan. Yet the alliances and treacheries, the battles and sieges, the incessant movement of forces, are seen only obliquely in his narrative, through a mist which is not dispersed by the false sunlight of the popular costume novel. The nightmarish facts of history compose a fitfully lighted background to the story of the servant Yaichi's devotion to Lady Oichi and her daughters, a devotion which is at last rewarded by cruelty.

All the characters of *A Blind Man's Tale* (except the narrator) figure in the historical records of the time. Familiar heroes such as Hideyoshi reveal new qualities to the novelist's imaginative perception, and there is even something enigmatic about the lovely women whose superficial calm is the mask of strange and complex emotions. A portrait of Lady Oichi, commissioned by her dutiful eldest daughter, has been preserved in a temple on Mount Koya. She sits in a serene formal pose, holding a sutra in her right hand. Her bland, expressionless face recalls the "face of classic oval outline and features so delicately modeled that they seem almost ethereal" in the faded photograph of Shunkin.

HOWARD HIBBETT

# CONTENTS

# SEVEN JAPANESE TALES

# A PORTRAIT OF SHUNKIN

Shunkin (born as Mozuya Koto, but better known by her professional name) was the daughter of an Osaka drug merchant. She died on the fourteenth of October in 1886—the nineteenth year of the Meiji era—and was buried in the grounds of a certain Buddhist temple of the Pure Land sect in the Shitadera district of Osaka.

Some days ago I happened to pass the temple, and stopped in to visit her grave. When I asked the caretaker how to find the Mozuya plot, he said "It's over this way, sir" and led me around the main hall. There, in the shade of a cluster of old camellias, stood the grave-stones of generation after generation of the Mozuya family—but none of them seemed to belong to Shunkin.

I told the caretaker about her, and suggested that she must have a grave somewhere. He considered this for a moment. "Well," he said at last, "maybe it's the one on the hill." And he took me to a flight of steps leading up a steep slope on the eastern side of the grounds.

As you may know, the Ikutama Shrine stands on a height overlooking Shitadera: the slope I mentioned rises from the temple grounds toward the shrine and is densely wooded, quite unusual for Osaka. We found Shunkin's gravestone in a little clearing about halfway up. It bore this inscription:

MOZUYA KOTO, also called SHUNKIN
Died October fourteenth
In the nineteenth year of Meiji
At the age of fifty-seven

On one side were carved the words: "Erected by her pupil, Nukui Sasuke." Perhaps the reason why Shunkin was buried apart from her family was that, although never legally married, she had lived with her "pupil," the celebrated samisen master Nukui Sasuke, as man and wife.

According to the caretaker, the Mozuya family was ruined long ago. The relatives hardly ever came to visit the graves any more, certainly not to Shunkin's. "I didn't think she belonged to the same family," he told me.

"So the grave is neglected, is it?" I asked.

5

"No," he said, "not really. An old lady from Haginochaya who looks to be about seventy comes here once or twice a year. She prays and offers flowers and incense, and then—" He paused, pointing to another grave at the left of Shunkin's. "You see that little stone next to it? As soon as she's finished she goes over and does the same thing there. She pays the temple to look after both graves, too."

I went to examine the other stone. It was about half the size of Shunkin's, and had this inscription:

NUKUI SASUKE, also called KINDAI
Pupil of Mozuya Shunkin
Died October fourteenth in the fortieth year of Meiji
At the age of eighty-two

So this was the grave of the famous virtuoso. The fact that his monument is smaller than Shunkin's and that he is described on it as her pupil shows that he wished to remain humble toward her even in death. As I stood there on the hillside, near the two stones glowing in the late-afternoon sun, I looked down at the city spread out below me. No doubt this hilly terrain, which stretches westward as far as the Tenno Temple, has had the same contour throughout the long history of Osaka. Today the grass and foliage are soot-stained, dead-looking; the great trees are withered and dusty, giving an air of drabness to the scene. But when these graves were dug it must have been a luxuriant setting; even now this is surely the most tranquil burial place in Osaka, and the one with the finest view. Here, high over the busiest

industrial city of the Orient, over the innumerable tall
buildings that pierce the evening haze, teacher and pupil
lie together in their eternal sleep, bound by a mysterious
fate. Osaka has changed almost beyond recognition since
Sasuke's day, but these two stones still testify to his love
for Shunkin.

The Nukui family belonged to the Nichiren sect of
Buddhism, and all of the family tombs except Sasuke's
are at a temple in Hino, his own birthplace, in the province of Omi. Yet because of his ardent wish to be buried
beside Shunkin, Sasuke abandoned the faith of his ancestors and joined the Pure Land sect. They say that all
arrangements for the two graves—including the size
and position of the stones—were made while Shunkin
was still alive. Shunkin's gravestone appeared to be about
six feet high, and Sasuke's less than four. The two were
side by side on low flagstone-covered bases, and a pine
tree, planted to the right of Shunkin, stretched its green
limbs protectingly over her. Sasuke's gravestone stood a
few feet to the left of hers, like a humble servant, just
beyond the tip of the pine branches. As I looked, I was
reminded how faithfully Sasuke had served his teacher,
following her like a shadow and attending to all her
needs. It seemed to me as if the stones had souls, and even
now he took pleasure in her happiness.

After kneeling at Shunkin's grave for a moment, I ran
my hand affectionately along the top of Sasuke's stone.
Then I wandered about on the hill until the sun had
dropped out of sight beyond the city.

7

Not long ago I acquired a slim volume called *The Life of Mozuya Shunkin,* which awakened my interest in her. The book has sixty pages, bound in the Japanese style, and is printed in large characters on pure handmade paper. I gathered that Sasuke had asked someone to compile his teacher's biography for private distribution on the second anniversary of her death. Although the text is written in the old-fashioned literary style and Sasuke himself is referred to in the third person, he undoubtedly supplied all the material and may well be regarded as the real author.

To quote from the *Life:*

For generations the Mozuya family has kept a pharmaceutical house in Dosho-machi in Osaka, under the name of Mozuya Yasuzaemon. Shunkin's father was the seventh in that line. Her mother, Shigé, came from the Atobé family of Kyoto, and bore her husband two sons and four daughters. Shunkin was the second daughter, and was born on the twenty-fourth of May, 1829, the twelfth year of the Bunsei era. . . . Even as a child, Shunkin was not only remarkably intelligent but gifted with an aristocratic grace and beauty quite beyond comparison. When she began learning to dance at about the age of three the correct movements seemed to come to her effortlessly; her gestures were more charming than those of any young professional dancing girl. They say that her teacher was astonished at her skill. "What a marvelous child!" he would murmur. "With her looks and ability she could become one of the most famous geisha in the country. It's a pity she was born into a respectable family!" Shunkin began to read and write at an early age too, and her progress was so extraordinary that she soon surpassed her older brothers.

Supposing that the source of this information was Sasuke, who seems to have idolized her, one hardly knows how much of it to believe. Still, there is a good deal of other evidence to suggest that she was indeed blessed with "aristocratic grace and beauty."

In those days most women were short in stature, and Shunkin is said to have been less than five feet tall, exquisitely formed, with very fine features and slender wrists and ankles. There is a photograph of her at thirty-six which shows a face of classic oval outline and features so delicately modeled that they seem almost ethereal. However, since it dates from the eighteen-sixties, the picture is speckled with age and as faded as an old memory. Possibly that is why it makes such a faint impression on me. In that misty photograph I can detect nothing more than the usual refinement of a lady from a well-to-do Osaka merchant family—beautiful, to be sure, but without any real individuality. She looks as if she might be thirty-six—or then again she might be ten years younger.

Although this picture was taken more than two decades after Shunkin lost her sight, she merely looks like a woman who has closed her eyes. It has been said that the deaf look like fools and the blind like sages: the deaf, in their effort to catch what others are saying, knit their brows, gape their mouths, and goggle their eyes, or cock their heads this way and that, all of which gives them an air of stupidity; while the blind, because they sit calmly with their heads bowed a trifle as if in meditation, appear to be extremely thoughtful. However that may be, we are so accustomed to seeing the half-closed "merciful eyes" with which Buddha and the Bodhisattvas gaze on all living things that closed eyes seem more benevolent to us than open ones—may even seem awe-inspiring. And Shunkin is such a meek, gentle-looking woman that one feels a sense of compassion in her veiled eyes, as one would in those of the merciful goddess Kannon.

As far as I know, this is the only photograph ever made of Shunkin. When she was younger the art had not yet been introduced to Japan, and in the same year that this one was made she suffered a calamity, after which she would certainly not have allowed herself to be photographed. Thus we have only one dim reflection of her to help us imagine her appearance. No doubt I have given a vague, inadequate impression of how she looked. Yet the photograph itself is perhaps even vaguer than the impression which my words convey.

It occurs to me that in the year Shunkin's picture was taken—when she was thirty-six—Sasuke himself became blind; the last time he saw her she must have looked rather like this. Was the picture of her which he carried in his memory in old age as faded as this photograph? Or did his imagination make up for a gradually failing memory? Did he create an image of another lovely woman, of one altogether different from the woman in the photograph?

The *Life of Shunkin* goes on with this passage:

Consequently, her parents regarded her as their precious jewel, and favored her over all of her five brothers and sisters. However, when Shunkin was eight years old she had the misfortune of contracting an eye disease; soon she lost her sight completely. Her parents were heartbroken: her mother seemed almost insane with grief, full of bitterness toward the whole world because of the misery of her child. From that time on Shunkin gave up dancing and devoted all her energy to the study of the koto and the samisen, and the allied art of singing. She dedicated her life to music.

It is not clear what sort of eye disease Shunkin had, and there is no further mention of it in the *Life*. But Sasuke once made this remark: "A tall tree is envied by the wind, as the saying goes. Just because she was more beautiful and more talented than the others, my teacher was the victim of jealousy twice in her life. All her troubles came from those two attacks." His words suggest that peculiar circumstances lay behind Shunkin's affliction.

Another time, Sasuke said that his teacher was blinded by purulent ophthalmia. Now, Shunkin had been more than a little spoiled by her pampered upbringing, but as a child she was so gay and charming and vivacious, so considerate to those who served her, that she got along very well with people. She was on the best of terms with her brothers and sisters, and seemed to be the darling of the household. However, her youngest sister's nurse is said to have secretly hated her out of resentment at the favoritism shown by her parents. Since purulent ophthalmia is a venereal infection of the mucous membranes of the eyes, Sasuke must have been hinting—whether or not he had any better grounds for thinking so—that the nurse had somehow managed to rob Shunkin of her sight. The later violence of Shunkin's temper does make one wonder if some such incident helped to shape her character; still, Sasuke's opinions are by no means to be trusted implicitly —this was not the only time that his grief over Shunkin seemed to poison his mind toward others. His suspicion of the nurse was probably quite unfounded.

In any case, rather than attempting to solve that problem, I need only record here that she lost her sight at the age of eight. And then: "From that time on Shunkin gave up dancing and devoted all her energy to the study of the koto and the samisen, and the allied art of singing. She dedicated her life to music." In other words, it was because of blindness that Shunkin turned to music. Sasuke said that she often told him her real talent was for dancing: those who praised her voice or her ability at the koto and samisen didn't know her true self—if only she could see, she would be a dancer. This sounds a little arrogant, as if she is pointing out how much she has achieved even in an art to which she is not really suited. But perhaps Sasuke exaggerated her words. At least, it seems possible that a chance remark of hers, uttered on a momentary impulse, made such a strong impression on him that he kept harking back to it as evidence of what a superior person she was.

. The old woman from Haginochaya who still comes to tend the two graves is Shigizawa Teru, a high-ranking member of the Ikuta school of koto players. To Shunkin in her late years, and then to Sasuke, she had given devoted service. "I've heard that my teacher was good at dancing," she told me, referring to Shunkin; "but she began studying the koto and samisen when she was only four or five, and practiced regularly from then on. She didn't just take up music because she went blind. In those days all proper young ladies started music lessons early. They say that when she was nine years old she memorized a long koto piece at a single hearing, and picked it out on the samisen all by herself. You can see she was a born genius—no ordinary person could do a thing like that! Once she was blind, I expect she studied harder than ever. She must have really put heart and soul into it."

Probably Teru is right, and Shunkin's true talent was for music. I am inclined to be dubious about her ability as a dancer.

Even if Shunkin "put heart and soul into it," she may not have intended to become a professional musician; there was no need for her to worry about making a living. It was for a different reason that she later opened her own establishment as a music teacher, and teaching was never her sole means of support. Her monthly allowance from her parents, though not enough to satisfy her luxurious tastes, was far greater than the income which she herself earned.

In the beginning, then, she must have practiced as hard

as she did simply for her own pleasure, with no thought of the future, developing her natural talent by this passion for music. It is probably true, as the *Life* tells us, that "by the time Shunkin was fourteen she had made such great progress that not one of her fellow pupils could compare with her."

According to Shigizawa Teru: "My teacher used to boast that her master Shunsho, who was very strict with his pupils, never gave her a real scolding. In fact, he often praised her. She told me he took a personal interest in her work, and was wonderfully kind and gentle—she couldn't imagine why people were afraid of him. I expect it was on account of her talent that he treated her so well. She didn't have to suffer for her training the way you usually do."

Since Shunkin was a daughter of the wealthy Mozuya family, no teacher, however strict, would have been as severe with her as with the children of professional musicians; besides, Shunsho must have felt a desire to protect the pitiful little girl whose happy childhood had so unexpectedly ended in blindness. Yet I suppose it was her ability, more than anything else, that won his admiration and his affection.

He worried about her more than about his own children: whenever she happened to miss a lesson because of illness he immediately sent someone to her house to ask how she was, or else set out to call on her himself. It was no secret that he took great pride in having Shunkin as his pupil. To the others he taught, the children of professionals, he would say: "Model yourselves after the little Mozuya girl, all of you! Soon you'll be making your living at it—and yet you're no match for the child." (He always spoke of Shunkin in intimate terms, possibly because he had also taught her elder sister and was a friend of the family.)

Once, when he was criticized for being entirely too kind to Shunkin, he told his pupils to stop talking nonsense. "The stricter a teacher is, the better," he said. "I'd have been kindest to that child if I'd scolded her. But she's so brilliant, she has so much natural ability, that she'd go right on learning even without any help from me. If I really drubbed it into her, she'd be so amazingly good that the rest of you would hang your heads in shame. But her family is well off, she'll never have to earn a living; so instead of giving her a thorough training I put all my energy into trying to make decent performers out of a bunch of blockheads. What are *you* complaining about?"

Shunsho's house was in Utsubo, over half a mile from the Mozuya establishment in Dosho-machi, but Shunkin went there for a lesson every day, led by the hand by her father's shopboy. The boy was Sasuke, and that was how his relationship with Shunkin began.

As I mentioned earlier, Sasuke was born in the village of Hino, in Omi. His parents kept a drugstore there, and both his father and his grandfather had learned their trade by working at the Mozuya house in Osaka. To Sasuke, therefore, serving the Mozuya family meant serving his hereditary master.

Since he began his apprenticeship at twelve, and was four years older than Shunkin, Sasuke came to the Mozuya house when she was eight—the age at which she lost her sight. By the time he arrived Shunkin's lovely eyes had been dimmed forever. Yet as long as he lived Sasuke considered himself fortunate that he had not once seen the light of her eyes. Had he known her before her blindness, her face might later have seemed imperfect to him, but happily he was never conscious of the least flaw in her beauty. From the very first her features seemed ideal.

Today, Osaka families of means are eagerly moving to the suburbs, and their sports-loving daughters are used to sunshine and open air. The old-fashioned sort of sheltered beauty, the girl brought up in hothouse seclusion, has quite disappeared. But even now, city children are usually pale and delicate, compared with boys and girls who grow up in the country. They are more refined—or, if you like, more sickly. In particular, Osaka and Kyoto people have traditionally prized a fair complexion and have been noted for the whiteness of their skins. The sons of old Osaka families are as slender and girlish-looking as their counterparts on the stage; only when they are about thirty do their faces become ruddy, their bodies plump, as they suddenly acquire the portly dignity befitting a prosperous gentleman. Until then they are as fair-skinned as women, and their taste in dress is rather effeminate too. And how much more extraordinary the gleaming whiteness, the translucent purity of the complexion of girls born into well-to-do merchant families before the Meiji era, girls brought up in the shadows of dark inner rooms! What strange, fascinating creatures they must have seemed to a boy like Sasuke!

At that time Shunkin's elder sister was eleven, and the next-younger was five. To Sasuke, fresh from the country, the little Mozuya girls seemed incredibly lovely. Most of all, he was struck by the mysterious charm of the blind Shunkin. Her closed eyes seemed to him more alive and beautiful than the open ones of her sisters; he felt that her face was perfectly natural, that it ought not to be any different.

Even if Shunkin was indeed the most beautiful of the four sisters, as everyone said, it may well be that pity had something to do with the general admiration for her. But Sasuke would have denied that. In later years, nothing offended him more than being told that his love for Shunkin sprang from pity. "That's ridiculous!" he would answer roughly. "When I look into my teacher's face I never dream of feeling sorry for her, or thinking of her as pitiful. We ordinary people are the wretched ones. Why would a lady so beautiful and so talented need anybody's sympathy? The fact is, she pities *me*, and calls me her 'poor Sasuke.' You and I have all our faculties, but she's far superior to us in every other way. *We're* the handicapped ones, in my opinion."

But that was later. At the beginning Sasuke was merely her faithful servant, though no doubt a secret flame of devotion was already burning in his heart. Perhaps he had not yet realized that he was in love with her—this innocent young girl who was the daughter of his hereditary master. He must have been overjoyed to become her companion, and to be able to go walking with her every day. It seems odd that a new shopboy was given the task of guiding the Mozuyas' precious daughter, but at first he was not the only one to be so entrusted. Sometimes one of the maidservants went along with her, and sometimes an older apprentice. But one day Shunkin said: "Let Sasuke take me," and thereafter it was his duty alone. He was thirteen at the time.

Beaming with pride at this great honor, Sasuke would walk along beside her, the palm of her little hand nestled in his, all the way to Shunsho's house. Then, after waiting until she had finished her lesson, he would escort her home again. Shunkin hardly ever spoke to him, and Sasuke kept silent as long as she did, devoting all his attention to guiding her safely along the street. Once, when Shunkin was asked why she had chosen him, she replied: "Because he's so well-behaved, and doesn't keep chattering away."

It is true, as I have said, that Shunkin originally had a great deal of charm and got along very well with people. But after losing her sight she became moody: she seemed almost taciturn, and seldom laughed. So perhaps what pleased her about Sasuke was that he fulfilled his duty faithfully and unobtrusively, without superfluous talk. (They say that Sasuke disliked seeing her laugh. I suppose he found it painful, since there is something poignant about a blind person's laughter.)

But was it really because Sasuke never bothered her that Shunkin chose him? Had she not become vaguely aware of his adoration and, young as she was, taken pleasure in it? Such a thing may seem out of the question in a little girl of nine; but when you consider that Shunkin, besides being such a clever, precocious child, had developed a kind of sixth sense as a result of her blindness, you cannot dismiss it as inconceivable. Even later, when Shunkin knew that she was in love, she was too proud to confess her feelings: it was a long time before she gave herself to him. Thus there is some doubt as to what she actually thought of him at the beginning. In any case she behaved as if she scarcely knew he existed—or so at least it seemed to Sasuke.

To guide her, Sasuke would raise his left hand as high as her shoulder, and Shunkin would rest the palm of her right hand in his upturned palm. He seemed to be no more than a hand to her. When she wanted him to do something she never told him plainly what it was; instead, she indicated it by a gesture, or by frowning, or by murmuring a hint as if she were talking to herself. Should one of these subtle hints escape his notice, she was certain to be very annoyed, and so Sasuke had to keep alert for her every movement and expression. He felt that she was testing him to see how attentive he was. Spoiled from infancy and warped by blindness, Shunkin never gave him a moment's rest.

Once, at her teacher's house, while they were waiting for her turn to take a lesson, Sasuke suddenly noticed that Shunkin had disappeared. Much alarmed, he began looking everywhere for her—and found that she had slipped out to the lavatory. Whenever she wanted to go there she would silently rise and leave the room, and Sasuke would hurry after her to lead her to the door of the lavatory; when she had finished, he would pour water over her hands at the washbasin. That day, however, Sasuke had been caught off guard and she had groped her way there alone. He came running up to her just as she was reaching for the ladle at the washbasin. "I'm awfully sorry!" he said, his voice trembling.

"Never mind," said Shunkin, shaking her head. But Sasuke knew that if he let her have her way it would be so much the worse for him later. Under the circumstances the best thing was to take the ladle from her, no matter how much she objected, and pour the water over her hands.

Again, one summer afternoon when they were awaiting her turn, with Sasuke sitting in his usual respectful attitude a little behind her, Shunkin murmured to herself: "It's hot."

"Yes, isn't it?" he agreed politely.

She was silent a few moments, and then repeated: "It's hot." Realizing what she wanted, Sasuke picked up a fan and began fanning her back. That seemed to satisfy her, but as soon as his fanning became a little less vigorous she repeated: "It's hot."

But it was chiefly to Sasuke, rather than to the other servants, that Shunkin displayed her stubbornness and willfulness. Since he did his best to cater to these tendencies in her, it was only with him that she could give full vent to such inclinations. That is one reason why she found him so useful. Sasuke, for his part, far from thinking himself abused, was pleased by the demands she made on him. Perhaps he took her extraordinary waywardness as a form of coquetry, interpreting it as a special favor.

The room in which Shunsho taught his pupils was on a mezzanine floor at the rear of the house up a short flight of stairs; when Shunkin's turn came, Sasuke would guide her up the steps and into the room to a seat facing her teacher. Then he would place her koto or samisen before her and go back downstairs to wait until the lesson was over. But while waiting he would remain alert, straining his ears to follow the music so that he could hurry back to get her as soon as the lesson ended. Naturally he became familiar with the pieces which Shunkin was learning to play and sing, and it was in this way that his own musical tastes were formed.

Of course Sasuke must have been born with a gift for music, since he eventually became a leading virtuoso. Still, except for his opportunity to serve Shunkin, except for the passionate love that made him share all her interests, he would no doubt have spent the rest of his life as an ordinary druggist. Even in his later years, when he was officially recognized as a master, he always maintained that his skill did not begin to compare with Shunkin's. "She taught me everything I know," he used to say. Such remarks cannot be taken at face value, since he was accustomed to humbling himself while praising her to the skies. But whatever their relative merits as artists, it seems undeniable that Shunkin had a touch of genius, and Sasuke a capacity for hard work.

Before the end of the year, while he was still thirteen, Sasuke secretly made up his mind to buy a samisen and began to save the small allowance his master gave him as well as the tips he got when he was out on errands. By the next summer he was at last able to buy a cheap practice-instrument, which he took apart, smuggling the neck and body separately up to his attic bedroom in order to escape the notice of the head clerk. Night after night, when the other apprentices were fast asleep, he practiced on his samisen.

At the beginning he had no confidence in his ability, nor did he intend to become a professional musician: it was only that he felt drawn to anything Shunkin liked, out of sheer loyalty. The fact that he did his best to conceal his interest in music from her shows that he was not learning to play the samisen as a means to win her love.

Sasuke shared a cramped, low-ceilinged attic room with five or six other clerks and apprentices; he asked them not to tell anyone about his practicing, and promised not to disturb them by it. They were all young enough to fall asleep as soon as their heads touched the pillow, and none of them ever complained. Even so, Sasuke would wait until he was sure they were sound asleep, then get up and practice in the closet where the bedding was kept. The attic room itself must have been hot and stuffy, and the heat inside that closet on a summer night almost unbearable. But by shutting himself up in it he could muffle the twang of the strings and at the same time avoid the distraction of outside noises, such as the snoring of his roommates. Of course he had to sing the vocal parts softly and pluck the strings with his fingers, instead of with a plectrum: sitting there in the pitch-dark closet, he played by his sense of touch alone.

But Sasuke never felt inconvenienced by the darkness. Blind people live in the dark like this all the time, he thought, and Shunkin has to play the samisen the same way. He was delighted to have found a place for himself in that dark world of hers. Even afterward, when he could practice freely, he was in the habit of closing his eyes whenever he took up the instrument, explaining that he felt he had to do exactly as Shunkin did. In short, he wanted to suffer the same handicap as Shunkin, to share all he could of the life of the blind. At times he obviously envied them. And these attitudes in which he persisted since boyhood help to account for his own later blindness. It was something that had to happen.

I suppose that all musical instruments are equally difficult when it comes to mastering their most profound secrets. However, the violin and the samisen offer special problems to the beginner, since they lack frets and must always be tuned before playing. They are the least suitable of instruments for self-teaching—and in those days there was no musical notation for the samisen. People say that with a good teacher it takes three months to learn to play the koto and three years for the samisen. But Sasuke could not afford to buy an instrument as expensive as a koto, nor could he possibly have smuggled in such a bulky object. He had to begin with the samisen. From the very first, though, he was able to tune it by himself, which not only suggests what a good ear for music he had, but how assiduously he listened while waiting at Shunsho's house. Everything he learned—the various modes, the words and melodies of the songs, the phrasing —he had to learn by remembering what he heard. There was no other way.

He went on practicing in secret for about half a year, managing to conceal it from everyone except his fellow roommates. Then early one winter morning (it was around four and as black as midnight) Shunkin's mother happened to get up to go to the lavatory, and heard the faint sound of a samisen filtering in from somewhere. In those days it was the custom for musicians to perform "midwinter exercises": that is, to get up before dawn during the cold season, bare themselves to the icy wind, and practice. But Dosho-machi was a commercial quarter, with staid business establishments lined up side by side, not the sort of place where you would find professional musicians or entertainers, or hear any gaiety at such an hour. In fact, it was still really night, much too early even for midwinter exercises; and the samisen was being played very softly, with the fingers, instead of loudly and energetically with a plectrum as one might have expected. And yet whoever it was seemed to be repeating the same passage over and over again, as if to perfect it. She could tell that he was a zealous student.

Shunkin's mother, though surprised to hear the music, paid no great attention to it and went back to bed. But she heard it again several times after that when she got up in the night; and others in the family said they had heard it too, and wondered where the sound could be coming from—surely this was no ghost! Thus the discussion went on, quite unknown to the clerks and apprentices.

All would have been well if Sasuke had continued to practice in the closet, but the fact that no one seemed to know what he was doing had made him bolder. Since he stole the night hours for his music he was bothered by loss of sleep, and being shut up in that airless closet soon made him drowsy. Toward the end of autumn, therefore, he had begun slipping out to the rooftop drying-platform to do his nightly practice in the open air. He always went to bed at ten o'clock along with the other shop employees, and would wake up at about three a.m., tuck his samisen under his arm, and go out on the platform, where, in the exhilarating cold, he would play on and on until the eastern sky began turning gray. It was during these hours of practice that Shunkin's mother heard him. Since the drying-platform was on the shop roof, directly over the attic where the apprentices slept, the sound carried over to the family quarters across the inner garden.

All the employees were questioned, and at last Sasuke's secret was out. The head clerk summoned him, scolded him severely, warning him never to do such a thing again, and took away his samisen. But then a helping hand was extended to him, most unexpectedly: Shunkin suggested that it might be interesting to hear what he could do.

Sasuke had felt sure that Shunkin would be offended if she learned of his practicing. She would think it presumptuous of him, a mere apprentice who ought to be contented fulfilling his duty as her guide. Whether she pitied or scorned him, he would be in for trouble. And he became all the more alarmed when he was told that she wished to hear him perform. I'd be so happy if she really cared, he thought. But he could only suppose that she was trying to make a laughingstock of him. Besides, he lacked the confidence to play and sing for others.

However, Shunkin insisted on hearing him, and by now her mother and sisters were curious too. Finally Sasuke was summoned to the family's private quarters and had to demonstrate how much he had managed to teach himself. It was a painfully formal debut.

By that time he could get through five or six pieces fairly well. Asked to play everything he knew, he screwed up his courage and did what he was told, playing and singing as if his life depended on it. Of course he had picked up all the tunes by ear, from the elementary "Black Hair" to the difficult "Teapickers' Song," and had learned his jumbled repertoire in a completely unsystematic way. Perhaps Shunkin and her family intended to make a laughingstock of him, as he suspected; but when they heard him perform they realized that for someone who had studied without a teacher, and only such a short time, both his instrumental technique and his voice were excellent. All of them were filled with admiration.

The *Life of Shunkin* says:

Thereupon, Shunkin began to sympathize with Sasuke in his ambition, and said to him: "In reward for your hard work I shall teach you myself from now on. Regard me as your teacher, and practice all you can in your spare time." At length Shunkin's father, Yasuzaemon, gave his consent to this arrangement, and Sasuke felt as if he had soared up to Heaven. Every day a fixed time was set aside during which he was freed from his duties as an apprentice and allowed to receive instruction. Thus there was the happy result that the ten-year-old girl and fourteen-year-old boy, besides being mistress and servant, formed the new and closer relationship of teacher and pupil.

But why did a difficult, temperamental girl like Shunkin suddenly begin to show such consideration for Sasuke? Some said that it was not really her idea, that those around her had persuaded her to act as she did. I suppose the blind little girl was often so lonely and melancholy, in spite of her happy home life, that even the maidservants (to say nothing of her parents) were at their wits' end, racking their brains to think of some way to amuse or divert her. And then they learned that Sasuke shared her taste for music. No doubt the servants, who had suffered bitterly from Shunkin's waywardness, wanted to lighten their own duties by having Sasuke spend more time with her. Might they not have appealed to her vanity by praising Sasuke and saying how wonderful it would be if she went to the trouble of teaching him, how gratefully he would receive such a favor? But since clumsy flattery only annoyed Shunkin it is not at all certain that she was responding to the influence of others. Perhaps she had at last begun to care for him, and to feel a strange new emotion stirring in her heart.

In any case, everyone was delighted when she proposed to take Sasuke as her pupil. No one asked whether a ten-year-old girl, however great a prodigy, was actually qualified to teach: it was enough that her boredom could be relieved in this way, and those around her spared. And so she was given this new game of "playing school," and Sasuke was ordered to be her pupil. Thus, the plan was intended for Shunkin's benefit, rather than Sasuke's; but as things turned out it was he who profited most.

According to the *Life*: "Every day a fixed time was set aside during which he was freed from his duties as an apprentice." But he was already spending at least several hours a day as her guide, so that being called regularly to her room for music lessons must have left him scarcely time to think of his work in the shop. Probably Yasuzaemon felt guilty toward Sasuke's parents for having made their son, whom he was supposed to be training to become a merchant, into a companion for his daughter. But keeping Shunkin in a good humor would have meant more to him than the future of one of his apprentices, and Sasuke himself was eager to do it. Apparently Yasuzaemon gave his tacit approval to the arrangement, feeling that it would do no harm to let matters take their course for the present.

This was when Sasuke began to call Shunkin "Madam,"

one of the formalities which she required of him during his lessons. She began to speak to him more brusquely, treating him precisely as her master Shunsho treated his own pupils and exacting the strictest obedience and respect. Thus they went on with their innocent "playing school," just as the adults had planned, and Shunkin found it highly diverting. But as the months went by the two showed no sign of abandoning their game. After two or three years had passed, both teacher and pupil had become so serious about it that there was no question of its being merely an amusement.

It was Shunkin's daily routine to set out for her teacher's house in Utsubo at about two o'clock in the afternoon, take a lesson which lasted half an hour to an hour, and then go home to spend the rest of the day practicing. After supper, if she happened to feel so inclined, she would summon Sasuke up to her room and give him a lesson. Eventually she taught him every day, without fail, sometimes not excusing him until nine or ten o'clock at night. Often the servants below were startled to hear the violent scoldings she would give him: "Sasuke! Is that what I taught you?" or "No, that won't do! Go over it till you can play it, even if it takes all night!" It was not unusual for the little girl to drive her pupil to tears, rapping him on the head with her plectrum and shouting: "Idiot! Why can't you learn?"

As is well known, teachers of the arts used to drill their pupils with brutal harshness, often inflicting physical punishment on them. For example, the famous chanter of puppet dramas Koshiji-dayu II had a large crescent-shaped scar between his eyebrows—a memento, so they say, of the time when his teacher cried "When will you ever learn?" and knocked him down with a blow of his heavy plectrum. Then there is the case of Yoshida Tamajiro of the Bunraku Theater. Once, during his apprenticeship, while he was helping his master Tamazo manipulate a puppet hero in rehearsing a climactic capture scene, he was unable to perfect a certain movement of the legs for which he was responsible. Suddenly his angry teacher shouted "Fool!" and, snatching up a puppet sword (one with a real blade), gave him a sharp blow on the back of the head. To this day he bears the scar of it. And Tamazo himself, who struck Tamajiro, once had his head split open when his own teacher struck him with a puppet. He begged his teacher for the broken-off, splintered legs of the puppet, which were crimson with his blood, and then wrapped them in silk floss and stored them away in a plain wooden box, such as is used for the ashes of the dead. Now and then he took the legs out and paid obeisance to them, as if he were worshipping the spirit of his dead mother. "Except for that beating," he would say with tears in his eyes, "I might have spent my whole life as a run-of-the-mill performer."

In his youth the late Osumi-dayu used to be called a plodder, since he often seemed slow to learn. His teacher was Toyozawa Dambei, known as "the Great Dambei." One sweltering night in midsummer while Osumi was taking a lesson at Dambei's house he stumbled over a few lines in the scene he was chanting. Again and again he repeated the passage, but as hard as he tried he could not satisfy Dambei, who prudently put up a mosquito net and retired within it to listen. While the mosquitoes fed on him, Osumi went on repeating it, hundreds and hundreds of times, till the early summer dawn began to light up the room, and even his teacher seemed to have tired and fallen asleep. Nevertheless, with the persistence of a true plodder, Osumi kept on chanting the passage as vigorously as ever, determined not to stop until it had been approved. Finally Dambei's voice came from the mosquito net: "You have it." He had listened intently all night long.

Anecdotes of this kind are not uncommon, nor are they confined to stories of puppet-theater chanters and manipulators. Similar incidents occurred in the teaching of the samisen and the koto. Moreover, these masters were usually blind men, many of whom had the stubbornness —and the streak of cruelty—so often found among persons with a physical handicap. Shunkin's master Shunsho was such a man.

Shunsho had long been known for the severity of his teaching methods. He often shouted curses at his pupils (many of whom were also blind) or even laid hands on them: whenever he scolded or lashed out at them they would back away a little—until sometimes a blind child, still clutching his samisen, would tumble over backward and fall clattering down the stairs. In later years, when Shunkin became a professional teacher, she was notorious for her strictness, which of course reflected Shunsho's influence. But she was already behaving that way as a child. What began as a little girl's game with Sasuke had gradually developed into the real thing.

One often hears of cruel teachers, but there can have been few women like Shunkin who went so far as to strike their male pupils. It has been suggested that she had sadistic tendencies, and that her teaching was only a pretext for enjoying a kind of perverse sexual pleasure. After all these years, we can hardly say whether that was true or not. Still, when children play house they always imitate grownups. Though Shunkin was her master's favorite and was never punished, she was aware of his usual method, and must have felt in her childish mind that that was how a master ought to behave. Inevitably she began to imitate him when she was playing with Sasuke. And the habit grew on her, until it became second nature.

Perhaps Sasuke cried easily, but they say that whenever Shunkin struck him he began to sob. And he sounded so wretched that everyone who heard him frowned, thinking: Shunkin is punishing him again! Her parents, who had only wanted to provide her with a new diversion, were extremely troubled by this state of affairs. Disturbing as it was to hear the samisen or the koto until far into the night, it was still worse when Shunkin gave him an angry scolding, as she often did, and when Sasuke's crying rang painfully in one's ears. Sometimes the maids felt so sorry for him—and so worried about the effect on Shunkin herself—that they would rush in to interrupt the lesson.

"What on earth are you doing?" they would say,

trying to pacify Shunkin. "You're being terribly hard on the poor boy, and not at all ladylike!"

But Shunkin would draw herself up haughtily and retort: "Go away! You don't know anything about this. I'm not just playing a game. I'm really teaching him—it's all for his own good. Teaching is teaching, no matter how mad I get or how hard I treat him. Can't you understand that?"

This is how the *Life of Shunkin* puts it:

"Do you look down on me because of my youth?" Shunkin would ask. "And do you dare to violate the sanctity of art? Young or old, anyone who sets out to teach ought to behave like a teacher. Giving lessons to Sasuke has never been merely a game with me. I think it is too bad that in spite of his love of music he has no chance to study under an expert; that is why I am doing my best to substitute for a teacher. I want to do all I can to help him fulfill his ambition. You couldn't possibly understand. Leave the room at once!" This firm declaration was delivered with such startling eloquence and such an awesome air of dignity that the intruders, much chastened, would make a hasty retreat.

One can easily imagine how spirited Shunkin's manner must have been. Although Sasuke was often brought to tears by her, he felt immense gratitude whenever he heard her talk like that. His tears were in part tears of gratitude for being spurred on so vehemently by the girl who was at once his mistress and his teacher. That is why he never fled from her maltreatment: even while weeping, he kept on with his lesson until she told him he could stop.

Shunkin's moods varied dramatically from day to day. When she burst out with a noisy scolding she was in one of her relatively good moods; but sometimes she only frowned and gave the third string of her samisen a loud twang, or had Sasuke go on playing as she sat listening without a word of criticism. It was on her silent days that he cried most.

One evening, when he was working on a samisen interlude from the "Teapickers' Song," Sasuke was being unusually dull-witted. Time and again he repeated the same mistake. Losing patience with him, Shunkin put her own instrument down and began beating time by slapping her knee briskly with her right hand as she sang out the notes: *Chiri-chiri-gan, chiri-gan* . . . Finally she gave up and sat there in stony silence.

Sasuke was helpless. Yet he had to go on somehow or other, doing his best to get through it. But as hard as he tried, Shunkin would not relent. Flushed and dizzy, he began making more mistakes than ever; his whole body was bathed in a cold sweat as he played on and on, quite at random. Shunkin remained silent, only tightening her lips a little more and deepening her frown. After some two hours of this Shunkin's mother came upstairs in her night kimono and stopped the lesson. "You mustn't be too eager," she told her daughter soothingly. "Going to extremes is bad for your health."

The next day Shunkin was summoned by her parents. "It's good of you to want to teach Sasuke how to play," they told her; "but shouting at pupils, or striking them, is only for an acknowledged master. After all, you're still taking lessons yourself. If you go on behaving like this it's bound to make you conceited—and conceited people don't become great artists. Furthermore, it's un-ladylike to hit a boy, or call him an idiot. Please don't do anything of that sort again! And from now on, set a time and stop at a decent hour. Sasuke's wailing gets on our nerves and none of us can sleep."

All this was put in such a gentle, kindly way by her parents, who had never been known to scold her, that even Shunkin seemed ready to listen to reason. But that was only on the surface. Actually, their words had no real effect on her.

"You're such a weakling!" she told Sasuke scornfully. "You're a boy, and yet you can't stand the least thing. It's all because of your crying that they blame me and think I'm being cruel to you. If you really want to become an artist you've got to grit your teeth and bear it, no matter how much it hurts. If you can't, I won't be your teacher."

After that, however badly she abused him, Sasuke never cried.

It seems to have worried Shunkin's parents that their daughter, whose blindness had already warped her character, had come to behave quite rudely now that she was teaching Sasuke. Having him as her companion was a mixed blessing. As grateful as they were to him for keeping her in a good humor, it distressed them to think that his habit of yielding to her every whim might gradually make her even more of a problem.

When Sasuke was seventeen his master arranged for him to take lessons from Shunsho himself, instead of from Shunkin; no doubt her parents felt that imitating her teacher had had an unhealthy influence on her. And the change decided Sasuke's future career. From then on he was freed from all his shop duties and went to Shunsho's house regularly both as Shunkin's guide and as a fellow pupil.

Nothing could have pleased Sasuke more; and it may be gathered that Yasuzaemon, on his part, worked very hard to persuade Sasuke's parents to consent to the arrangement, assuring them that, having caused their son to abandon his trade, he would guarantee the boy's future. I suppose Yasuzaemon and his wife were already beginning to think that Sasuke would make a good husband for Shunkin. In view of her handicap, they could scarcely hope to marry her to someone of equal social position. Sasuke might be the best possible match for her.

Two years later (when Shunkin was fifteen and Sasuke nineteen) her parents suggested that she consider such a marriage. To their surprise, she flatly refused. "I don't intend to marry as long as I live," she announced, looking much displeased; "and I wouldn't dream of having a man like Sasuke."

However, about another year later her mother noticed a curious change in Shunkin's figure. Surely not! she told herself; but the longer she watched, the more her suspicions seemed to be confirmed. The servants will begin to talk, she thought; we must act quickly if we are to save the situation. But when she asked her daughter about it one day as discreetly as possible, the girl told her she hadn't the faintest idea what she was talking about. Finding it awkward to pursue the matter further, Shunkin's mother let it go for a month or two. By then her daughter's condition was obvious.

Now, Shunkin frankly admitted to her parents that she was pregnant, but refused to name her lover. Pressed for an answer, she declared: "We promised each other to keep it a secret."

When they asked if the man was Sasuke she denied it indignantly. "Don't be absurd!" she said. "An apprentice like that?"

Naturally anyone would have suspected Sasuke, but Shunkin's parents, remembering what she had said last year, thought it most unlikely. Then too, a relationship of that kind could scarcely have been such a well-kept secret: an inexperienced boy and girl would have given themselves away. Furthermore, ever since Sasuke began studying under her teacher he had no reason to stay up late with her as he used to. Sometimes Shunkin would help him review his lessons; except for that, she was always the haughty young lady, treating him merely as her guide. None of the employees had the slightest suspicion of any misconduct between them—indeed, they felt that Shunkin was too distant, too cold toward him.

But surely Sasuke will know *something* about it, her

parents thought. The man must have been one of the other pupils. Sasuke, however, denied any knowledge of the matter. "I can't imagine who it could be," he said. Still, he seemed so nervous and guilty-looking that they became increasingly suspicious. As they questioned him more closely he began to contradict himself. At last he said: "If I tell you, she'll be angry with me!" And he burst into tears.

"No, no!" they insisted. "It's kind of you to want to protect her, but why do you disobey our orders? If you keep it secret you'll only make things worse. Do tell us the man's name!" Despite their urging, he refused to answer. Finally they realized that the man in question was Sasuke. He talked as if he had promised Shunkin never to confess, and yet wanted them to know that he was guilty.

Troubled as they were, Shunkin's parents felt relieved. What's done is done, they thought; at least we can be glad that it's Sasuke. But in that case why had she tried to deceive them last year, when they were encouraging her to marry him? Young girls were certainly unpredictable! Now that things had gone this far it would be best for her to marry as soon as possible, before people began to talk. But when they brought the subject up with Shunkin once more, she again refused. "I don't want to hear another word about it," she said, coloring. "As I told you last year, I wouldn't have a man like Sasuke. I'm grateful to you for taking pity on me, but even if I *am* handicapped I won't stoop so low as to marry a servant. Besides, it would be an insult to the father of my child."

"Well then, who *is* the father?"

"Please don't ask me that," she replied. "Anyway, I don't intend to marry him."

By now Sasuke's words seemed more baffling than ever. What were they to believe? Still, they could hardly think that she had been involved with anyone else; she must have denied it out of sheer embarrassment. Feeling sure that she would confess before long, Shunkin's parents decided to give up any further attempt at questioning her and sent her off immediately to the hot-spring resort at Arima to have her baby.

That was in May of Shunkin's sixteenth year. Sasuke stayed behind in Osaka; and she left with two maids for Arima, where she remained until her safe delivery of a baby boy in October. Since the baby's face was the very image of Sasuke's, it seemed that at last the mystery had been solved. But still Shunkin refused to listen to any talk of marriage—and denied that Sasuke was the father. When the two were forced to confront each other before her parents, she drew herself up stiffly and demanded: "Sasuke, what have you said to create suspicion? It's causing me a lot of trouble, and I wish you'd make it perfectly clear that you're innocent."

At this warning, Sasuke shrank back in alarm, and exclaimed: "How could I be involved with my master's daughter? From the time I was a child I've owed everything to the Mozuya family—I wouldn't dream of behaving so ungratefully! It's really absurd!" Thus he joined Shunkin in wholehearted denial. The matter seemed as far from a solution as ever.

"But don't you have any feeling for your own baby?" her parents asked Shunkin. "After all, we can hardly rear a fatherless child. If you positively refuse to marry we have no choice but to give the child away."

Shunkin was unmoved by this appeal to her maternal instincts. "Please do give it to anyone you like," she replied calmly. "Since I shall never marry, it would only be a burden to me."

Soon the baby was sent out for adoption. (That was in 1845, and nothing is known of its later life; presumably Shunkin's parents made suitable arrangements for the child's welfare.) Thus Shunkin managed to have her own way and hush up the whole incident of her illegitimate child. Before long she was nonchalantly going to her lessons again, with Sasuke as her guide. By then, however, it seems that their relations were an open secret. Yet whenever a formal union was suggested they both denied that there was anything between them. Knowing their daughter's temperament, Shunkin's parents were obliged to ignore what was going on.

This ambiguous state of affairs—they were at once mistress and servant, fellow pupils, and lovers—continued for two or three years, until Shunkin was nineteen. Then her master Shunsho died, and she herself became a teacher. Leaving her parents, she set up a household in Yodoyabashi, and Sasuke went along with her.

Of course her ability had long been recognized by

Shunsho, and before he died he had licensed her to teach. It was he who had given her the very name of Shunkin, which incorporated part of his own name; and he did all he could to further her career, often playing duets with her in public recitals and having her perform the leading parts. So perhaps it was only natural that she opened a studio of her own. Still, considering her age and circumstances, I find it odd that she made herself independent so soon. Probably her relations with Sasuke had something to do with it. Her parents may have decided that if this unsavory and by now quite open relationship was to continue, setting a bad example for the other employees, it would be best to have the two of them go and live elsewhere. Shunkin could scarcely object to *that.*

Yet she behaved as coldly toward Sasuke as ever. Even when they were living together at Yodoyabashi he was treated as her servant. Also, now that their teacher had died, he began to receive instruction from her again— and this time they maintained the roles of teacher and pupil in the presence of others. Shunkin intensely disliked any appearance of being Sasuke's wife. She was very strict in requiring him to observe proper decorum both as a pupil and as a servant; she made a point of prescribing the correct forms of speech for him, down to the most trivial niceties of usage. When he happened to violate one of these rules, she upbraided him relentlessly for his rudeness, and would not easily accept his apologies, however abject. As a result, Shunkin's new pupils were slow to realize that the two were lovers. And it seems that the servants would gossip among themselves, saying: "How do you suppose she acts when they're in bed together? I'd like to spy on them sometime!"

Why did Shunkin treat Sasuke in this fashion? To be sure, Osaka people have always been more concerned about questions of family background, property, and status, when it comes to marriage, than those of Tokyo: Osaka is famous for its proud old merchant families—and how much prouder they must have been in the feudal days before Meiji! A girl like Shunkin would doubtless have regarded Sasuke, whose family had served hers for generations, as someone immeasurably beneath her. Then too, with the typically embittered attitude of a blind person, she must have been determined not to show any weakness, or let anyone make a fool of her.

I suppose she felt that she would be insulting herself irreparably by taking Sasuke as her husband. Probably she was ashamed of sleeping with an inferior, and reacted by behaving coldly toward him. Then did she consider him nothing more than a physiological necessity? As far as she was aware of her own feelings, I dare say she did.

To quote again from the *Life:*

Shunkin was a woman of fastidious habits and immaculate dress. She changed into fresh undergarments daily, and insisted on having her rooms thoroughly cleaned morning and evening: before sitting down she would run her fingertips carefully over the cushions and the floor matting—she loathed even the least speck of dust. They say that a pupil of hers who suffered from indigestion once came for his lesson on a day when his breath was bad. Shunkin gave the third string of her samisen an ominous twang, laid the instrument down before her, and sat there frowning without a word. The embarrassed pupil timidly asked if anything was the matter. When he asked a second time, she replied: "I may be blind, but there is nothing wrong with my nose. Go wash out your mouth!"

Perhaps it was because of her lack of sight that Shunkin had a morbid love of cleanliness, but when a fastidious woman happens also to be blind the difficulties of those who take care of her are endless. The task of being her guide was not confined to leading her here and there by the hand; one had to see to all the little details of her daily life—eating and drinking, getting up and going to bed, taking baths, going to the lavatory, and the like. And because Sasuke had been responsible for these duties ever since her childhood, and understood all her idiosyncrasies, no one else could manage them to suit her. It was in this sense, rather than the physiological, that Sasuke was indispensable.

Moreover, at home in Dosho-machi Shunkin had been subject to the restraining influence of her parents and her brothers and sisters, but as the head of her own household her fastidiousness and waywardness went from bad to worse. Sasuke's duties became still more demanding. For certain further details, which were naturally omitted from the *Life*, I am indebted to Shigizawa Teru. "Even in the lavatory my mistress never washed her own hands," she told me. "Shunkin was not in the habit of doing things like that for herself—they were all done by Sasuke. He even bathed her. They say great ladies think nothing of having themselves washed from head to toe by their servants, and don't feel a bit of shame about it; my teacher's attitude toward Sasuke was like that. Maybe it's because she was blind, but I expect she was so used to being cared for, after all those years, that she didn't give it a second thought. She was a very stylish woman too. Even if she hadn't seen herself in a mirror since she was a little girl, she didn't have the faintest doubt of her own beauty. She spent as much time choosing her clothes, or doing her hair and making up, as any woman."

I imagine that Shunkin's powerful memory retained for many years the picture of her own good looks when she was a child of eight. Besides, after constantly receiving compliments and hearing herself praised, she knew very well that she was beautiful. As a result, she devoted an extraordinary amount of time to cultivating her appearance.

Shunkin always kept a number of nightingales, and would mix their droppings with rice bran to use as a sort of pumice for the skin; she also set great store by the juice of the snake gourd as a cosmetic. Unless her face and body were satin-smooth, she felt quite uncomfortable—a rough skin was her chief aversion. People who play stringed instruments keep their left-hand fingernails short, since the strings are pressed with those fingers; but Shunkin had the nails of both her hands (and both feet as well) trimmed and filed regularly every three days. Of course they hardly seemed to have grown in that time, but she insisted that they must always look the same. Afterwards, she would carefully feel each of her fingernails and toenails, and would never permit the slightest variation from their proper size and shape. All such services as manicuring her nails were performed by Sasuke alone. During what time he had left, he received lessons from her, and even, occasionally, took her place in teaching one of the younger pupils.

Sexual relations are infinite in their variety. Sasuke, for example, knew Shunkin's body in the most exhaustive detail: he was bound up with her in an intimacy beyond the dreams of any ordinary husband and wife or pair of lovers. It is not surprising that in his later years when he himself was blind he still cared for her personal needs with no great difficulty. To the end of his long life (he died at eighty-two) Sasuke never married or formed a second liaison, or indeed had any experience with a woman other than Shunkin. Though scarcely qualified to make critical comparisons, he took to boasting about her in his old age, the years after her death, and he would never tire of telling his friends about her incredibly smooth skin, her soft, pliant legs and arms. It was the one topic on which he rambled as interminably as any garrulous old man. Sometimes he would hold out his hand and say: "Her dainty little foot was just big enough to nestle into my palm." Or again, stroking his cheek: "Even her heel was softer and smoother than this."

I have mentioned that Shunkin was small in stature. But she was not so slender as she appeared to be when dressed: in the nude, her body was unexpectedly voluptuous. And she was dazzlingly fair—her skin kept its youthful gloss and freshness throughout her life. Perhaps that was because of her epicurean tastes, so remarkable for a lady of those days. They say that she was fond of chicken and fish, particularly fillets of sea bream, and that she enjoyed *saké* too, never failing to have a few cups of it with her evening meal.

(There is something painful about watching a blind person eat, especially a beautiful young woman. Whether Shunkin was aware of this or not, she disliked eating in the presence of anyone but Sasuke. When invited out to dinner she seemed excessively refined, barely touching her food; but the truth was that she had luxurious tastes. Not that she ate heavily: only a scant two bowls of rice, together with a morsel from each of the various other dishes. But because she took so little there had to be a number of different courses. She seemed to be deliberately trying to make work for Sasuke. He became very skillful at boning sea bream or shelling crabs and lobsters, and could extract the bones neatly through the tail of a small fish without altering its shape.)

Shunkin had a mass of soft, silky hair. Her hands were slender and supple, with a strength that must have come from years of practice on the koto and samisen—one of her slaps left a real sting. Though subject to fits of feverish dizziness, she was also highly sensitive to cold: even in midsummer her feet were icy and she never perspired. All the year round she slept in a thickly quilted robe of satin or silk crepe, with her feet wrapped securely in its long, trailing skirt; and she lay so still that it was never disarranged. Fearing that the blood might rush to her head, she avoided using hot-water bottles and other warming devices: when her feet were too cold Sasuke would lie down and clasp them against his bosom, the chief effect of which was to chill him to the bone. When she took a bath she had the windows of the bathroom thrown wide open (even in winter) to disperse the steam. She got in and out of the tub repeatedly, staying only a few minutes, though the water was never more than lukewarm. Since a long soaking caused her heart to palpitate and the steam made her dizzy, she had to warm herself by spending as little time as possible in the water, and then have her body washed with the utmost haste. As one learns more and more about Shunkin, one begins to realize how much trouble she gave Sasuke.

Yet his material compensation was very small. As to wages, he received only an occasional allowance, so little that he often lacked tobacco money; and he had no new clothing except that provided by his mistress at the midsummer Bon Festival and the end of the year, in the traditional feudal manner. Although he sometimes gave lessons in place of Shunkin, he was not accorded any special status. Pupils and maidservants were ordered to address him as one of themselves, and whenever he accompanied Shunkin to a pupil's house he had to wait for her at the door.

One day Sasuke had such a bad toothache that his right cheek was greatly swollen. By nightfall the pain was almost unbearable, but he forced himself to hide his suffering. Now and then he would stealthily rinse his mouth, and he was careful to keep his breath away from Shunkin as he served her. At last she retired, and told him to massage her shoulders and back. After a while she said: "That's enough. Now you can warm my feet." Obediently he lay down, opened his kimono, and pressed the soles of her ice-cold feet against his chest. But his face, smothered in the bedclothes, was flaming hot—and his toothache worse than ever. Finally, in desperation, he put his swollen cheek against one of her feet.

Suddenly Shunkin gave the cheek a sharp kick, and Sasuke leaped up with a cry of pain. "You needn't bother any more!" she said witheringly. "I told you to warm my feet—not cool your face! Do you think you can trick me just because I'm blind? I knew you had a toothache all day. Even with the sole of my foot I can tell that your right cheek is puffed and feverish. If it hurts so much you ought to say so—I'm not a tyrant who mistreats servants. But you pretend to be so devoted, and then have the impudence to use me for your own comfort. I suppose you think that's clever. You ought to be ashamed of yourself!"

This was not unusual behavior for her. But what particularly annoyed Shunkin was for Sasuke to pay any attention whatever to the young girls among her pupils, to be kind to them, or help them with their lessons. The more she tried to conceal her jealousy, the more cruelly she treated him. It was at such times that he suffered worst of all.

When a woman is blind and never marries, there are limits to her extravagance. Even if she has expensive tastes in food and clothing, and indulges them, the sums involved are not likely to be very great. However, Shunkin's household included half a dozen servants, and the monthly expenses were substantial. As to why she spent so much money and kept such a large establishment, it was chiefly because she was a bird fancier, with a weakness for nightingales.

Today, a nightingale that sings beautifully will cost up to ten thousand yen; no doubt that was true even in Shunkin's time. Meanwhile, bird fanciers seem to have changed their tastes somewhat; but in current practice the most valuable nightingales are those which, apart from their natural call of *hōhokekyō*, can sing both the "valley-flying call" of *kekkyo-kekkyo* and the "high notes" of *hōkiibekakon*. Wild nightingales cannot produce these two melodies. At best, they may achieve an unpleasant *hōkiibecha*—to become capable of the lovely, lingering bell-like note of *kon* they require intensive training. Baby nightingales must be caught before their tail feathers are grown, and then trained by another nightingale, a "teaching bird." If their tails are already grown out, they will have learned the unmelodious calls of their parents, and nothing more can be done.

Teaching birds are trained from the beginning in this artificial way, and famous ones have names, such as Phoenix or Eternal Companion. So when it is learned that a certain gentleman has a marvelous nightingale, other nightingale fanciers come from far and wide, bringing their own birds to be "given a voice" by it. This training usually occurs early in the morning, and goes on day after day. Sometimes a teaching bird is taken out to a special place, and its pupils gather around it, like any singing class. Of course each nightingale has its own unique qualities, its own kind of song: there are infinite degrees of skill at turning a melody, or holding a long, trailing note, even when it comes to producing the same call. First-rate nightingales are hard to find, and, in view of the profit from training fees, command a high price.

Shunkin gave the finest of her nightingales the name Tenko, or Drum of Heaven, and loved to listen to it from morning till night. Tenko's voice was really superb. Its clear, ringing high notes made one think of some exquisite musical instrument: it was a voice of steady, sustained power, as well as of great charm and sweetness. And so, Tenko was handled with meticulous care, every precaution being taken as to its diet. Now, a nightingale's feed is prepared by parching soy beans and unpolished rice, grinding them together, and adding rice bran to make a "white meal," after which a "carp meal" is made, by grinding up dried carp or dace or other fresh-water fish; then the two are mixed (in equal parts) and thoroughly blended with the juice of grated radish leaves. And besides all this, which is trouble enough, the bird must be given a few insects every day—the insects living in the stem of the wild grape vine are the only ones that will do—in order to improve its song. Shunkin had about half a dozen birds that required this sort of care, and one or two of her servants were kept busy looking after them.

Since nightingales never sing while people are watching, they are housed in special cages of paulownia wood, closely fitted with sliding paper screens which admit only a faint glow of light. These screens have decorative panels of rosewood, ebony, or the like, elaborately carved, or worked in gold lacquer and inlaid with mother of pearl. Some of the cages have considerable artistic value—even now people often pay large sums of money for them. Tenko's cage was fitted with handsome panels, said to have come from China: the frames were rosewood and the lower part was set with jade plaques of landscapes and palaces in delicate relief. It was a very elegant piece.

Shunkin kept this cage in the window beside the alcove in her sitting room, where she could listen to Tenko whenever it sang. Since Tenko's lovely voice always put her in a good humor, the servants would do their best (even dashing water over it) to get the bird to sing. It sang best on sunny days, so that Shunkin's mood brightened with the weather. Tenko's voice was heard most frequently from late winter through spring; by summer its silences began to lengthen, and Shunkin became more and more gloomy.

Nightingales are often long-lived if properly cared for, but they require constant attention. Left to an inexperienced person they soon die. As pampered as it was, Tenko died at the age of seven, and Shunkin, like most owners who lose their birds, tried to find a worthy successor. After several years she managed to train another splendid nightingale, which she also called Tenko and prized as highly.

Tenko the Second, too, had a voice of such marvelous beauty that it might have sung in Paradise. Shunkin loved the bird dearly and kept its cage by her side night and day. She used to make her pupils be quiet when it sang, and then admonish them in this fashion: "Listen to Tenko, all of you! It was only an ordinary fledgling at first, but you can see what long training has done for it. No wild nightingale has a voice as beautiful as that. Some people may say that it is merely an artificial beauty; nothing is more lovely, they will tell you, than the song of the wild nightingale bursting suddenly out of the mist over a stream, as you wander through deep valleys looking for the flowers of spring. I cannot agree with them. It is only the time and place that make the call of the wild nightingale so moving; if you stop to listen, you realize that its voice is far from beautiful. But when you hear a bird as accomplished as Tenko, on the other hand, you are reminded of the tranquil charm of a secluded ravine—a rushing stream murmurs to you, clouds of cherry blossoms float up before your eyes. Blossoms and mist alike are within that song, and we forget that we are still in the dusty city. This is where art rivals nature. And here too is the secret of music."

Often she would make the slower pupils feel ashamed, asking derisively if even the little birds had not penetrated the mysteries of art. "You are really no match for them," she would say.

To be sure, there was a degree of truth in what Shunkin said. Still, Sasuke and the other pupils must have found it trying to be so often—and so unflatteringly—held up for comparison with a bird.

Next to her nightingales, Shunkin was fondest of her larks. It is the instinct of this bird to soar up to the heavens; even within its cage it always flies as high as it can. That is why lark's cages are built tall and narrow, as much as four or five feet high.

For the true appreciation of the lark's song, however, one must release it from its cage, let it fly up out of sight, and listen to it sing as it soars among the clouds. That is what is called its "cloud-piercing" virtuosity. Usually a lark will come back to its cage after remaining in the air for a certain fixed length of time, between ten minutes and half an hour; the longer it stays aloft, the better the lark. Hence, when contests are held, the cages are lined up in a row, their doors opened simultaneously,

and the birds released. The last one to return to its cage
is the winner. Inferior birds sometimes fly back to the
wrong cage, and the worst of them alight as far as one
or two hundred yards away. But larks seldom make mistakes of that kind: no doubt it is because they fly
vertically up into the sky, hover in one place, and then
descend vertically again, that they naturally return to
their own cage. In spite of the term "cloud-piercing,"
larks do not actually fly into clouds—they only seem
to because the clouds drift past them.

On a beautiful spring day those who lived near
Shunkin's house in Yodoyabashi often saw the blind
music teacher go out on her rooftop drying-platform
and send one of her larks up into the sky. Sasuke would
always be standing there beside her, along with a maid
who took care of the cage. When Shunkin gave the
order, her maid would open the cage door and the lark
would rush out joyously, singing *tsun-tsun* as it climbed
higher and higher, until it vanished into the spring haze.
Shunkin would lift her head to follow the bird's path
with her blind eyes, and then listen in ecstasy as the long,
wailing melody came down through the clouds. Sometimes other bird lovers would join them, each with his
favorite lark, and they would amuse themselves by having a contest.

On such occasions the people of the neighborhood
would go up to their own rooftops and enjoy the singing of the larks. But some of them were not so much
interested in the birds as in the good-looking music
teacher. Although the young men who lived nearby

must have seen her the year round, there were the inevitable libertines among them, who, as soon as they heard the larks, would hurry up to the roof, thinking: There she is! Perhaps it was her blindness that fascinated them, stimulating their lecherous curiosity. Or perhaps she seemed especially beautiful when she was flying her larks, since she was then so animated and smiling, instead of glum and silent as when Sasuke led her out to give a lesson.

Besides larks and nightingales, Shunkin often kept robins, white-eyes, buntings, and other birds, sometimes half a dozen each of a number of different species. All of this entailed a good deal of expense.

Shunkin was the sort of person whose bad temper is reserved for home. Away, she was surprisingly pleasant; when invited to dinner, for instance, her whole manner was so gracious and appealing that no one would have taken her for the woman who, in her own home, tormented Sasuke or scolded and slapped her pupils. When it came to her social obligations she tended to be ostentatious. Her gift-giving at the Bon Festival or at the New Year, or on any occasion whatever, displayed all the generosity that one might have expected from the daughter of a prosperous family. Even her tips to teahouse maids, palanquin bearers, and ricksha men were astonishingly liberal.

Yet it should not be supposed that Shunkin was a reckless spendthrift. Osaka people have frugal habits. Their apparent love of luxury is unlike the out-and-out extravagance of people in Tokyo: they maintain a tight control over their affairs, and economize whenever they can do it unobtrusively. And Shunkin too, as the daughter of an old merchant family of Dosho-machi, had her wits about her. Her fondness for luxury was combined with miserliness and greed. It was because of her naturally competitive spirit that she vied with others in extravagance; she never squandered her money unless it served that purpose. Rather than wasting money, or frittering it away on a moment's impulse, she planned her expenditures carefully. In that respect, she was cool and calculating. But sometimes her competitiveness turned into sheer rapacity. The fees which she charged her pupils, for example, were quite out of keeping with those of other women teachers; she demanded to be paid every bit as much as a master of the first rank.

Moreover, Shunkin let it be known to her pupils by persistent hinting that she expected the traditional midsummer and year-end presents to be as substantial as possible. Once she had a blind pupil whose family was so poor that he often fell behind in paying his monthly fees. At midsummer, because a suitable gift was entirely beyond his means, he brought a box of rice cakes as a token of gratitude. Appealing to Sasuke to intercede for him, he said: "Please ask my teacher to accept this insignificant present."

Sasuke felt sorry for him, and timidly apologized to Shunkin on the boy's behalf. But she paled with anger, and declared: "Perhaps you think I am being greedy when I insist on having the proper fees and gifts, but that is quite wrong. The money itself means nothing to me: it is only that unless standards of some kind are set, the correct relationship between teacher and pupil cannot be established. That boy even neglects to pay his monthly fees, and now he has the insolence to bring me a miserable box of rice cakes! I can hardly be blamed for thinking that he lacks respect for his teacher. It's too bad, but if he is as poor as all that, he really has no hope of accomplishing anything in music. Of course if he had exceptional talent I might even teach him without charge. But he would have to be a prodigy with a brilliant future in store for him. Very few are able to overcome poverty and win success in the arts—you can't do it by hard work alone. The only thing outstanding about that boy is his impudence, I can't believe he shows any special promise. How presumptuous of him to ask for sympathy! Instead of shaming himself and troubling others, he should quit the field. If he still wants to keep on studying there are plenty of good teachers in Osaka —let him go elsewhere. But this is the end as far as I'm concerned. I don't want to have any more to do with him." And Shunkin was as good as her word. Further apologies were of no avail.

However, when someone brought her a particularly expensive present, Shunkin relaxed her usual strictness. All that day she would smile at him, and flatter him, until the favored pupil began to feel distinctly uneasy. "Madam's compliments" became something to dread.

Shunkin took care to examine every one of her presents personally, even opening and inspecting the smallest box of cakes. Similarly, she would check the settlement of all the monthly accounts, sending for Sasuke and having him run the figures off on the abacus for her. She was clever at arithmetic, and once she heard a figure it stuck in her mind: two or three months later she would remember the precise amount of a rice dealer's or a *saké* dealer's bill. Her extravagances were purely selfish ones, and the money she spent satisfying her own tastes had to be made up by economies elsewhere—specifically, by victimizing the servants. In Shunkin's household, she alone lived royally; Sasuke and the others had to live like mice in order to cut expenses. Even their daily rice allotment would vary, often dwindling to the point where they left the table hungry. Behind her back, the servants would criticize their mistress. "She tells us her larks and nightingales are more devoted to her than we are. But is it any wonder? Think how much better she treats them!"

As long as her father was alive Shunkin received all the money she wanted; but after his death, when her elder brother succeeded him as head of the family, she was put on a limited allowance. Today, self-indulgent ladies of leisure are hardly rare, but in former times even aristocratic gentlemen were accustomed to refrain from luxury. Members of fine old families, however affluent, lived in modest fashion, disliking to be classed with the newly rich or thought ostentatious. Shunkin's parents were generous with her out of natural sympathy, since her blindness cut her off from so many pleasures; but once her brother became responsible there was family criticism of her conduct, and a sum was fixed as the maximum for her monthly allowance. Demands for greater amounts were simply turned down. No doubt this helps to account for Shunkin's miserliness.

Yet her allowance must have been large enough to live on without eking it out by teaching. She could afford to be arrogant toward her pupils. In fact, few came to study under her, and she led a lonely, secluded life, which is why she had so much time to devote to her birds. But Shunkin was not merely being conceited when she regarded herself as one of the leading musicians in Osaka, both on the samisen and on the koto. No one could fairly deny that. Even those who detested her arrogance were secretly envious of her skill, or stood in awe of it. One of my friends is an old musician who, in his youth, often heard her perform on the samisen. Although his own specialty was theatrical music, rather than the lyrical kind that Shunkin played, he told me there was no one alive who could rival her subtlety of tone. And he said that Dambei, who once heard her, lamented that she was not a man, saying: "What a master she would have been on the large samisen!" Did Dambei regret that Shunkin, with all her talent, lacked the strength to play the large theatrical samisen, the noblest of these instruments? Was he, rather, expressing admiration for the masculine vigor of her playing? According to my friend, her tone had the brilliant clarity of a man's. "But it wasn't just a beautiful tone," he said. "It was so expressive that sometimes she made you want to cry." She does seem to have been a remarkable performer.

If Shunkin had been a little more tactful and modest in professional circles she would probably have become a great success. But having been brought up in luxury, ignorant of the problems of earning a living, she behaved so selfishly that other musicians shunned her; her very talent only made more enemies. It was indeed a misfortune, though one largely brought on by herself, that she spent her whole life in obscurity.

And so Shunkin's pupils were those who were already won over by her artistry, who were obsessed with the idea that she was the only teacher for them, and who came prepared to submit to the most rigorous discipline —even to verbal or physical abuse—for the privilege of studying under her. At that, few put up with it for long. Usually they found that her methods were more than they could bear; the dilettantes among them would quit within a month.

I suppose that Shunkin's awareness of being a master artist had something to do with the malicious, if not sadistic, punishment she administered. That is to say, because she was known for her cruelty she must have felt that the more she mistreated her pupils, the more she proved her high standing as an artist. Gradually becoming more and more vain, she ended by losing all self-control.

Shigizawa Teru told me that Shunkin had only a small number of pupils. "Some of them came just because of her good looks," she said. "That's what drew most of the ones who didn't intend to make a career of it."

Beautiful, unmarried, and the daughter of a wealthy family—it is not surprising that she attracted men who were scarcely motivated by a love of music. They say that her severity was partly a means of driving off these pursuers. Ironically enough, her very cruelty seems to have had its attraction. I suspect that even among her serious pupils there were those who found the most intriguing part of their studies to be the strangely pleasurable sensation of being punished by the beautiful blind woman.

Now that I come to the second great calamity that befell Shunkin, I regret that, since the *Life* avoids giving a clear account of it, I cannot be sure why she was injured or who her attacker was. But it seems reasonable to think that she had made an enemy of one of her pupils, and that he retaliated by harming her.

One incident of possible relevance concerns a young man named Ritaro, the son of a well-to-do grain merchant of Tosabori. Ritaro had long prided himself on his musical ability, and had been taking lessons on the koto and the samisen from Shunkin for some time. Boastful of his father's fortune and accustomed to lord it over others wherever he went, he regarded his fellow pupils with contempt, treating them as if they were his father's shop clerks. Although Shunkin privately disliked him, he gave her such lavish presents that she did her best to be agreeable.

However, Ritaro began telling everyone that their

stern teacher had a weakness for him; and he showed particular scorn for Sasuke, refusing to accept his instruction in Shunkin's place. He became so bold and presumptuous that Shunkin found it hard to put up with him. Early one spring, just as matters were coming to a head, he invited her to a blossom-viewing party in Tengajaya, where his father had built a rustic cottage, set among lovely old plum trees in a quiet garden.

The whole affair had been arranged by young Ritaro, who was surrounded by a swarm of geisha and other entertainers. As usual, Shunkin was accompanied by Sasuke. That day Ritaro and his friends were so hospitable that Sasuke felt quite embarrassed. He was not much of a drinker: lately he had become accustomed to having a little *saké* at supper with Shunkin, but he was forbidden to touch a drop of it elsewhere without her express permission. Since getting drunk would make him unfit for his duties as her guide, he was only pretending to sip from his cup.

But Ritaro saw through his trick, and called out to Shunkin in a thick, insinuating voice: "Madam, Sasuke won't drink unless you say it's all right. But this is a party—let him have the day off! If he can't hold it, there are two or three other fellows who wouldn't mind being your guide!"

"I suppose a little won't hurt," said Shunkin politely, forcing a smile. "Only please don't make him drink too much."

When they heard this, Ritaro and the others cried: "Come on! She says it's all right!" and began pressing cups of wine on him from all sides. Still, Sasuke kept himself under control, and managed to empty most of them into a nearby vase.

It seems that all the attending gay-quarter jesters and geisha were astonished at the voluptuous charm of the samisen teacher of whom they had heard so much. They saw with their own eyes that rumor had not exaggerated her beauty, and they were full of praise for her. Perhaps some flattered her in order to curry favor with Ritaro, but there is no doubt of her fascination. At thirty-six, as she then was, Shunkin looked a full ten years younger; her complexion was extraordinarily fair, and a glimpse of her neck and shoulders gave the onlooker a sudden shiver of pleasure. As she sat there modestly, her exquisite hands resting in her lap, her head tilted slightly forward, the loveliness of Shunkin's blind face captivated everyone.

That afternoon while they were all out strolling in the garden Sasuke led Shunkin among the plum blossoms, guiding her slowly from tree to tree and stopping before each of them. "Here is another!" he would say, as he held her hand out to stroke the trunk. Like all blind people, Shunkin depended on her sense of touch to make sure that something was really there; it was also her way of enjoying the beauty of flowers and trees. But when one of the jesters saw her eagerly caressing the rough bark of an old plum tree with her delicate hands, he cried out in a queer, shrill voice: "Ooh, I envy that tree!" Then another jester ran up in front of Shunkin, threw himself into a grotesque pose, arms and legs aslant, and announced: "I'm a plum tree too!" Everyone burst out laughing.

All this was meant as a compliment, there was no intention of making fun of her. However, not being used to the boisterous pranks of the gay quarter, Shunkin was offended. Since she always wanted to be treated as if she were normal a joke of this sort annoyed her intensely.

Finally it began to get dark and they went inside to carry on with the party. "You must be tired, Sasuke," Ritaro told him. "I'll look after Shunkin for you. Your supper is ready in the other room—go in and have another drink too!"

Thinking it best to fortify himself with a good meal, Sasuke did as he was told and retired to the next room to have his own supper before the others. Though he asked for rice immediately, an old geisha stayed close at his side and insisted on pouring *saké* for him, one cup after another. Thus he spent more time at his meal than he had expected, but even after finishing it he had to wait to be summoned. Meanwhile, something happened in the other room: perhaps Shunkin got up to go to the lavatory and asked for Sasuke, only to have Ritaro block her way and tell her that if that's what she wanted, he'd take her himself. And perhaps he was trying to lead her forcibly out into the corridor. In any case, Shunkin was heard to cry: "No! Please call Sasuke!" She had shaken herself free from Ritaro and was standing there cowering when Sasuke came hurrying to her. With one glance at her face, he understood the situation.

After that, Shunkin felt relieved to think that she

would be spared any further trouble with Ritaro. But apparently he could not accept such a blow to his reputation for being irresistible to women. He had the impudence to come for a lesson the very next day, as nonchalantly as ever. This led to a sudden change of attitude on Shunkin's part. If that's what he wants, I'll drum it into him, she thought; let's see if he can stand real discipline. From then on she was merciless.

Day after day, the bewildered Ritaro found himself working till the sweat ran and he had to gasp for breath. Having supposed himself to be an expert, he had thrived on flattery; but when he was sharply reprimanded for every slip, it became evident that his playing was riddled with errors. Now that Shunkin heaped abuse on him he began to lose heart for his lessons—which, in the first place, had been a mere pretext for seeking to fulfill a quite different aspiration. When she drove him even harder he deliberately played in a dull, listless manner. At last Shunkin cried: "You idiot!" and struck out at him with her plectrum, wounding him between his eyebrows. Ritaro gave a howl of pain, daubed at the blood trickling down from his forehead, and, as he left the room, muttered angrily: "You'll pay for this!" He never appeared again.

According to one opinion, the person who injured Shunkin was the father of a girl who was in training to become a geisha, and who put up with Shunkin's severity in order to benefit from the thoroughness of her teaching. But one day Shunkin struck her on the head with a plectrum, and the girl ran home crying. Because the wound left a visible scar, her father took the matter very seriously indeed. Furious with anger, he went to Shunkin to demand satisfaction. "You can talk all you want about discipline, but you have no right to torture people!" he told her roughly. "This child's face is her fortune, and now you've scarred her! You won't get away with that. What are you going to do about it?"

His strong language immediately aroused Shunkin's stubbornness. "People come to me because I'm strict," she retorted. "If you don't like it, why did you send her here?"

But the girl's father refused to let it go at that. "It's bad enough for a teacher to hit a pupil, but when she can't see what she's doing it's positively criminal! A blind person ought to behave like one!"

Because the man seemed on the point of violence, Sasuke intervened and, after a good deal of talking, persuaded him to go home. Meanwhile, Shunkin sat there in silence, pale and trembling; she never uttered a word of apology. Some say that this man took revenge by disfiguring her.

However, the girl's scar was probably only a tiny one on the forehead or behind the ear. To ruin Shunkin's looks for life on that account would have been incredibly vengeful, even for an agitated doting father. And Shunkin was unable to see her own face, so that if the aim had been to punish her alone, spoiling her beauty would hardly have seemed the best way to accomplish it.

I wonder if the aim of the attacker might not also

have been to cause grief to Sasuke, which would presumably make Shunkin suffer even more. If we follow this line of reasoning, perhaps our heaviest suspicion must fall on Ritaro after all. We have no way of telling how passionately he desired her, but young men are likely to be attracted to the ripe beauty of women older than themselves. No doubt the beautiful blind woman had a peculiar glamor for him, whetting an appetite jaded by long dissipation. Even if he had begun with a casual attempt to seduce her, the fact that he had not only been snubbed by her but slashed across his manly brow might well have made him seek a really vicious revenge.

Still, Shunkin had so many other enemies that it is hard to say who had the worst grudge against her, or why. We cannot safely conclude that Ritaro was the guilty one. Nor was it necessarily the usual affair of passion: perhaps money was at the root of it, since more than one pupil had been heartlessly rejected because of his poverty. Then there were said to be others who, though not so brazen about it as Ritaro, were jealous of Sasuke. The fact that Sasuke was a "guide" who occupied an equivocal position in Shunkin's household could not be concealed for long. All the pupils eventually found out what was going on, and those who had fallen in love with Shunkin secretly envied Sasuke's happiness—some of them even resented his devotion in serving her. If he had been her legal husband, or at least her accepted lover, they would have had no reason to object. But to all appearances he was merely her guide, her servant: he took care of her every need, even massaging and bathing her, like a faithful slave. To those who knew what went on in private between them, his humility must have seemed ridiculous. Some remarked sarcastically: "It might be a little taxing, but I wouldn't mind being *that* kind of a companion! There's nothing self-sacrificing about him." And so one of the other pupils may have hated Sasuke, and said to himself: "How do you suppose he'd take it if her pretty face turned hideous over night? I wonder if he'd still be the perfect servant, and go to all that trouble for her. That's something I'd like to see!" Quite possibly the real motive was a desire to strike at Sasuke.

Indeed, there are so many theories about the crime that it is hard to choose among them. Some think the attacker was not one of Shunkin's pupils at all, but one of her professional rivals. Although there is no particular evidence for such a view, it may yet be the most perceptive. Shunkin's customary arrogance and high regard for her own ability—a regard which the more discriminating members of the public tended to accept —may have wounded the self-esteem of other artists, even seemed to menace their position. Among blind musicians, some of the men held official rank as "Master," a title which was still granted by the Court in those days and which permitted them to enjoy special privileges as well as public acclaim far beyond that of ordinary performers. When the rumor began to circulate that these favored artists were less gifted than Shunkin, they must have felt deeply resentful, not least because of their own blindness. Perhaps they tried to think of some devious way to finish her career once and for all. Jealous artists have been known to poison their rivals with mercury; but since Shunkin was a singer as well as an instrumentalist, and extremely proud of her good looks, an enemy may have decided to disfigure her so that she would never dare perform in public again. If her enemy was another woman teacher, she must have hated the very sight of the vain, lovely Shunkin, and taken all the more pleasure in destroying her beauty.

When we consider how many people had reasons for hating Shunkin, we can see that sooner or later someone was sure to injure her. Without realizing it, she had sown the seeds of her own misfortune.

It happened around three o'clock one morning at the end of April, six weeks after the plum-viewing party at Tengajaya:

Startled awake by Shunkin's moaning, Sasuke ran in from the next room and hastily lighted a lamp. Apparently someone had forced open the shutters and entered her bedroom, but, hearing Sasuke, fled without taking anything. By the time Sasuke arrived it was already too late to catch a glimpse of him.

Meanwhile, the frightened thief had snatched up a nearby kettle and dashed it at Shunkin's head, splashing her lovely snow-white cheek with a few drops of scalding water. Regrettably, they left a scar. Of course it was only a tiny flaw; her face was actually as beautiful as ever. But from then on Shunkin was acutely embarrassed by that trifling scar, and always concealed it by wearing a silken hood. She would spend the whole day shut up in her room, never venturing out into company, so that even pupils and close relatives hardly saw her face. As a result, there were all sorts of rumors and speculation about it.

That is how the incident is described in the *Life of Shunkin*, which goes on to say:

After all, it was only an insignificant blemish, but because of her extreme concern for her appearance she disliked having it seen. Perhaps, with the morbid sensitivity of the blind, she thought of it as a cause for shame.

And then:

By some strange turn of fate, within a few weeks Sasuke began to suffer from cataracts, and soon lost his sight altogether. At a time when his eyes were beginning to fail and everything around seemed to be getting hazy, he groped his way to Shunkin, and declared exultantly: "Madam, I am going blind too! Now I shall never see your scar as long as I live—how lucky that my blindness comes just at this time! It must be the will of Heaven!"

For a long while afterward Shunkin seemed depressed.

Much as one may sympathize with Sasuke's wish to conceal the truth, there is no denying that this account has been deliberately falsified. I cannot believe that he merely happened to develop cataracts, or that Shunkin—however great her concern for her appearance or her morbid sensitivity—would hide her face and shrink from the sight of others because of a minor scar. The fact is that her beautiful face had suffered a tragic change.

According to Shigizawa Teru (as well as several other sources), the intruder went immediately to the kitchen, made a fire, and boiled a kettleful of water, which he then took into Shunkin's bedroom and with deliberate care poured full in her face. That was what he had come to do—he was no ordinary thief, nor did he act out of desperation. The wound was a severe one: Shunkin lost consciousness until the next morning, and it took more than two months for the skin to heal. That explains why there were so many rumors about a hideous change in her looks; perhaps there is even some truth to the report that her hair fell out, leaving one side of her head completely bald. Sasuke's own blindness may have kept him from seeing Shunkin in her disfigurement; but how could it be true that "even pupils and close relatives hardly saw her face"? Surely someone like Shigizawa Teru must have seen it. But even Teru, out of respect for Sasuke's feelings, never revealed the secret of Shunkin's looks. Once I asked her point-blank, but she only said: "Sasuke always thought of her as a very beautiful lady, so that's the way I thought of her too."

It was more than ten years after Shunkin's death when Sasuke finally told a few people closest to him a more detailed—and more trustworthy—story of how he lost his sight.

On the night that Shunkin was attacked he was sleeping in the little room next to her bedroom, as usual. Awakened by a noise, he noticed that the night light had gone out. Then he heard a groan coming from her pitch-dark room. Startled, he jumped up, relit the lamp, and hurried with it over to Shunkin's bed, which was behind a folding screen. The room itself seemed undisturbed, as he glanced around it in the weak lamplight reflected from the gold ground of the screen. The only thing out of place was a teakettle near her pillow. Shunkin was lying on her back, under the covers, but for some reason she was moaning. At first Sasuke thought she was having a nightmare, and tried to rouse her by asking what was wrong. Just as he was about to shake her, he cried out in sudden horror and clapped his hands over his eyes.

"Sasuke, Sasuke!" Shunkin gasped. "I'm hideous! Don't look at me!" Writhing in pain, she frantically tried to cover her face with her hands.

"Please don't worry," he said, moving the lamp away. "I won't look at you—my eyes are shut." When she heard this Shunkin seemed to relax and slip into unconsciousness.

But she kept on murmuring deliriously: "Don't let anyone see my face! . . . Don't tell anyone. . . ."

And Sasuke would try to comfort her. "You mustn't worry. As soon as the blistering heals you'll look the same as ever."

But after she regained consciousness, she became more and more vehement. "How can I be the same after such an awful burn?" she would exclaim. "Stop trying to console me—just don't look at my face!" She refused to let anyone but the doctor see her condition: when the dressing had to be changed, she allowed no one else— not even Sasuke—to stay in the room.

Thus, it seems that although Sasuke did have a glimpse of her red, scalded face when he rushed to her bedside that night, what he saw was so appalling that he instantly shut his eyes, leaving in his mind nothing more than a hazy memory of some weird hallucination there in the flickering lamplight. After that her whole face was bandaged, except for her mouth and nostrils. I suppose that Sasuke was as afraid of seeing her as Shunkin was of being seen. Whenever he approached her bed he closed his eyes or looked away, so determined was he to remain unaware of her changed appearance.

But one day, when Shunkin's convalescence was well along and the wound almost healed, she suddenly turned to him as he was sitting alone at her bedside. "Sasuke," she asked, in a voice charged with feeling, "did you see my face?"

"No, of course not!" he replied quickly. "I wouldn't disobey you by looking, when you told me not to."

But even the strong-willed Shunkin seemed to have lost all her spirit. "It won't be long till the bandages have to be taken off," she said. "The doctor won't come any more either. So I'll have to let *you* see this face of mine, even if you're the only one who does." She began to cry—something almost unheard-of for her—and dabbed at the tears through her bandages.

Sasuke was speechless with grief, and the two wept together. At last he spoke up in a firm voice, as if he had come to a decision. "Please don't worry," he told her. "It'll be all right—I'll make sure that I never see your face."

A few days later Shunkin was able to leave her bed: the time had come to remove the bandages. Early that morning Sasuke stealthily took a mirror and a sewing needle from the maids' room, went back to his bed, and there, sitting bolt upright and peering into the mirror, tried to thrust the needle into the pupil of his left eye. He had no real knowledge that pricking his eyes with a needle would make him blind, but he thought that this might be the easiest and least painful method. Difficult as it was to aim such a thrust into the pupil, the white of the eye was too tough to be readily pierced; and after a few attempts he succeeded in puncturing the soft pupil to a depth of about a quarter of an inch. Instantly the whole surface of the eyeball clouded, and he realized that he was losing his sight. There was neither bleeding nor fever; he scarcely felt any pain. No doubt he had ruptured the crystalline lens tissue, causing a traumatic cataract. Next, Sasuke used the same method on his right eye—within a few moments he had destroyed both eyes. To be sure, he could still see dim outlines for about a week afterward. Then he was totally blind.

Later that morning, when Shunkin was up, he groped his way to her room. Bowing humbly before her, he said: "I have gone blind. I shall never see your face again as long as I live."

All Shunkin replied was: "Really, Sasuke?" She sat there a long while, sunk in thought. Never before or since did Sasuke experience such happiness as during those moments of silence.

Centuries ago, it is said, the warrior Kagekiyo was so touched by the magnanimity of his arch-enemy Yoritomo that he gave up his desire for revenge, swore never to look on Yoritomo again, and gouged out his own eyes. Though its motive was different, Sasuke's deed was equally heroic. But was that what Shunkin wanted of him? Had her tearful appeal a few days before meant: "Now that I've suffered this calamity, I want you to be blind too"? That is hard to say; yet the words "Really, Sasuke?" had seemed to him to have a quaver of joy.

As they sat facing each other in silence, Sasuke began to feel the quickening of that sixth sense which only the blind possess, and he could tell that there was nothing but the deepest gratitude in Shunkin's heart. Always before, even while they were making love, they had been separated by the gulf between teacher and pupil. But now Sasuke felt that they were truly united, locked in a tight embrace. Youthful memories of the dark world of the closet where he used to practice came flooding into his mind, but the darkness in which he now found himself seemed completely different. Most blind people can sense the direction from which light is coming; they live in a faintly luminous world, not one of unrelieved blackness. Now Sasuke knew that he had found an inner vision in place of the vision he had lost. Ah, he thought, this is the world my teacher lives in— at last I have reached it! He could no longer clearly distinguish the objects around him, or the way Shunkin herself looked; all he could detect was the pale, blurred image of her bandage-swathed face. But he had no thought of the bandages. It was Shunkin's exquisite white face—as it had looked until only two months ago —that hovered before him in a circle of dim light, like the radiant halo of the Buddha.

"Did it hurt much, Sasuke?" she asked him.

"No," he said, turning his blinded eyes toward the pale, glowing disk that was Shunkin's face. "It was nothing, compared with what you have suffered. I couldn't forgive myself for being asleep when that evil person stole in. It's my duty to stay in the next room every night so that I can protect you—and yet I went unharmed, even though it was my fault that you suffered such pain. I felt I ought to be punished. Day and night I prayed to the spirits of my ancestors, begging for some affliction, since there was no other way for me to atone for my negligence. When I woke up this morning the gods had taken pity on me and I was going blind. Dear Madam! I shall never see how you have changed! All I can see now is the image of your beautiful face—that lovely image that has haunted me for the past thirty years. Please let me go on serving you as I always have. Since I'm not used to blindness I'm afraid I won't be able to get around very well, and I'll be unsteady when I wait on you; but still I want to be the one who cares for all your needs."

"I admire your courage," Shunkin replied. "You have made me very happy. I don't know who hated me enough to do this to me, but I must confess that I couldn't stand to have you, of all people, see me as I am now. I am grateful to you for realizing it."

"Ah," Sasuke cried, "blindness is a small price for the joy of hearing you say that! I don't know who could have been so cruel to us, and caused us so much grief; but if he meant to attack me by disfiguring you his wicked scheme has failed. Now that I'm blind, it's as if nothing happened to you. Actually, it's anything but a misfortune for me—I've never had such a stroke of good luck. My heart leaps when I think how I've triumphed over that coward!"

"Sasuke!"

And the blind lovers embraced, weeping.

Shigizawa Teru is the only person who has an intimate knowledge of their life together after they turned their misfortune into a blessing. This year she is seventy, and it was in 1874, when she was only eleven, that she went to live at Shunkin's house as a servant and pupil. Besides studying the samisen under Sasuke, Teru helped the blind couple in many ways, both as a guide and as a kind of link between them. No doubt they needed some third person to assist them in this way, since one was recently blind and the other, though blind since childhood, was a lady accustomed to luxury, who never lifted her hand to the slightest task. They had decided to hire a little girl, with whom they would feel at ease; and from the time she came to them, Teru's honesty and trustworthiness won their confidence completely. She remained in their service for many years. After Shunkin's death Sasuke had her stay on with him until 1890, the year in which he received official rank as a master.

When Teru first came to Shunkin's house in 1874 Shunkin was already forty-five, on the verge of old age. Nine years had passed since her disfigurement. Teru was told that, for certain reasons, her mistress never showed her face to others, and that she must never try to see it. Shunkin's entire head, except for a little of her nose, was covered by a bluish-gray crepe silk hood.

Sasuke was forty when he pierced his eyes with the needle. To become blind in middle age must have been difficult enough, and yet he was touchingly solicitous in caring for Shunkin—anticipating her wishes and sparing her every possible inconvenience. Shunkin disliked having anyone else serve her. "Ordinary people are quite unable to take care of me," she would say. "Sasuke does it best, since he's been with me for years." She still depended on him to dress, bathe, and massage her, and to escort her to the lavatory.

As a result, Teru's duties were mainly on behalf of Sasuke; she seldom had occasion to come into physical contact with her mistress. Only at mealtime were her services indispensable. For the rest, she would merely fetch and carry things for Shunkin, or be of indirect use by helping Sasuke. When Shunkin took a bath Teru went with her and Sasuke as far as the bathroom door, then left them alone until she heard Sasuke clap his hands to summon her, by which time Shunkin would already be out of the tub, and wearing her light bath-gown and hood. Meanwhile everything had been done by Sasuke. How would he have gone about it? He must have touched her as sensitively as Shunkin had caressed the trunks of the old plum trees—certainly it was no easy task for him. People wondered how he could put up with all the trouble she caused him, how the two could get along so well. But Sasuke and Shunkin seemed to enjoy the very difficulties, expressing their unspoken love in this way. I suppose we cannot imagine how much pleasure the two sightless lovers took in the world re-vealed to them by their sense of touch. Perhaps it is no wonder that Sasuke served Shunkin with such devotion, that she delighted in having him serve her, and that they never tired of each other's company.

In addition, Sasuke taught a great many pupils during the time he could be away from Shunkin, who spent the whole day shut up in her room. She gave him the pro-fessional name of Kindai, and turned over all instruction to him: his new name was added (in smaller characters) beside her own on the sign in front of the house. Sasuke's loyalty and gentleness had long since earned him the sympathy of the neighborhood, and more pupils came to him than had ever come to Shunkin. While Sasuke was teaching, Shunkin would stay in her inner room, listening to her nightingales. But whenever she needed his help, even if he was in the midst of a lesson, she would call out: "Sasuke!" and he would stop at once and hurry to her side. For that reason he was anxious to be near her, and insisted on doing all his teaching at home.

Here I should mention that around this time the fortunes of the Mozuya establishment in Dosho-machi were declining, and Shunkin's monthly allowance often failed to arrive. Except for this, would Sasuke have chosen to teach? Whenever he had a moment free he went to her, and even while busy teaching he must have felt impatient to be at her side. Perhaps Shunkin herself felt lost without him.

Now that Sasuke had taken over all the teaching and was in effect supporting the household, why did he not become Shunkin's legal husband? Was her pride still the obstacle? According to Teru, Sasuke told her that Shunkin had become quite dejected, and that it grieved him— he could not bear to think of her as pitiable, someone to feel sorry for. Apparently the blind Sasuke had given himself up to his imperishable ideal. To him, there was only the world of his old memories. If Shunkin had actually changed in character because of her misfortune she would no longer have been Shunkin. He wanted to think of her as the proud, haughty girl of the past; otherwise, the beautiful Shunkin of his imagination would have been destroyed. And so it seems that it was he who had the stronger reason for not wishing to marry.

Because Sasuke used the real Shunkin to call to mind the Shunkin of his memories, he was careful to observe the proper etiquette between servant and mistress. Indeed, he humbled himself more than ever, serving her with the utmost devotion so that she might soon forget her misery and regain her old self-confidence. Contented with the same bare pittance, with the same coarse food and clothing, he gave all he earned to Shunkin. In addition, among many other economies, he reduced the number of servants who helped him. Yet he saw to it that nothing was lacking for Shunkin's comfort, though he now had to work twice as hard as before his blindness.

Teru says that some of his pupils felt sorry for him because he looked so shabby, and hinted that he ought to be a little more concerned about his appearance. But Sasuke paid no attention. Also, he insisted that they go on calling him Sasuke, rather than "Master"; but this embarrassed them so much that they tried not to address him at all. Teru, however, with her numerous household duties, could not be so discreet. She always called Sasuke by his name, and called Shunkin "Mistress."

It was because of her special relation to them that Sasuke, after Shunkin's death, began to confide in Teru. Occasionally he reminisced about Shunkin with her. Later, when his talent was officially recognized and everyone called him "Master," he still wanted Teru to use his ordinary name. He would not allow her to be more formal with him.

Once he said to her: "I suppose people consider blindness a terrible misfortune, but I've never felt that way. On the contrary, it made this world into a paradise, where my mistress and I were alone together. When you lose your sight you become aware of all sorts of things you never noticed before. It was only after I went blind that I realized how beautiful she was. At last I could fully appreciate the softness of her body, the fine texture of her skin, her exquisite voice. . . . Why had I never before been so moved by her loveliness? But most of all I was amazed by the sudden revelation of her artistry on the samisen. I'd always said she was a genius, far above my own modest level, but the true measure of her superiority astonished me. How stupid of me not to have realized it earlier, I thought. Even if the gods had offered to give me back my sight, I believe I would have refused. It was because both of us were blind that we experienced a happiness ordinary people never know."

Of course one hesitates to take Sasuke too literally. But as far as Shunkin's music is concerned, might not her second calamity have been a turning point in her development? However blessed with talent, she could scarcely have attained the ultimate mastery of her art without tasting the bitterness of life. Shunkin had always been coddled. Though severe in her demands on others, she herself had never known hardship or humiliation. There had been no one to humble her. But then Heaven had subjected her to a cruel ordeal, endangering her life and smashing her stubborn pride.

I am inclined to think that the destruction of her beauty had its compensations for Shunkin in various ways. Both in love and in art she must have discovered undreamed-of ecstasies. Teru says that Shunkin used to play the samisen for hours on end, while Sasuke sat beside her, his head bowed, listening in rapture. Often the pupils marveled at the subtle tones that filtered to their ears from the inner room, whispering among themselves that this must be no ordinary instrument.

In those days Shunkin not only played the samisen but spent a great deal of time composing for it. Even at night she would quietly pick out new melodies with her finger-tips. Teru remembers two of her songs: "A Nightingale in Spring" and "Snowflakes." The other day I had her play them for me. They were full of originality, and left no doubt of Shunkin's talent as a composer.

Shunkin fell ill early in June of 1886. A few days before, she and Sasuke had gone out to the garden and opened the cage of her prized lark, letting it soar up into the sky. While Teru watched, the blind couple stood hand in hand, their faces lifted toward the lark's song that came down to them from far above. Still singing vigorously, the lark soared higher and higher until it was lost in the clouds. It was out of sight for such a long time that Sasuke and Shunkin began to worry. They waited more than an hour, but the lark never returned.

From that day Shunkin was despondent. Soon she contracted beriberi, and by autumn her condition was serious. She died of a heart attack on the fourteenth of October.

Besides her lark, Shunkin had been keeping a nightin-gale which she called Tenko the Third. For years after-ward, Sasuke wept when he heard Tenko sing. Often he burned incense before Shunkin's memorial tablet, and took up his koto or samisen to play "A Nightingale in Spring."

The song begins with the phrase: "A singing nightin-gale alights in the hills." Probably it is Shunkin's finest work, one she put herself into heart and soul. Though not long, it has some very complicated instrumental passages—Shunkin conceived the idea for it while she was listening to Tenko. The melodies of these passages suggest all the poetic associations of the bird's song, as it flies from valley to valley, from branch to branch, tempting one out to enjoy the varied charms of spring. There is the first faint warmth, when the snow deep in the hills—"the frozen tears of nightingales"—begins to melt, and then the rippling of swollen mountain streams, the soughing of pines in the east wind, mists over hill and field, the fragrance of the plum blossom, clouds of cherry trees in bloom. . . . Whenever Shunkin played it Tenko sang out joyously, straining its voice to rival the beauty of her samisen.

Perhaps the song made Tenko yearn for the sunlight and freedom of its native valley. But what memories did it evoke for Sasuke while he played it? For years he had known his ideal Shunkin through sound and touch—did he now fill the void in his life with music? As long as we remember them, we can see the dead in dreams; but for Sasuke, who saw his lover only in dreams even while she was still alive, it may have been hard to realize when the separation came.

Two boys and a girl were born to Sasuke and Shun-kin, besides the child mentioned earlier. The girl died soon after her birth, and both of the boys were adopted in infancy by a farmer in Kawachi. Even after Shunkin's death Sasuke seemed to feel no attachment to them, and made no effort to get them back; nor did his sons want to return to their blind father.

Thus Sasuke spent his later years without wife or children, and died, attended only by his pupils, on the fourteenth of October (the anniversary of Shunkin's death) in 1907, at the advanced age of eighty-two. I suppose that during the two decades in which he lived alone he created a Shunkin quite remote from the actual woman, yet more and more vivid in his mind.

It seems that when the priest Gazan of the Tenryu Temple heard the story of Sasuke's self-immolation, he praised him for the Zen spirit with which he changed his whole life in an instant, turning the ugly into the beautiful, and said that it was very nearly the act of a saint. I wonder how many of us would agree with him.

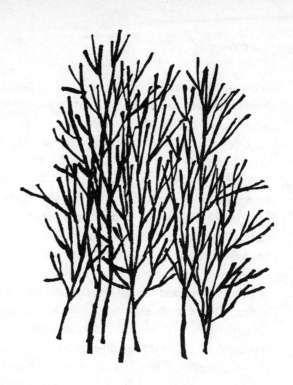

# TERROR

It was early last June while I was in Kyoto that the illness menaced me. Of course I had had attacks in Tokyo, but, what with giving up alcohol, having cold baths and rubdowns, and consuming pills, I seemed to have recovered. Then after coming to Kyoto I began leading an irregular life once more, spending most of my nights in bars and geisha houses, and I found myself slipping into a relapse.

According to a friend, this ailment of mine—this tormenting, idiotic ailment that I hate to think of even now

—is probably a type of neurosis called *Eisenbahnkrank-heit* (railroad phobia). My seizures are nothing like the nausea and vertigo of motion sickness: I suffer the agony of pure terror. The moment I board a train, the moment the whistle shrills and the wheels begin to turn and the cars lurch forward—at that moment the pulse in all my arteries speeds up as if stimulated by strong drink, and blood mounts to the top of my head. A cold sweat stands out on my whole body, my arms and legs begin to shake as if from the ague. I feel that unless I am given emergency treatment all my blood—every drop of it—will rush into that small hard round vessel above my neck, till the cranium itself, like a toy balloon blown up beyond its capacity, will have to explode. And yet the train, with its utter indifference and its tremendous energy, hurtles down the track at full speed. "What's the life of one human being?" it seems to ask. Belching sooty smoke like a volcano and roaring along in its bold, heartless way, it dashes forward relentlessly into jet-black tunnels, over long, rickety steel bridges, across rivers, through meadows, around forests. The passengers, too, seem excessively casual as they read, smoke, steal a nap, or even gaze out of the window at the dizzyingly unreeling scene.

"Help! I'm dying!" I scream within myself, turning pale and gasping as if in a fatal paroxysm. I run into the lavatory and douse my head with cold water, or grip the window sill and stamp my feet, thrashing around in frantic desperation.

Intent on bursting out of the train in one way or another, I batter fiercely at the paneling in my compartment, oblivious of my bleeding fists, and rage like a criminal thrown into a cell. At the height of my fit I can hardly keep from opening a door and leaping from the train, or reaching blindly for the emergency cord. Yet somehow I manage to contain myself until the next stop, stumble out, a piteous, wretched sight to behold, and make my way laboriously from the platform to the ticket gate. As soon as I leave the station my pulse calms down with absurd promptness and the shadows of anxiety fall away one by one.

This phobia of mine is not limited to trains. It can come over me in streetcars, automobiles, theaters—anywhere that movement and color and the noise and bustle of crowds seem to threaten my morbidly excitable nerves. I am subject to an attack at any place and at any time. However, in streetcars and theaters, since I can easily escape, I have never been brought so close to the brink of madness.

And so it was in early June, when I rode a swaying Kyoto streetcar, that I knew the illness still held me in its grip. In the meantime I had scrupulously avoided trains and given up all thought of returning to Tokyo until I felt sure that my phobia would not recur. I wanted to take my conscription examination, which had to be done before the summer was over, somewhere near Kyoto, at a place I could get to without going by train.

Unfortunately, I found that I was too late for any of the examination centers in the Kyoto area; but thanks to a friend of mine in Osaka it was arranged for me to go to one in a fishing village on the Osaka-Kobe car line, provided that I transferred my legal residence there two or three days in advance. The examinations in that village were scheduled for the middle of June.

I was delighted that I could get there by electric car— without even boarding a train, let alone having to go all the way home to Tokyo. And around noon on the twelfth, with my official seal and a copy of our family register (forwarded to me from Tokyo) in my pocket, I set out for the Gojo Street station of the Osaka–Kobe line.

The midsummer-like sunshine glittered off the dry, dusty Kyoto streets; the clear sky looked poisonously sleek, a smooth expanse of dense indigo blue. I was wearing a silk gauze cloak over a plain unlined kimono, and on the way to the station by ricksha I could feel the sweat ooze like sticky drops of blood from the longish hair at my temples and trickle down my cheeks to soak into my collar. Looking off toward Mount Atago from Gojo Bridge, I saw heat waves billowing in the foothills as if fanned up from the bowels of a blast furnace. The distant fields and woods were obscured by a steamy haze; while in the foreground the tiled roofs and checkered stone walls and the waters of the Kamo River were dyed in such vivid hues, as vivid as fresh paint, that it hurt my eyes to look at them. When I started to get down from the ricksha at the station my kimono skirts clung to my perspiration-drenched legs, binding them so tightly I nearly fell.

I'll be all right if it's just an electric car—that was what

I had told myself, trying to build up a little confidence, but already my nerves were strained by this oppressive heat. After buying a ticket to Osaka I decided to rest until my nerves were calmer, and sagged down on a bench, where I sat staring vacantly at the street like a beggar.

Car after car of the Osaka-Kobe line—built more solidly than city streetcars, as dark and massive as cages for wild beasts—came up, hooted its whistle, and spewed forth one crowd of passengers in exchange for another, which it immediately swallowed, and retreated toward Osaka. A car arrived every few minutes. Summoning all my courage, I stood up and went as far as the ticket gate —but then my heart beat wildly and my legs refused to carry me any further. I seemed to have been paralyzed by some fearful spell. I tottered back to the bench.

"Ricksha, sir?"

"No, I'm waiting for someone," I told the man. "I'm going to Osaka." But after getting rid of him I stayed where I was. "I'm going to Osaka," I had replied, but somehow it rang in my ears as "I'm going to die." How stunned that ricksha man would have been if I had rolled my eyes and collapsed on the spot—as abruptly as Svidrigailoff did in *Crime and Punishment* ("If anyone should ask you, say I've gone to America!") when he clapped a pistol to his forehead and shot himself!

When I looked at my watch I saw that it was about one o'clock. The village office probably closed at three or four, and I had to register by the end of the day to be eligible for the examination. Otherwise, the kind efforts of my friend would be wasted. On a sudden inspiration, I bought a pocket flask of whiskey from a nearby liquor store. Then I sat down on the bench again, leaned back, and began emptying the flask in little gulps.

According to past experience the whiskey would deaden my nerves long enough to let me escape the worst of the terror. I had an almost superstitious faith in it. I thought that if I drank myself into a stupor before boarding the car I might be able to reach Osaka safely.

Numbness slowly seeped through my heavy body. As I sat there patiently, I was conscious of an insane drunkenness splendidly rotting away my mind and blunting all my senses. Soon I was staring dull-eyed and languid at the bright, noisy thoroughfare, watching the flux of swirling lights and shadows.

Passers-by at the foot of Gojo Bridge were flushed pink and beaded with sweat, like melting jelly-sculpture. Even beautiful young girls draped in filmy summer garments suffered visibly from the unrelenting heat, their flesh grossly swollen. Perspiration . . . the perspiration of huge throngs of people seemed to exude ceaselessly into the sultry atmosphere, hovering over everything, stickily clinging to walls and surfaces everywhere. It reminded me of a line of decadent verse: "Over the city hangs a mist of sweat. . . ."

Like a wrinkling movie screen, the street seemed to waver back and forth, now warped, now caving in, blurring, doubled. . . . The knowledge that I was drunk beyond control was the only thing that emboldened me, that gave me courage.

Finally I made up my mind to board the next car, and took the precaution of buying another bottle of whiskey. Also, to be ready to cool my head if by any chance I should feel an attack coming on, I bought some cracked ice and wrapped it in my handkerchief.

Thus armed, I let myself be squeezed and shoved toward the gate by the milling crowd, had my ticket punched, and was just reaching the platform when I found myself once again under the spell. In the presence of that furiously snorting and hooting car, so impatient to go roaring off, my nerves were shattered of their protective glaze of alcohol, and my suddenly clear head jerked up and began to quake and tremble. I was seized by an overpowering terror, as if my mind would crack, as if I might be plunged into a black coma, or into the limbo of madness. Instinctively I fled back to the gate.

"I'm sorry," I blurted out to the clerk. "I just had my ticket punched, but I have to wait for a friend, so I'll take the next car." Pressing the ice pack to my forehead, I battled my way through the opposing current of people and, completely unnerved, bolted out of the station as if pursued by some evil spirit. Sinking down limply on a bench, I finally managed to begin breathing easily again. I felt as if someone were laughing scornfully at me behind my back.

"It shouldn't have turned out like this," I told myself. "I thought I was drunk enough to get away with it—what the devil went wrong today? Are my nerves so raw that even whiskey can't deaden them?"

At last it was two o'clock. If I dawdle any longer I

may be too late, I thought. And if I let this chance slip
I'll soon have to go back to Tokyo. . . . But suppose I
write a letter explaining my trouble to the authorities:
"Since a train trip will either kill me or drive me mad, I
cannot return to Tokyo in time for the examination."
Perhaps they will reply: "Even if it kills you or drives
you mad, do not fail to be here in time for the examination." That would make me feel like forcing myself to
take the train, and going back to Tokyo a raving maniac.
. . . I'd want to charge in on them the day of the examination and make a scene. "You see?" I'd tell them between sobs. "You're so unreasonable I've lost my mind!
It's a fact, I'm really out of my mind!" What would the
army doctor say then, I wonder? Perhaps he'd compliment me coolly. "That's all right. You did well to come
back. You did well to come back even if it meant losing
your mind. I admire your sense of duty."

Still brimming over with whiskey, I let my thoughts
drift from one idiotic notion to another as I sat there
laughing to myself, getting angry, raging, or feeling
disgusted.

After considering the situation seriously, I decided I
had only three choices: to die, to go mad, or to stay
away from Tokyo. If I didn't want to die or go mad I
had to conquer my phobia and leave for Osaka immediately.

But suppose I lost consciousness in the car. . . .

Sighing helplessly, I glowered at an approaching car
and got up from the bench. Maybe I should rush off
to forget my troubles in a geisha house—or should I

stick it out here a little longer and wait till I calm down? The sun will set, gradually night will deepen. If I wait here dumbly until the last car pulls out and then go back to my apartment with nothing accomplished, perhaps I will resign myself to my fate—and feel a certain relief.

"Well there, T. Where are you off to?"

It was my friend K. He was wearing a cool-looking summer kimono, with a Panama hat tilted jauntily on the back of his head, shading his clean-cut features and handsome crop of hair.

Startled, as if some crime of mine had been discovered, I mumbled: "Just to Osaka . . ." and grinned stupidly.

"Oh, that army physical you mentioned the other day." K. nodded understandingly. "I'm going as far as Fushimi myself. We can leave together."

"Well—"

"I want you to meet a friend of mine." K. promptly introduced his companion, who was a doctor: a fair-complexioned, slightly rotund man in his early thirties, with a charming little neatly trimmed mustache.

"Shall we be on our way? Please go ahead."

"Yes, thank you," I responded, still hesitating. But I let myself be urged toward that ferocious car.

"Please, please, after you," K. insisted, almost pushing me aboard.

"Well, then." Resolutely I closed my eyes and climbed briskly into the car. No sooner was I inside than I clutched a strap with one hand, lifted my whiskey bottle to my mouth with the other, and took a stiff drink.

Standing and hanging on to a strap gave me the feeling that I still had some control over my fate.

"Quite a tippler, aren't you?" said the doctor.

"No, it's just that I hate trains. I have to get drunk or I can't ride them." It struck me that my explanation might sound a bit illogical, especially to a doctor.

With a last hoot from the whistle, the electric car started to move.

"Am I going to die now?" a voice inside me whispered. This must have been how it felt to be waiting for the guillotine.

"What do you think, Doctor? Do you think he'll pass the physical?"

"Let's see. Oh, you'll pass all right. A fine husky fellow like you."

Already the Kyoto streets were behind us: speeding by the windows were the fresh young leaves of surburban trees and shrubs, the highway, the low hills outside the city. It was then that a tiny bud of confidence began to unfold within me. Perhaps I would reach Osaka safely after all.

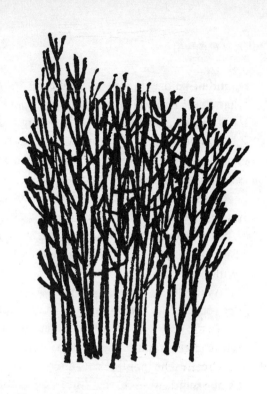

# THE BRIDGE OF DREAMS

*On reading the last chapter of* The Tale of Genji:

> *Today when the summer thrush*
> *Came to sing at Heron's Nest*
> *I crossed the Bridge of Dreams.*

This poem was written by my mother. But I have had two mothers—the second was a stepmother—and although I am inclined to think my real mother wrote it, I cannot be sure. The reasons for this uncertainty will become clear later: one of them is that both women went

by the name of Chinu. I remember hearing as a child that
Mother was named after the Bay of Chinu, since she was
born nearby at Hamadera, where her family, who were
Kyoto people, had a seaside villa. She is listed as Chinu
in the official city records. My second mother was also
called Chinu from the time she came to our house. She
never used her real name, Tsuneko, again. Even my
father's letters to her were invariably addressed to
"Chinu"; you can't tell by the name which of the two
he meant. And the "Bridge of Dreams" poem is simply
signed "Chinu."

Anyway, I know of no other poems by either woman.
I happen to be acquainted with this one because the
square slip of wave-patterned paper on which it is written
was reverently mounted in a hanging scroll to be kept
as a family heirloom. According to my old nurse, who
is now in her sixties, this kind of handmade paper was
decorated by the ancient "flowing ink" process (that
is, by dipping it in water and letting it absorb a swirl of
ink) and had to be ordered all the way from Echizen.
My mother must have gone to a great deal of trouble to
get it. For years I puzzled over the Konoé-style calligraphy of the poem, and the many unusual Chinese characters that even an adult—let alone a child—would find
hard to read. No one uses such characters nowadays.
I am reminded that we have a set of poem cards which
seem to have been written by one of my mothers in that
same esoteric style.

As for the quality of the hand, I am not really able
to judge. "They tell me nobody else wrote such a beauti-

ful Konoé style," my nurse used to say; and to my own amateur taste, for whatever that is worth, it appears to be the work of quite an accomplished calligrapher. But you would expect a woman to choose the slender, graceful style of the Kozei school. It seems odd that she preferred the thick, fleshy Konoé line, with its heavy sprinkling of Chinese characters. Probably that reveals something of her personality.

When it comes to poetry I am even less qualified to speak, but I hardly think this verse has any special merit. The line "I crossed the Bridge of Dreams" must mean "Today I read 'The Bridge of Dreams'—the last chapter of *The Tale of Genji*." Since that is only a short chapter, one that would take very little time to read, no doubt she is saying that today she at last finished the whole of *Genji*. "Heron's Nest" is the name by which our house has been known ever since my grandfather's time, a name given to it because night herons often alighted in its garden. Even now, herons occasionally come swooping down. Although I have seldom actually seen them, I have often heard their long, strident cry.

Heron's Nest is on a lane running eastward through the woods below the Shimogamo Shrine in Kyoto. When you go into the woods a little way, with the main building of the shrine on your left, you come to a narrow stone bridge over a stream: our gate is just beyond it. People who live in the neighborhood say that the stream flowing under this bridge is the subject of the famous poem by Chomei:

*The stony Shallow Stream—*
*So pure that even the moon*
*Seeks it out to dwell in it.*

But this seems doubtful. Yoshida Togo's gazetteer describes our "Shallow Stream" as "the brook that flows southward, east of the Shimogamo Shrine, into the Kamo River." Then it adds: "However, the 'Shallow Stream' mentioned in ancient topographical writings was the Kamo River itself, of which the brook in question is merely a tributary having its source in Matsugasaki." That is probably right, since Chomei is quoted elsewhere as saying that "Shallow Stream" is the old name of the Kamo River. The Kamo is also mentioned by that name in a poem by Jozan, which I will cite later, and the poet's prefatory note explains: "On refusing to cross the Kamo River into Kyoto." Of course our little stream is no longer especially pure and limpid, but until my childhood it was as clear as Chomei's poem might suggest. I remember that in mid-June, during the ceremony of purification, people bathed in its shallow waters.

The garden pond at Heron's Nest was linked to this stream by earthen drainage pipes to prevent it from overflowing. Once inside our main gate, with its two thick cedar pillars, you went down a flagstone walk to an inner gate. Dwarf bamboo were planted along both sides of the walk, and a pair of stone figures of Korean court officials (apparently of the Yi Dynasty) stood face to face on either side of it. The inner gate, which was always kept closed, had a roof thatched with cypress bark in an elegant rustic style. Each gate pillar bore a narrow bamboo tablet inscribed with one line of a Chinese couplet:

*Deep in the grove the many birds are gay.*
*Far from the dust the pine and bamboo are clean.*

But my father said he had no idea whose poem or whose calligraphy it was.

When you rang the doorbell (the button was beside one of the poem tablets) someone came out to open the gate for you. Then you went along under the shade of a large chestnut tree to the front door; in the main entrance hall, you saw mounted over the transom a piece of calligraphy from the brush of the scholar-poet Rai Sanyo:

*The hawk soars, the fish dives.*

What gave Heron's Nest its value was its landscape garden of almost an acre; the house itself was low and rambling but not particularly large. There were only some eight rooms, including the maids' room and the smaller entrance hall; but the kitchen was a spacious one, big enough for an average restaurant, and there was an artesian well next to the sink. Originally my grandfather lived on Muromachi Street near the Bukko Temple, and used Heron's Nest as his villa. Later, though, he sold the Muromachi Street house and made this his home, adding a sizable storehouse at its northwest corner. Going back and forth to the storehouse for a scroll or vase was quite inconvenient, since you had to go through the kitchen. Our household consisted of seven persons—my parents and me, my nurse Okane, and three maids—and we found the house comfortable enough. Father liked a quiet life. He put in an appearance at his bank now and then, but spent most of his time at home, seldom inviting guests. It seems that my grandfather enjoyed the tea ceremony and led an active social life: he had a fine old teahouse brought in by the side of the pond, and built another small place for entertaining, which he called the Silk-Tree Pavilion, in the southeast corner of the garden. But after his death his prized teahouse and pavilion were no longer used, except as a place to take an afternoon nap or read or practice calligraphy.

All of my father's love was concentrated on my mother. With this house, this garden, and this wife, he seemed perfectly happy. Sometimes he would have her play the koto for him, and he would listen intently, but that was almost his only amusement at home. A garden of less than an acre seems a little cramped to be called a true landscape garden, but it had been laid out with the greatest care and gave the impression of being far deeper and more secluded than it actually was.

When you went through the sliding doors on the other side of the main entrance hall you found yourself in an average-sized room of eight mats, beyond which was a wide, twelve-mat chamber, the largest room in the house. The twelve-mat room was somewhat after the fashion of the Palace style, with a veranda along the eastern and southern sides, enclosed by a formal balustrade. On the south, in order to screen out the sun, the wide eaves were extended by latticework with a luxuriant growth of wild akebia vine hanging out over the pond; the water came lapping up under the vine leaves to the edge of the veranda. If you leaned on the rail and gazed across the pond you saw a waterfall plunging out of a densely wooded hill, its waters flowing under double globeflowers in the spring or begonias in autumn, emerging as a rippling stream for a little way, and then dropping into the pond. Just at the point where the stream entered the pond a bamboo device called a "water mortar" was set up: as soon as the water filled its bamboo tube, which was pivoted off-center, the tube would drop with a hollow clack against a block of wood set below it and the water would run out. Since the tube was supposed to be of fresh green bamboo, with a cleanly cut open end, the gardener had to replace it often. This sort of device is mentioned in a fourteenth-century poem:

> *Has the water upstream*
> *Become a lazy current?*
> *The sound of the mortar is rarely heard.*

Even today, the sound of a water mortar echoes through the garden of the well-known Hall of Poets, the home of the early Edo poet Ishikawa Jozan in the northern suburbs of Kyoto. There, too, is displayed an explanatory text written in Chinese by Jozan. I suppose the reason why we had a water mortar is that my grandfather went there, read the description, and got the impulse to copy the device for his own house. It is said that Jozan's poem about not wishing to cross the Kamo River was written as a polite way of declining an invitation from the Emperor:

> *Alas, I am ashamed to cross it—*
> *Though only a Shallow Stream*
> *It would mirror my wrinkled age.*

A rubbing of the poem hangs in an alcove in the Hall of Poets, and we had one at our house too.

When I was about three or four, I was enchanted by the clack, clack of our water mortar.

"Tadasu!" Mother would call. "Don't go over there or you'll fall in the pond!" But no matter how often she stopped me, I would run out into the garden and make my way through the tall bamboo grass of the artificial hill, trying to get to the edge of the stream.

"Wait! It's dangerous! You mustn't go there alone!" Mother or Okane would hurry after me in alarm and seize me by the back of my sash. Squirming forward while one of them held fast to me, I would peer down into the stream. As I watched, the green bamboo tube of the mortar slowly filled, dropped with a sharp rap against the block of wood, spilling its water into the pond, and then sprang back into place. After a few minutes it was full again, repeating the process. I suppose this clacking noise is my earliest memory of our house. Day and night it echoed in my ears, all the while that I was growing up.

Okane was always on her guard with me, hardly daring to let me out of her sight. Yet my mother often scolded her. "Do be careful, Okane!" she would say. There was an earth-covered footbridge over the pond, and whenever I tried to cross it Okane was sure to stop me. Sometimes Mother came running after me too. Most of the pond was shallow, but it was over six feet deep at one place, where a hole had been sunk so that the fish could survive if the rest of the water dried up. The hole was near the bridge, and Mother warned me about it time and again. "It would be dreadful if you fell in there," she used to say. "Even a grownup couldn't get out."

On the other side of the bridge was an arbor, and next to it the teahouse, my favorite playroom.

"Wait outside, Okane!" I would tell my nurse. "You mustn't come in after me." I was delighted with the low-roofed, narrow little building because it seemed exactly like a toy house for a child. I would play there for hours: sprawling out on its straw-matted floor, going through the tiny doorways, turning the water on and off in the pantry, untying the braided cords of the wooden boxes I found and taking out the tea objects, or putting on one of the wide rush hats the guests wore when coming to the tea ceremony in the rain.

Okane, who was standing outside, would begin to worry. "Tadasu!" she would call. "Don't stay any longer —your mother won't like it." Or again: "Look! There's a great big centipede here! It's terrible if a centipede bites you!" I actually did see large centipedes in the teahouse a few times, but I was never bitten.

I was far more afraid of the half dozen stone figures of Buddhist saints which stood here and there on the hill and around the pond. These were only three or four feet high, considerably smaller than the Korean statues before the inner gate, but their ugly, grotesque faces seemed somehow very Japanese. Some of them had hideously distorted noses and seemed to be staring at you out of the corners of their eyes; others seemed on the verge of a sly, malicious laugh. I never went near them after sunset.

Now and then Mother called me over to the veranda when she fed crumbs to the fish.

"Here, little fish," she said, scattering crumbs out into the pond as the carp and crucian came swimming up from their hiding place in that deep hollow. Sometimes I sat close to her on the edge of the veranda, leaning against the low rail and tossing crumbs to them too; or else I sat on her lap, feeling the warm, resilient touch of her rather full thighs as she held me snugly in her embrace.

In the summer my parents and I used to have supper by the pond, and sit there to enjoy the cool of evening. Occasionally we ordered food from a restaurant or had a man come in from a caterer, bringing all the ingredients and cooking them in our huge kitchen. Father would put a bottle of beer under the spout of the bamboo mortar. Mother would sit at the edge of the pond and dangle her feet in the water, where they looked more beautiful than ever. She was a small, delicately built woman, with plump, white little dumpling-like feet which she held quite motionless as she soaked them in the water, letting the coolness seep through her body. Years later, after I was grown up, I came across this line of Chinese verse:

*When she washes the inkstone,*
*the fish come to swallow ink.*

Even as a young child I thought how pleasant it would be if the fish in our pond came gliding playfully around her beautiful feet, instead of coming only when we fed them.

I remember that on one of those summer evenings I noticed some long, thin, slippery-looking leaves in my soup, and asked Mother what they were.

"That's called *nenunawa*," she said.

"Oh? What's *that*?"

"A kind of water plant, like a lotus—they gather it at Mizoro Pond," she explained in her soft, well-bred voice.

Father laughed. "If you say it's *nenunawa* people won't know what you're talking about," he told her. "They call it *junsai* nowadays."

"But doesn't *nenunawa* sound long and slippery, just the way it is? That's the name for it in all the old poems, you know." And she began reciting one of them. From that time on it was always called *nenunawa* at our house, even by the maids and by the men who came to cook for us.

At nine o'clock I would be told that it was bedtime, and be taken away by my nurse. I don't know how late my parents stayed up; they slept in the room with the veranda around it, while Okane and I were in a small room of six mats on the north side, across the corridor from them. Sometimes I fretted and lay awake a long time, pleading: "Let me sleep with Mama!"

Then Mother would come to look in at me. "My, what a little baby I have tonight," she would say, taking me up in her arms and carrying me to her bedroom. Even though the bed had already been prepared for sleeping, father would not be in it—perhaps he was still out in the pavilion. Mother herself had yet to dress for bed. She lay down beside me just as she was, not taking off her sash, and held me so that my head nestled under her chin. The light was on, but I buried my face inside the neck opening of her kimono and had a blurred impression of being swathed in darkness. The faint scent of her hair, which was done up in a chignon, wafted into my nostrils. Seeking out her nipples with my mouth, I played with them like an infant, took them between my lips, ran my tongue over them. She always let me do that as long as I wanted, without a word of reproach. I believe I used to suckle at her breasts until I was a fairly large child, perhaps because in those days people were not at all strict about weaning their children. When I used my tongue as hard as I could, licking her nipples and pressing around them, the milk flowed out nicely. The mingled scents of her hair and milk hovered there in her bosom, around my face. As dark as it was, I could still dimly see her white breasts.

"Go to sleep now," she would murmur; and as she comforted me, patting me on the head and stroking my back, she began to sing her usual lullaby:

> *"Go to sleep, go to sleep.*
> *Don't cry, there's a good child, go to sleep.*
> *It's Mother cuddling you,*
> *Mother cradling you,*
> *Don't cry, there's a good child, go to sleep."*

She would sing it over and over while I drifted off into a peaceful sleep, still clutching her breasts and running my tongue around her nipples. Often my dreams were penetrated by the distant clack of the water mortar, far beyond my shuttered windows.

Okane also knew a number of lullabies, such as this one:

> *When I asked the pillow, "Is he asleep?"*
> *The honest pillow said, "He is!"*

She sang many others for me too, but I was never easily lulled asleep by her songs. (Nor, in the room I shared with her, could I hear the sound of the water mortar.) Mother's voice had a seductive rhythm all its own, a rhythm that filled my mind with pleasant fancies and quickly put me to sleep.

Although I have thus far written "mother" without specifying which of the two I meant, my intention has been to relate only memories of my true mother. Yet it occurs to me that these recollections seem a little too detailed for a child of three or four. Seeing her dangle her feet in the pond, or hearing her talk about *nenunawa*, for instance—would such things, if they had really happened when I was a child of that age, have left any impression whatever? Possibly impressions of the first mother were overlaid by those of the second, confusing my memory. For early one autumn, just as the chestnut tree at our doorway was beginning to shed its leaves, my twenty-two-year-old mother, who was with child, contracted an infection of the womb and died. I was five at the time. A few years later I had a stepmother.

I cannot recall my first mother's features distinctly. According to Okane, she was very beautiful, but all that I can summon to my mind's eye is the vague image of a full, round face. Since I often looked up at her as she held me in her arms, I could see her nostrils clearly. The lamplight gave a pink luminosity to her lovely nose: seen from that angle, it appeared to be all the more exquisitely proportioned—not in the least like Okane's nose, or anyone else's. But when I try to remember her other features—her eyes, her mouth—I can only visualize them in a very general way. Here too I am perhaps being misled by the superimposed image of my second mother. After my real mother's death Father used to read the sutras and say prayers for her every morning and evening before her memorial tablet, and I often sat beside him praying too. But as hard as I stared at her photograph, which stood beside the tablet on our Buddhist altar, I never had the sudden poignant feeling that this was my own mother—the woman who had suckled me at her breasts.

All I could tell from the picture was that she wore her hair in an old-fashioned style, and that she seemed even plumper than I had remembered. It was too faded to re-create in my mind the way she actually looked.

"Papa," I asked, "is that really Mama's picture?"

"Yes, of course it is," he said. "It was taken before we were married, when she was about sixteen."

"But it doesn't look like her, does it? Why don't you

put up something better? Don't you have another one?"

"Your mother didn't like to be photographed, so this is the only one I could find of her by herself. After we were married we had some pictures taken together, but the man did such a bad job retouching them that she thought they spoiled her face. Now this one shows her when she was a very young girl, and she may seem different from the way you remember her. But that was how she really looked at the time."

I could see then that it did bear a certain resemblance to her, though by no means enough to bring the forgotten image of my mother back to life.

I would think of her wistfully as I leaned on the balustrade and watched the carp swimming in the pond, yearn for her as I listened to the clack of the bamboo mortar. But it was especially at night, when I was lying in bed in my nurse's arms, that I felt an indescribable longing for my dead mother. That sweet, dimly white dream world there in her warm bosom among the mingled scents of her hair and her milk—why had it disappeared? Was this what "death" meant? Where could she have gone? Okane tried to console me by singing Mother's lullabies, but that made my grief all the worse. "No, no!" I cried, thrashing about in bed. "I don't like you to sing for me! I want Mama!" Kicking off the covers, I howled and wept.

At last my father would come in to say: "Tadasu, you mustn't give Okane so much trouble. Now be a good boy and go to sleep." But I cried even harder.

"Your mother has died," he would tell me, his voice

thickening and faltering. "It doesn't do any good to cry about it. I feel as much like crying as you do—maybe more—but I'm being brave. You try to be brave too."

Then Okane would say: "If you want to see your mama, you ought to pray as hard as you can. If you do, she'll come to you in a dream, and say: 'Tadasu, you're such a good little boy!' But if you cry she won't come!"

Sometimes Father would give up in despair at my incessant wailing and screaming, and say: "All right then, come sleep with me." Taking me along to his room, he would lie down with me in his arms. But I found his masculine smell so different from my mother's fragrance that I was inconsolable. Rather than sleep with him, I preferred to sleep with my nurse.

"Papa, you make me feel sick. I want to go back to Okane."

"Well, go sleep in the other room then."

But Okane would scold me for it when I got back into bed with her. "Even if your father *does* make you feel sick, why do you have to say such an awful thing?" She used to say I looked exactly like him, not like my mother. That made me unhappy too.

Father always spent an hour morning and evening reading aloud from the sutras before the memorial tablet. As soon as I thought he was going to stop I would steal up to the altar and sit beside him for the few remaining minutes, running my little string of prayer beads through my fingers. But sometimes he led me there by the hand, saying: "Come to pray for your mother"; and I had to sit still beside him for the whole hour.

The next spring, when I was six, I entered elementary school, and from that time on I seldom made a nuisance of myself at night. But I longed for Mother all the more. Even my unsociable father, who had never cared for any company except my mother's, seemed to feel lonely, and began going out occasionally for diversion. On Sundays he often took Okane and me along to dine at a riverside restaurant in Yamabana, or on an excursion to the hills west of the city.

One day he said to me: "When your mother was alive we often used to go out to Yamabana for dinner. Do you remember that, Tadasu?"

"I only remember once. Weren't some frogs croaking in the river behind us?"

"That's right. Do you remember hearing your mother sing a song there one evening?"

"I don't think so."

Then, as if it had suddenly occurred to him: "Tadasu, suppose there was someone just like your mother, and suppose she was willing to come and *be* your mother—how would you feel about that?"

"Do you really think there *is* such a person?" I asked dubiously. "Do you know anyone, Papa?"

"No," he replied hastily, "I only said 'suppose.'" He seemed anxious to drop the subject.

I am not sure exactly how old I was when Father and I had that conversation. Nor have I any way of knowing whether he already had someone in mind, or whether it was simply a chance remark. But when I was in the second grade—in the spring, when the double globe-

flowers at the mouth of the waterfall were in full bloom
—I came home from school one day and was startled to
hear the sound of a koto from the inner room. Who
could be playing? My mother had been an accomplished
musician of the Ikuta school, and I had often seen
Father sitting beside her on the veranda, listening ab-
sorbedly as she played for him on her six-foot-long koto,
which was decorated with a pine-tree pattern worked
in gold lacquer. After her death, her beloved koto was
wrapped in a cloth dyed with our family crest of
paulownia leaves and flowers, placed in a black-lacquered
box, and put away in the storehouse, where it had remained undisturbed ever since. Could that be her koto?
I wondered, as I came in through the side entrance. Just
then Okane appeared, and whispered into my ear.
"Tadasu, be very quiet and peek in the other room.
There's a pretty young lady here today!"

When I went through the eight-mat room to the other
side, pushed open the sliding doors a little, and peered
in, Father noticed me at once and beckoned. The strange
lady was engrossed in her koto; even after I came up
beside her she kept on playing without so much as turning her head. She sat where my mother used to sit, and
in the very same pose, her instrument laid out at the same
angle, her left hand stretched out in the same way as she
pressed the strings. The koto was not Mother's—it was a
plain one, completely unadorned. But Father's position
and attitude as he sat there listening so attentively were
exactly the same as in my mother's time. It was only

after she finished and took off the ivory finger picks that the strange lady turned to smile at me.

"Are you Tadasu?" she inquired politely, in a well-bred Kyoto accent. "You look just like your father."

"Make a nice bow," Father said, putting his hand on my head.

"Did you just come home from school?" she asked. Then she slipped the picks back on her fingers and began to play again. I didn't recognize the piece, but it sounded extremely difficult. Meanwhile I sat obediently beside my father and watched her every movement, hardly daring to breathe. Even after she stopped playing for us, she made no attempt to shower me with compliments— all she did was smile when our eyes met. She talked to Father in a calm, relaxed way, and seemed to have an air of composure. Soon a ricksha came for her; she was gone before dusk. But she left her koto with us. We stood it up against the wall in the alcove of the eight-mat room.

I was sure that Father would ask me what I thought of her, whether I didn't agree that she looked like my mother. But he said nothing, nor did I try to find out how they happened to become acquainted. Somehow I hesitated to bring the matter up. To tell the truth, if I'd been asked whether or not she looked like my mother I would scarcely have known what to say. At least, my first glimpse of her had not given me the impression that here indeed was the reincarnation of my mother. And yet her soft, round face, her delicate body, her calm, unhurried speech, in particular her polite reserve and utter

lack of flattery when we met, together with her inde-
finable attractiveness and charm—in all this she seemed
to resemble my mother, and I felt friendly toward her.

"Who was that?" I asked Okane later.

"I really don't know," she said. Possibly she had been
warned not to tell me.

"Is this the first time she's come here?"

"No, she was here about twice before. . . . It's the
first time she's played the koto, though."

I saw the woman once more that summer, around the
season when you begin to hear the song of the thrush.
That time she seemed even more at ease, staying to feed
crumbs to the fish with Father and me after playing the
koto. But she left before supper. Again her koto was put
in the alcove—maybe she came to the house more often
than I knew.

One day in March, when I was eight years old, Father
called me into the veranda room to talk to me. I think it
was after supper, about eight o'clock in the evening,
when no one else was around.

"I have something to discuss with you, Tadasu," he
began, in an unusually solemn tone. "I don't know how
you feel about the lady who's been coming to visit us,
but for various reasons—reasons that concern you as
well as me—I'm thinking of marrying her. You'll be
in the third grade this year, so I want you to try to
understand what I'm saying. As you know, I had the
greatest love for your mother. If she were only alive
today I wouldn't want anyone else. Her death was a
terrible blow to me—I couldn't get over it. But then

I happened to meet this lady. You say you don't remember your mother's face very clearly, but you'll soon find that this lady resembles her in all sorts of ways. Of course no two people are quite alike, unless they're twins. That isn't what I mean by resembling her. I mean the impression she makes, the way she talks, the way she carries herself, her quiet, easygoing personality, sweet and gentle, and yet deep—that's why I say she's like your mother. If I hadn't met her I'd never have wanted to marry again. It's only because there *is* such a person that I've come to feel this way. Maybe your mother saw to it that I happened to find this lady, for your sake as well as mine. If she'll come and stay with us, she'll be a wonderful help to you as you grow up. And now that the second anniversary of your mother's death has passed, this seems like a proper time for marrying her. What do you think, Tadasu? You understand what I've been telling you, don't you?"

Curiously enough, I had already given my consent long before he finished what he intended to say. Seeing my face light up, he added: "There's one thing more I'd like you to remember. When she comes you mustn't think of her as your second mother. Think that your mother has been away somewhere for a while and has just come home. Even if I didn't tell you so, you'd soon begin to look at it that way. Your two mothers will become one, with no distinction between them. Your first mother's name was Chinu, and your new mother's name is Chinu too. And in everything she says and does, your new mother will behave the way the first one did."

After that, Father stopped taking me in to sit beside him during his morning and evening worship at the memorial tablet. The time he spent reading the sutras gradually became shorter. Then one evening in April the wedding ceremony was held in the veranda room. Maybe there was a reception afterward, in some restaurant, but I have no remembrance of that. The ceremony itself was a very quiet affair: only a few close relatives attended on either side. From that day on Father called his bride "Chinu," and I, having been told to call her "Mama," found that the word came to my lips with surprising ease.

For the past two or three years I had been accustomed to sleeping in the room next to Father's, but from the night my new mother arrived I went back to sharing the little room across the corridor with Okane. Father seemed to be truly happy, and began living the same kind of tranquil domestic life he had enjoyed with my first mother. Even Okane and the maids, who had been with us for years and who might have been expected to gossip and criticize their new mistress, were won over completely by her. Probably it was because of her natural kindness and warmth—anyway, they served her as faithfully as they had her predecessor.

Our household returned to its old routine. Father would sit listening attentively while Mother played the koto, just as he used to when my real mother was alive; and he always had the gold-lacquered koto brought out for the occasion. In summer the three of us would have supper beside the pond. Father would take his beer to cool under the spout of the bamboo mortar. Mother would dangle her feet in the pond. As I looked at her feet through the water I found myself remembering my real mother's feet. I felt as if they were the same; or rather, to put it more accurately, whenever I caught a glimpse of my new mother's feet I recalled that those of my own mother, the memory of which had long ago faded, had had the same lovely shape.

My stepmother also called the water plant we had in soup *nenunawa*, and told me how it was gathered at Mizoro Pond.

"I imagine that sooner or later you'll hear at school about the Court anthologies," she remarked one day. "Well, there's a poem in the earliest one that goes like this." And she recited a poem which had a pun on the word *nenunawa*.

As I have said before, I suspect that these incidents occurred during my real mother's lifetime and were only being repeated. No doubt Father had instructed my present mother how to behave, and was trying his best to confuse me about what my two mothers had said or done, so that I would identify them in my mind.

One evening—I believe it was that autumn—Mother came into my room just as I was about to go to sleep with Okane.

"Tadasu," she asked, "do you remember how your mama used to nurse you till you were about four years old?"

"Yes," I said.

"And do you remember how she always sang lullabies to you?"

"I remember."

"Wouldn't you still like to have your mama do those things?"

"I suppose so. . . ." I answered, flushing, aware that my heart had begun to pound.

"Then come and sleep with me tonight."

She took my hand and led me to the veranda room. The bed was ready for sleeping, but Father had not yet come in. Mother herself was still fully dressed, still wearing her usual sash. The light was shining overhead. I could hear the clack of the bamboo mortar. Everything was the way it used to be. Mother got into bed first, propped her head on the wooden pillow (her hair was done up in an old-fashioned chignon), and lifted the covers for me to crawl in after her. I was already too tall to bury myself easily under her chin, but being face to face with her made me feel so awkward that I shrank as far as I could under the covers. When I did, the neckline of her kimono was just at my nose.

Then I heard her whisper: "Tadasu, do you want some milk?" As she spoke, she bent her head down to look at me. Her cool hair brushed against my forehead.

"You must've been awfully lonely, with no one but Okane to sleep with for such a long time. If you wanted to sleep with Mama, why didn't you say so earlier? Were you feeling shy about it?"

I nodded.

"What a funny little boy you are! Now, hurry up and see if you can find the milk!"

I drew the top of her kimono open, pressed my face between her breasts, and played with her nipples with both hands. Because she was still looking down at me, a beam of light shone in over the edge of the bedclothes. I held one nipple and then the other in my mouth, sucking and using my tongue avidly to start the flow of milk. But as hard as I tried, it wouldn't come.

"Ooh, that tickles!" Mother exclaimed.

"I can't get a drop," I told her. "Maybe I've forgotten how."

"I'm sorry," she said. "Just be patient—I'll have a baby one of these days, and then there'll be lots of milk for you."

Even so, I wouldn't let go of her breasts, and kept sucking at them. I knew it was hopeless, but still I enjoyed the sensation of rolling around in my mouth those firm little buds at the tips of her soft, full breasts.

"I'm terribly sorry—and you've worked so hard at it! Do you want to go on trying anyway?"

Nodding my head, I kept on suckling. Once again, by some strange association, I seemed to drift among the mingled scents of hair oil and milk that had hovered in my mother's bosom so long ago. That warm, dimly white dream world—the world I thought had disappeared for-ever—had unexpectedly returned.

Then Mother began to sing the old lullaby, in the very rhythm that I knew so well:

> *"Go to sleep, go to sleep,*
> *Don't cry, there's a good child, go to sleep. . . ."*

But in spite of her singing I was too excited to relax that night, and I went on sucking away greedily at her nipples.

Within half a year, though I hadn't forgotten my

real mother, I could no longer distinguish sharply between her and the present one. When I tried to remember my real mother's face, my stepmother's appeared before me; when I tried to remember her voice, my stepmother's echoed in my ears. Gradually the two images merged: I found it hard to believe that I had ever had a different mother. Everything turned out just as Father had planned.

When I reached the age of twelve or thirteen, I began sleeping alone at night. But even then I would sometimes long to be held in my mother's bosom. "Mama, let me sleep with you!" I would beg. Drawing open her kimono, I would suck at her milkless breasts, and listen to her lullabies. And after drifting peacefully asleep I would awaken the next morning to find that in the meantime—I had no idea when—someone had carried me back and put me to bed alone in my own small room. Whenever I said: "Let me sleep with you!" Mother was glad to do as I wished, and Father made no objection.

For a long time I didn't know where this second mother was born, what her background was, or how she happened to marry my father; such subjects were never brought up in my presence. I knew I might have found some clue in the city records, but I obeyed my father's orders: "Think of her as your real mother. You musn't take the attitude that she's a stepmother." Also, I had some qualms about what I might find. However, when I was about to enter higher school I had to get an abstract from the records, and at that time I learned that my stepmother's real name was not Chinu but Tsuneko.

The following year my nurse Okane, who was then fifty-seven, ended her long service with us and retired to her home town of Nagahama. One day in late October before she left I went along with her to visit the Shimogamo Shrine. She made an offering, prayed briefly before the main altar, and then said in a voice filled with emotion: "I don't know when I'll see this shrine again. . . ." After that she suggested we go for a little walk through the shrine forest, toward the Aoi Bridge.

As we were walking along she suddenly turned to me and said: "You know all about it, Tadasu, don't you?"

"Know about what?" I asked, surprised.

"If you haven't heard, I won't say any more. . . ."

"What are you talking about?"

"I wonder if I ought to tell you," she said, hesitating. Then, still strangely evasive: "Tadasu, do you know much about your stepmother?"

"No," I answered. "I know that her real name is Tsuneko."

"How did you find that out?"

"I had to get an abstract from the city records last year."

"Is that really all you know?"

"That's all. Father said I shouldn't be too inquisitive about her, and you didn't tell me anything either, so I decided not to ask."

"As long as I was working at your house I didn't want to mention it, but once I go back to the country I can't say when I'll set eyes on you again. So I think maybe I ought to tell you after all. You mustn't let your father hear about it, though."

"Never mind then," I said, without really meaning it. "Don't tell me—I think I ought to do what Father says."

But she insisted. "Anyway, you're bound to find out sooner or later. It's something you ought to know."

I couldn't help being fascinated by her long, rambling story, told to me bit by bit as we walked along the shrine road.

"I've only heard this at second hand, so I can't be sure," Okane began, and went on to give me a full account of my stepmother's past.

It seems that she was born into a Kyoto family that owned a large stationery shop in the Nijo district, specializing in decorative papers and writing brushes. But when she was about nine years old the family went bankrupt; by the time of Okane's story their shop no longer existed. At eleven, she was taken in as an apprentice geisha at one of the houses in Gion; from twelve to fifteen she entertained at parties as a dancer. You could probably have discovered the professional name she used at that time, the name of the geisha house, and so on; but Okane didn't know. Then, at fifteen, she is supposed to have had her debts paid off by the son of a wholesale cotton merchant, and to have been taken into the family as his bride. Opinions differ as to whether or not she was his legal wife, some declaring that her name was never entered in the official records.

Anyhow, she enjoyed all the privileges of a wife, and for about three years lived comfortably as the young mistress of a prosperous household. But at eighteen, for one reason or another, she was divorced. Some say that family pressure drove her out; others that her dissipated husband simply tired of her. No doubt she received a considerable sum of money at the time, but she went back to her parents' drab little house in Rokujo, turned the upstairs room into a studio, and made her living by teaching flower arrangement and the tea ceremony to the young women of the neighborhood.

Apparently it was during those days that my father became acquainted with her. But no one knew how he happened to meet her, or where they were seeing each other before she came to Heron's Nest as his bride. Two and a half years passed from the time of my mother's death until father's second marriage. As vividly as the girl may have reminded him of his lost wife, he could hardly have fallen in love with her less than a year after the death of the woman he had so much adored; probably he made his mind up only a few months before the wedding took place. His first wife had died at twenty-two; his second was twenty when she married him; father himself was thirty-three, thirteen years her senior; and I, at eight, was almost that much younger.

Learning about my stepmother's background aroused strong curiosity in me, along with all sorts of other feelings. I had never dreamed that she was once a professional entertainer in Gion. Of course she was very different from the ordinary girl of that kind: she came from a respectable family, and had left the gay quarter after only a few years to take up the life of the young mistress of a well-to-do household, during which time she seems to have acquired a number of polite feminine accomplishments. Yet I had to admire her for preserving her unaffected charm and graciousness, in spite of having been a Gion dancer. But what of the evident refinement of her voice, that soft speech in the tradition of the old Kyoto merchant class? Even if she had only spent two or three years in Gion one would expect to find some trace of it in her speech. Did her first husband and his parents make a point of correcting her?

I suppose it was natural for my father, at a time when he was sad and lonely, to be attracted by such a woman. And it was natural, too, for him to come to believe that a woman like her would have all the fine qualities of his former wife and could help me forget the sorrow of having lost my mother. I began to realize how much thought he had given to this, not merely for his own sake but for mine. Even if my stepmother shared his wish to make me think of my two mothers as a single woman, it was his own extraordinary effort that enabled him to mold her in the image of my real mother. I could see that the love he lavished on my stepmother and me only strengthened his love for his first wife all the more. And so, while it might seem that exposing the secrets of my new mother's earlier life had frustrated all of Father's patient efforts, the result was to deepen my gratitude to him and my respect for my stepmother.

After Okane left we added another maid, so that there were four in all. And in January of the following year I learned that Mother was pregnant. It was in the eleventh year of her marriage to my father. Since she had never had a child before, even by her former husband, both Father and she seemed to be surprised that such a thing could happen, after all these years.

"I feel ashamed to be getting big like this, at my age," she used to say. Or again: "When you're past thirty it's hard to give birth for the first time, I hear." Both Mother and Father had concentrated all their parental love on me, and perhaps they worried about my reaction to this event. If they did, they needn't have: I cannot describe how pleased I was to think that, after all these years as an only child, I was about to have a little brother or sister. I suppose, too, that Father's heart was darkened now and then by the ominous memory of my first mother's death in pregnancy. But what struck me as odd was that neither Father nor Mother seemed to want to bring up the matter; I began to notice that they looked strangely gloomy whenever the subject was mentioned.

"Since I have Tadasu I don't need another child," she would say, half-jokingly. "I'm too old to have a baby." Knowing her as I did, I thought it unlikely that she said such a thing merely to hide her embarrassment at being pregnant.

"What are you talking about, Mother?" I would object. "You mustn't say foolish things like that!" But somehow Father seemed to agree with her.

The doctor who examined her said that Mother's heart was rather weak, but that it was not bad enough to be a cause for concern—on the whole, she had a strong constitution. And in May of that year she gave birth to a baby boy. Her delivery took place at our house: the little six-mat room that I had been using was given over to her. The baby was a healthy one, and in due time Father gave it the name Takeshi. But when I came home from school one day—I believe it was about two weeks later—I was startled to find that Takeshi wasn't there.

"Father, where is Takeshi?" I asked.

"We've sent him out to Shizuichino for adoption," he told me. "Someday I think you'll understand, but for the present, please don't ask too many questions. I didn't plan this by myself—from the time we knew the child was coming your mother and I discussed it together every night. She wanted to do it even more than I did. Maybe we shouldn't have gone ahead without a word to you, but I was afraid that talking to you about it might do more harm than good."

For a moment I looked at him incredulously. Mother, who had left her bed only the day before, seemed to have deliberately slipped off somewhere, to leave us alone, "Where's Mother?" I asked.

"I think she may have gone out to the garden," he said, as if he didn't know.

I went out to look for her at once. She was in the middle of the bridge, clapping her hands and calling the fish, and scattering food to them. When she saw me, she went over to the other side of the pond, sat down on a celadon porcelain drum beside one of those sinister-looking stone saints, and beckoned me to come and sit on the other drum, facing her.

"I was just talking to Father," I said. "What on earth is the meaning of this?"

"Were you surprised, Tadasu?" Her soft, round face dimpled in a smile. The expression in her eyes was far too serene for a mother struggling to hold back her grief at having just been robbed of her beloved newborn infant.

"Of course I was."

"But haven't I always said that Tadasu is the only child I need?" Her calm expression remained unchanged. "Your father and I both thought it was for the best. Let's talk about it another time."

That night the room I had given up to Mother and her baby was once again my bedroom. The more I thought about what had happened, the more puzzled I became. It was dawn before I fell asleep.

Here I should like to say a little about Shizuichino, the place to which Takeshi had been sent.

Shizuichino is the modern name for the Ichiharano district, where the legendary hero Raiko is supposed to have killed the two robber chiefs. Even now one of its villages is called Ichihara, and that is also the name of the local station on the electric-car line to Mount Kurama. However, it was only in recent years that the car line opened; before that, you had to make the six- or seven-mile trip from Kyoto to Shizuichino by ricksha, or go by carriage as far as Miyake-Hachiman and then walk about three and a half miles. For several generations we had had close ties with a family named Nosé who were prosperous farmers in this district—I suppose one of my ancestors had been sent out to nurse at their house. Even in Father's time, the head of the Nosé family and his wife would come to pay their respects to us at the Bon Festival and at New Year's, bringing with them a cartload of fresh vegetables. Their Kamo eggplants and green soybeans were unobtainable at the market; we were always delighted to see them coming with their little handcart. Since we often went to stay overnight with them in the fall, to go mushroom hunting, I had been familiar with that region since childhood.

The road from the Nosé house to the mushroom hill led along the Kurama River, one of the sources of the Kamo. We were already well above Kyoto: as we climbed still higher we could see the city lying below us. They say that the great scholar Fujiwara Seika retired here, after declining the invitation of the Shogun Ieyasu to come to Edo. The mountain villa Seika lived in has long since disappeared, but its site was in a wide bend of the meandering Kurama River. Not far away were the places he chose as the "Eight Scenic Beauties," to which he gave such names as Pillow-Stream Grotto and Flying-Bird Pool.

Another nearby point of interest was the Fudaraku Temple, popularly known as the Komachi Temple, where Ono no Komachi and her tormented suitor are said to lie buried. According to the *Illustrated Guide to the Capital*, this is also the temple which the Emperor Go-Shirakawa visited during his journey to Ohara, as related in *The Tale of the Heiké*. There is a passage in one of the Nō plays about Komachi saying that many years ago a man who happened to be passing Ichiharano heard a voice from a clump of tall *susuki* grass recite this poem:

> *When the autumn wind blows,*
> *Eyeless Komachi wails in pain.*
> *But where is her lovely face*
> *In this wilderness of susuki?*

Whereupon the priest who recalls the poem decides to go to Ichiharano and pray for the repose of Komachi's soul. I have seen an old painting which shows *susuki* growing out of the eye sockets of what is presumably Komachi's skull; and in the Komachi Temple there was a "wailing stone" on which was carved the poem I have quoted. In my childhood, that whole area was a lonely waste covered with a rank growth of *susuki* grass.

A few days after I learned the astonishing news about Takeshi I decided that I had to make a secret visit to the Nosé family in Shizuichino. Not that I was determined to steal Takeshi away from them and bring him home again. I am not the sort of person to do a thing like that on my own initiative. It was simply that I felt an over-powering rush of pity for my poor little brother, taken from his mother's arms to a house far away in the country. At least I could make sure that he was well, I thought, and then go home and urge Father and Mother to reconsider. If they didn't listen to me at first, I meant to go on visiting Takeshi regularly, keeping our link with him intact. Sooner or later they would understand how I felt.

I set out early in the morning and reached the house a little before noon. Fortunately, Nosé and his wife had just returned from the fields, but when I asked to see Takeshi they seemed embarrassed.

"Takeshi isn't here," they told me.

"He isn't? Then where is he?"

"Well, now . . ." they began, exchanging worried glances as if they were at a loss for an answer.

But after I repeated my question several times, Nosé's wife broke down and said: "We left him with some people a little farther out." Then they explained that because there wasn't anyone in the house just then to nurse a baby, and because my parents wanted Takeshi further away, they took him out to live with some old friends of theirs, people you could trust.

When I asked where "a little farther out" was, Nosé seemed even more embarrassed. "Your parents know where it is," he said; "so please ask them. It wouldn't do for me to tell you myself."

His wife chimed in: "They said if you ever happened to ask us we shouldn't tell you!" But I was finally able to worm it out of them that the place in question was a village called Seriu.

There is a folk song with the line "Out beyond Kyoto, by Ohara and Seriu"; and the Kabuki play *The Village School* has a passage about "hiding their lord's child in the village of Seriu, nestled in the hills." But this Seriu is over the Ebumi Pass on the road from Shizuichino to Ohara, and now has a different name. The Seriu that Nosé and his wife were talking about is a mountain village in Tamba, even more remote and isolated. To go there, you take the electric car to Kibune, the second stop after Shizuichino, and cross the Seriu Pass into Tamba. The pass is a difficult one, more than twice as high as the Ebumi Pass, and there is not a single house in the five miles from Kibune to Seriu.

Why would my parents have sent my little brother to such a place? Even the Seriu in the play—the village "nestled in the hills" where a lord's child was kept in hiding—wasn't that far from Kyoto. Why had Takeshi been hidden away deep in the mountains of Tamba? I felt that I should try to find him that very day, but since all I knew was the name of the village I would have had to look for him from house to house. Anyway, there was hardly time for me to go on to Kibune and cross that steep mountain pass. Giving up for the time being, I went back home, thoroughly dejected, along the same road I had come that morning.

For the next two or three days my relations with my parents were strained; even at supper we seldom talked. Whether or not they had heard from the Nosé family, they never said a word about my trip to Shizuichino, nor did I mention having gone. Mother was bothered by the swelling of her breasts and often secluded herself in the teahouse to use a milking device to relieve the pressure, or call one of the maids to massage her. Around this time my father seemed to be in poor health, and began taking afternoon naps in the veranda room, his head on a Chinese pillow of crimson papier-mâché. He seemed feverish too; I often saw him with a thermometer in his mouth.

I intended to go to Seriu as soon as possible, and was

trying to think of an excuse to be away from home overnight. But one afternoon—it must have been late spring,
since the silk tree my grandfather had been so proud of
was in blossom—I decided to spend a little time reading
in the pavilion. Taking along a novel, I went through the
garden, past the flowering tree, and up the pavilion steps.
Suddenly I noticed that Mother was sitting there on a
cushion before me, busily milking her breasts. That was
something she did in the teahouse, I thought. I had never
imagined I'd find her on the pavilion veranda in that state:
leaning over in a languid pose, her kimono open so that
her naked breasts were bared to my view. Startled, I
turned to leave, but she called after me in her usual calm
voice: "Don't go away, Tadasu."

"I'll come again later," I said. "I didn't mean to disturb
you."

"It's stifling in the teahouse, so I thought I'd sit out
here. Did you want to read?"

"I'll come later," I repeated, feeling very uncomfortable. But again she stopped me from leaving.

"You needn't go—I'll be done in a moment. Just stay
where you are." And then: "Look! My breasts are so
full they hurt!"

I said nothing, and she continued: "You must remember how you tried to nurse at them till you were twelve
or thirteen. You used to fret because nothing would come
out, no matter how hard you sucked."

Mother removed the milking device from her left
nipple and placed it over the right one. Her breast swelled
up inside the glass receptacle, almost filling it, and a

number of tiny streams of milk spurted from her nipple. She emptied the milk into a drinking glass and held it up to show me.

"I told you I'd have a baby someday and there'd be lots of milk for you too, didn't I?" I had somewhat recovered from my initial shock and was watching her fixedly, though I hardly knew what to say.

"Do you remember how it tastes?" she asked. I lowered my gaze and shook my head.

"Then try a little," she said, holding the glass out to me. "Go on and try it!"

The next moment, before I realized what I was doing, my hand reached out for the glass, and I took a sip of the sweet white liquid.

"How is it? Does it remind you of how it used to taste? Your mother nursed you till you were four, I think." It was extraordinary for my stepmother to say "your mother" to me, distinguishing between herself and my father's first wife.

"I wonder if you remember how to nurse," she went on. "You can try, if you like." Mother held one of her breasts in her hand and offered me the nipple. "Just try it and see!"

I sat down before her so close that our knees were touching, bent my head toward her, and took one of her nipples between my lips. At first it was hard for me to get any milk, but as I kept on suckling, my tongue began to recover its old skill. I was several inches taller than she was, but I leaned down and buried my face in her bosom, greedily sucking up the milk that came gushing out. "Mama," I began murmuring instinctively, in a spoiled, childish voice.

I suppose Mother and I were in each other's embrace for about half an hour. At last she said: "That's enough for today, isn't it?" and drew her breast away from my mouth. I thrust her aside without a word, jumped down from the veranda, and ran off into the garden.

But what was the meaning of her behavior that afternoon? I knew she hadn't deliberately planned it, since we met in the pavilion by accident. Did our sudden encounter give her the impulse to embarrass and upset me? If our meeting was as much a surprise to her as it was to me, perhaps she merely yielded to a passing whim. Yet she had seemed far too cool to be playing such a mischievous trick: she had acted as if this were nothing out of the ordinary. Maybe she would have been just as calm even if someone had come upon us. Maybe, in spite of my having grown up, she still thought of me as a child. Mother's state of mind was a mystery to me, but my own actions had been equally abnormal. The moment I saw her breasts there before me, so unexpectedly revealed, I was back in the dream world that I had longed for, back in the power of the old memories that had haunted me for so many years. Then, because she lured me into it by having me drink her milk, I ended by doing the crazy thing I did. In an agony of shame, wondering how I could have harbored such insane feelings, I paced back and forth around the pond alone. But at the same time that I regretted my behavior, and tortured myself for it, I felt that I wanted to do it again—not once, but over and over. I knew that if I were placed in those circumstances again—if I were lured by her that way—I would not have the will power to resist.

After that I stayed away from the pavilion; and Mother, possibly aware of how I felt, seemed to be using only the teahouse. Somehow the desire that had occupied such a large place in my heart—the desire to go to Seriu to see Takeshi—was no longer quite so strong. First of all, I wanted to find out why my parents had disposed of him in that way. Was it Father's idea or Mother's? As far as I could judge, it seemed likely that my stepmother—out of deference to my own mother—had decided that she ought not to keep her child here with us. And perhaps Father shared her scruples. Undoubtedly his love for his former wife was still intense, and he may well have thought it wrong for him to have any other child than the one she left him. Perhaps that is why my stepmother gave up her baby. For her, such an act would have shown self-sacrificing devotion to my father—and wasn't she more attached to me than to her own son? I could only suppose that they had come to their decision for reasons of this sort. But why hadn't they confided in me, or at least given me some hint of their intentions? Why had they kept Takeshi's whereabouts such a dark secret?

I have mentioned that Father's health seemed to be failing, and it occurred to me that that might have influenced his decision. Since about the end of the last year he had begun to look pale, and had become noticeably thinner. Although he seldom coughed or cleared his throat, he seemed to have a low fever, which made me suspect that he was suffering from some kind of chest trouble. Our family doctor was a man named Kato, whose office was on Teramachi at Imadegawa. During the early stages of his illness Father never had him come to the house. "I'm going for a walk," he would say, and then take the streetcar to visit Dr. Kato. It was not until after the episode in the pavilion that I managed to find out where he was going.

"Father," I asked, "is anything wrong with you?"

"No, not in particular," he answered vaguely.

"But why do you have a prescription from Dr. Kato?"

"It isn't serious. I'm just having a little trouble passing water."

"Then it's inflammation of the bladder?"

"Yes," he said. "Something like that."

At last it became obvious to everyone that Father had to urinate frequently. You could see that he was always going to relieve himself. Also, his coloring was worse than ever, and he had lost his appetite completely. That summer, after the rainy season, he began to spend most of the day resting, as if he felt exhausted; in the evening he sometimes came out to have dinner with us beside the pond, but even then he was listless and seemed to be making the effort out of consideration for Mother and me.

I felt suspicious because he was so evasive about his illness, even concealing his regular visits to his doctor. One day I made a visit of my own to Dr. Kato's office and asked him about it.

"Father tells me he has inflammation of the bladder," I said. "I wonder if that's really all it is."

"It's true that he has an inflamed bladder," said Dr. Kato, who had known me all my life. "But hasn't he told you any more than that?" He looked a little surprised.

"You know how retiring and secretive Father is. He doesn't like to talk about his illness."

"That puts me in a difficult position," Dr. Kato said. "Of course I haven't been too blunt with your father about it, but I've let him know his condition is serious. So I suppose that he and your mother are pretty well prepared for the worst—I can't understand why they've kept it from you. Probably they want to spare you any unnecessary grief. To my own way of thinking, I'm not sure it's wise to hide the truth from you, since you're already so worried. I've known your family for a good many years—your grandfather was a patient of mine—and so I don't think there should be any objection if I take it on myself to inform you." He paused a moment, and went on: "I'm sorry to have to say this, but as you must have gathered by now your father's condition is not at all hopeful." Then he told me the whole story.

It was last autumn that Father noticed a change in the state of his health and went to be examined by Dr. Kato. He complained of various symptoms—fever, blood in his urine, pain after urinating, a sensation of pressure in his lower abdomen—and Dr. Kato found immediately, by touch, that both of his kidneys were swollen. He also discovered tuberculous bacilli in the urine. This is very serious, he thought; and he urged Father to go to the urology department at the university hospital for a special examination, with X-rays. Father seems to have been reluctant. However, he finally went, after Dr. Kato urged him repeatedly and gave him a letter of introduction to a friend of his at the hospital.

Two days later Dr. Kato learned the results of the examination from his friend: just as he had feared, both the cystoscope and the X-rays showed clearly that the disease was tuberculosis of the kidneys, and that Father's condition was fatal. If only one of his kidneys had been attacked he could probably have been saved by its removal. Even in such cases, the prognosis was bad: thirty or forty per cent of the patients died. Unfortunately both of my father's kidneys were affected, so nothing could be done for him. Though he still didn't seem to be a very sick man, he would soon have to take to his bed—at the longest, he might live another year or two.

"This isn't the kind of thing you can afford to neglect," Dr. Kato had warned him at the time, in a roundabout way. "From now on I'll come to see you once or twice a week—you ought to stay at home and rest as much as possible." And he added: "I must ask you to refrain from sexual intercourse. There's no danger of respiratory contagion at present, so you needn't worry as far as the rest of the family is concerned. But your wife will have to be careful."

"Is it some kind of tuberculosis?"

"Well, yes. But it isn't tuberculosis of the lungs."

"Then what is it?"

"The bacilli have attacked the kidney. Since you have two kidneys, it's nothing to be so alarmed about."

Dr. Kato managed to gloss it over for the moment in that way, and Father quietly accepted his advice. "I understand," he said. "I'll do as you've told me. But I like going out for walks, and as long as I'm able to get around I'll come to your office."

Father continued to visit Dr. Kato as usual, apparently not wishing to have him call at our house. Most of the time he came alone, but now and then Mother accompanied him. Although Dr. Kato felt an obligation to inform her frankly of her husband's condition, he had not yet found an opportunity to do so.

Then one day Father surprised him by saying: "Doctor, how much longer do I have, the way things are going?"

"Why do you talk like that?" Dr. Kato asked him.

Father smiled faintly. "You needn't keep anything from me. I've had a premonition about it all along."

"But why?"

"I don't know . . . maybe you'd call it instinct. It's just a feeling I've had. How about it, Doctor? I know what to expect, so please tell me the truth."

Dr. Kato was well acquainted with Father's character and took him at his word. Father had always been an acutely perceptive man; possibly he had been able to guess the nature of his illness from the way the specialists at the university treated him. Sooner or later I'll have to tell him or tell someone in his family, Dr. Kato thought; if he's so well prepared for it maybe I'd better do it now and get it over with. Indirectly, but without trying to evade my father's questions any longer, he confirmed his fears.

This is what Dr. Kato reported to me. Then he warned me that, since the disease often ended by invading the lungs, all of us—not just my mother—had to be careful.

I come now to the part of my narrative that I find most difficult.

I have tentatively given this narrative the title of *The Bridge of Dreams*, and have written it, however amateurishly, in the form of a novel. But everything that I have set forth actually happened—there is not one falsehood in it. Still, if I were asked why I took it into my head to write at all, I should be unable to reply. I am not writing out of any desire to have others read this. At least, I don't intend to let anyone see it as long as I am alive. If someone happens across it after my death, there will be no harm in that; but even if it is lost in oblivion, if no one ever reads it, I shall have no regret. I write for the sake of writing, simply because I enjoy looking back at the events of the past and trying to remember them one by one. Of course, all that I record here is true: I do not allow myself the slightest falsehood or distortion. But there are limits even to telling the truth; there is a line one ought not to cross. And so, although I certainly never write anything untrue, neither do I write the whole of the truth. Perhaps I leave part of it unwritten out of consideration for my father, for my mother, for myself. . . . If anyone says that not to

tell the whole truth is in fact to lie, that is his own inter-
pretation. I shall not venture to deny it.

What Dr. Kato revealed to me about my father's
physical condition filled my mind with wild, nightmarish
fancies. If it was last fall that Father became aware of
his unhappy fate, he was then forty-three years old,
Mother was thirty, and I was eighteen. At thirty, however, Mother looked four or five years younger—people
took her for my sister. Suddenly I recalled the story of
her earlier life, which Okane had told me as we walked
through the shrine forest before she left us last year.
"You mustn't let your father hear about it," she had said,
but might she not have done so on his instructions? Perhaps he had reason to want to sever the connection between my real mother and my stepmother, who had
become so closely linked in my mind.

Also, I thought of what had happened not long ago in
the Silk-Tree Pavilion. Perhaps Father had had something to do with *that*. I hardly think Mother would have
tried to tantalize me so shamelessly without his permission. The fact is, although I stayed away from the
pavilion for several weeks after that incident, I went
there to suckle at Mother's breast more than once. Sometimes Father was away, sometimes at home: it seems
unlikely that he didn't realize what she was doing, or
that she concealed it from him. Possibly, knowing he
hadn't long to live, he was trying to create a deeper
intimacy between Mother and me, so that she would
think of me as taking his place—and she made no objection. That is all I can bring myself to say. However, such

a theory would explain why they sent Takeshi to Seriu.
. . . It may seem that I have imagined the most pre-
posterous things about my parents, but what Father told
me on his deathbed, as I shall relate presently, appears to
bear me out.

I don't know when Mother learned that Father's days
were numbered; perhaps he told her as soon as he knew.
But that afternoon in the pavilion when she used the
phrase "your mother"—was it really by chance, as it
seemed then, or had she intended to say that? Indeed,
Father must have told her about his illness even before
she gave birth to Takeshi in May. Once they anticipated
what the future held in store for them they may have
come to an understanding—even if they never discussed
the matter openly—and sent Takeshi off for adoption.

What seemed strange was that, as far as I could tell,
Mother showed no sign of gloom or depression at the
impending separation from her husband. It would have
been contrary to her nature to display her emotions
plainly—but was there even a shadow of secret grief
across that bland, lovely face? Was she forcibly sup-
pressing her tears, thinking she must not let me see her
lose control of herself? Whenever I looked at them, her
eyes were dry and clear. Even now I cannot say that I
really understand how she felt, the complex emotions
that seem to have existed beneath her surface calm. Until
Father was at his dying hour she never tried to talk to
me about his death.

It was in August that Father lost the strength to get
out of bed. By then his entire body was swollen. Dr.

Kato came to see him almost every day. Father grew steadily weaker, losing even the will to sit up to eat. Mother hardly left his bedside.

"You ought to hire a nurse," Dr. Kato told her.

But Mother said: "I'll take care of him myself." She let no one else touch him. Evidently that was also my father's wish. All his meals—though he ate only a few bites—were carefully planned by her; she would order his favorite delicacies, such as sweetfish or sea eel, and serve them to him. As his urination became more and more frequent she had to be always ready to give him the bedpan. It was during the midsummer heat, and he suffered from bedsores, which she also cared for. Often, too, she had to wipe his body with a solution of alcohol. Mother never spared herself any pains at these tasks, all of which she did with her own hands. Father grumbled if anyone else tried to help him, but he never uttered a word of complaint about what she did. His nerves became so tense that the least sound seemed to bother him: even the bamboo mortar in the garden was too noisy, and he had us stop it. Toward the end he spoke only when he needed something, and then only to Mother. Occasionally friends or relatives came to visit him, but he didn't seem to want to see them. Mother was busy with him day and night; whenever she was too exhausted to go on, her place was taken by my old nurse, Okane, who had come back to help us. I was amazed to discover that Mother had so much stamina and perseverance.

It was one day in late September, the day after an

unusually heavy rainstorm when the "Shallow Stream" overflowed its banks and backed up into our pond, clouding the water, that Mother and I were summoned to Father's bedside. He was lying on his back, but he had us turn him over on his side so that he could look into our faces more easily. Beckoning me to sit close to him, he said: "Come here, Tadasu. Your mother can listen from where she is." He kept his gaze fixed on me all the while he spoke, as if he were seeking something in the depths of my eyes.

"I haven't much longer," he said. "But this was meant to be, so I am resigned to it. When I go to the other world your mother will be waiting for me, and I'm happy at the thought of meeting her again after all these years. What worries me most is your poor step-mother. She still has a long life ahead of her, but once I'm gone she'll have only you to rely on. So please take good care of her—give her all your love. Everyone says you resemble me. I think so myself. As you get older you'll look even more like me. If she has you, she'll feel as if I am still alive. I want you to think of taking my place with her as your chief aim in life, as the only kind of happiness you need."

Never had he looked at me that way before, deep into my eyes. Though I felt I could not fully understand the meaning of his gaze, I nodded my consent; and he gave a sigh of relief. Then, after pausing a few minutes until he was breathing easily once more, he went on:

"In order to make her happy you'll have to marry, but instead of marrying for your own sake you must marry for your mother's, to have someone who will help you take care of her. I've been thinking of Kajikawa's daughter Sawako. . . ."

Kajikawa was a gardener who had come to our house regularly for many years. (His father had been an apprentice of the man who laid out the garden at Heron's Nest.) We saw him frequently, since he and his helpers still worked in our garden several days a week. And we knew his daughter Sawako too: ever since she had been in Girls' High School she used to call on us once a year, on the day of the Aoi Festival.

Sawako had a fair complexion and a slender, oval face of the classic melon-seed shape, the kind of face you see in ukiyoye woodblock prints. I suppose some people would consider her beautiful. After graduating from high school, she began wearing extremely heavy make-up, and was even more striking. It had seemed to me that a girl with a lovely white skin needn't paint herself so; but the year before last she stopped by during the midsummer festival, after viewing the great bonfire in the Eastern Hills from the Kamo riverbank, and since she said she was hot we invited her to have a bath, which she did, reappearing later and passing so near me that I noticed a few freckles on her cheeks. That explains why she wears so much make-up, I thought. After that I didn't see her for a long time, but about ten days ago she and Kajikawa had come to pay a sick call. I found their visit rather disturbing. Father, who usually refused to see any visitors, asked that they be brought to his room and spent over twenty minutes talking with them. Realizing that something was up, I half expected what he had to say to me.

"I dare say you know a good deal about the girl," Father continued; and he gave me a brief description of how Sawako had been brought up and what she was like. But there was nothing particularly new to me, since I had been hearing about her for years. She was nineteen, my own age, having also been born in 1906; she was intelligent and talented, and had been graduated from Girls' High School three years ago with an excellent record; after graduation she had kept busy taking lessons of one kind or another, acquiring a range of accomplishments far beyond what one might have expected of a gardener's daughter. Thus she had all the qualifications to make a fine bride for any family—except that 1906 was the Year of the Fiery Horse, by the old calendar, and she was a victim of the superstition that women born in that year are shrews. As a result, she had not yet received an attractive offer of marriage.

All this was long since familiar to me, and Father concluded by asking me to take her as my wife. Then he added that both the girl and her parents would be delighted to accept such a proposal. "If you'll only agree to it, everything will be settled," he said. "But in that case there's one thing more I'd like to ask of you. If you have a child, send it elsewhere, just as your mother gave up her own child for your sake. There's no need to say anything to Sawako or her parents right away— you might as well keep this to yourself until the time comes when you have to tell them. The earlier you're married, the better. Have the ceremony as soon as the year of mourning is over. I can't think of a suitable go-between at the moment, but you and your mother can discuss that with Kajikawa and decide on someone."

After having talked for such a long time, Father closed his eyes and drew a deep breath. He seemed suddenly reassured that I would obey his wishes. Mother and I turned him on his back again.

The next day Father began to show symptoms of uremia. He could eat nothing whatever, his mind was hazy, and now and then he talked deliriously. He lived about three more days, until the beginning of October; but all that we could catch of his incoherent speech was my mother's name, "Chinu," and the broken phrase "the bridge . . . of dreams," a phrase he repeated over and over. Those were the last words I heard my father utter.

Okane had come back from the country in August to help us, and as soon as the Buddhist service of the Seventh Day was over she went home. Relatives we hadn't seen for years gathered at the house even for the services of the Thirty-fifth and Forty-ninth Days; but their number gradually dwindled until, on the Hundredth Day, only two or three people made an appearance.

The following spring I was graduated from higher school and entered the law department of the university. After the death of my unsociable father the guests who called at Heron's Nest, never very many, became so rare that at last there was hardly anyone but Sawako and her parents, who came about once a week. Mother would spend the whole day indoors, worshipping before Father's memorial tablet or, if she needed diversion, taking out my first mother's koto and playing it for a while. Because our house seemed so lonely and quiet now, she decided to start the bamboo mortar up again after its long silence; and she had Kajikawa cut a piece of green bamboo for it. Once again I could hear the familiar clack, clack that I had always loved.

Mother had borne up well while she was nursing Father the year before; even throughout the long series of Buddhist services that followed his death she always received our guests with dignity and self-control, and looked as full-cheeked and glowing with health as ever. But lately she seemed to show signs of fatigue, and sometimes had one of the maids massage her. Sawako offered her services whenever she was there.

One day when the silk tree was beginning to blossom I went out to the pavilion, knowing that I would find Mother and Sawako. Mother was lying in her usual place, on two cushions, while Sawako was energetically rubbing her arms.

"Sawako's good at massaging, isn't she?" I said.

"She's really wonderful!" Mother replied. "I don't know anyone who can equal her. She makes me so drowsy I almost drop off to sleep—it's a delicious feeling!"

"She *does* seem to know how to use her hands. Sawako, did you ever take lessons at this?"

"No, no lessons," she answered; "but I'm used to massaging my parents every day."

"That's what I thought," Mother said. "No wonder she'd put even a professional to shame. Tadasu, let her try it on you."

"I don't need a massage. But maybe I'll be her pupil and learn how to do it."

"Why should you learn?" asked Mother.

"Then I can massage you too. I ought to be able to learn that much."

"But your hands are too rough—"

"They're not rough, for a man. Isn't that so, Sawako? Just feel them!"

"Let's see," Sawako said, clasping my fingers in her own, and then stroking my palms. "My, you really do have nice smooth hands! You'll be fine!"

"It's because I've never gone in much for sports."

"Once you get the knack of it you'll soon be an expert!"

For some weeks after that I had Sawako teach me the various massaging techniques, and practiced them on Mother. Sometimes she got so ticklish that she shrieked with laughter.

In July the three of us would sit by the pond together to enjoy the cool of evening. Like my father, I would take a few bottles of beer to put under the spout of the bamboo mortar. Mother drank too, several glasses if I urged her; but Sawako always refused.

Mother would dangle her bare feet in the water, saying: "Sawako, you ought to try this. It makes you delightfully cool!"

But Sawako would sit there primly in her rather formal summer dress, with a heavy silk sash bound tightly around her waist. "Your feet are so pretty!" she would say. "I couldn't possibly show ugly ones like mine beside them!"

It seemed to me that she was too reserved. She might have been a little freer and more intimate with someone who would eventually become her mother-in-law. But she seemed too solicitous, too eager to please; often her words had a tinge of insincerity. Even her attitude toward me was curiously old-fashioned, for a girl who had been graduated from high school. Perhaps marriage would change her, but at the moment I couldn't help feeling that our relations were those of master and servant. Of course, it may have been precisely that quality in her which appealed to my father, and no doubt Mother's strength and firmness made her seem retiring, by contrast. Yet she seemed inadequate, somehow, for a young girl who was to become the third member of our small family.

A month or two after the silk-tree and pomegranate blossoms had fallen, when the crape myrtle was beginning to bloom and the plantain ripening, I had become fairly skillful at massaging and often asked Mother to come out to the pavilion for a treatment.

"A few minutes then, if you like," she would reply.

Naturally I took Sawako's place whenever she wasn't there, but even when she was with us I would brush her aside and say: "Let me try it—you watch!" Unable to forget the days when Mother had given her breasts to me, I now found my sole pleasure in massaging her. It was around then that Sawako, who had always worn her hair in Western style, began having it done up in a traditional high-piled Shimada, a coiffure that set off beautifully her ukiyoye-like face. She appeared to be getting ready for the Buddhist service that would be held on the first anniversary of my father's death, a time which was drawing near. Mother herself ordered new clothes for the occasion: among them, a formal robe of dark purple figured satin with a hollyhock pattern on the skirt, and a broad sash of thick-woven white silk dyed with a pattern of the seven autumn flowers.

The anniversary service was held at a temple at Hyakumamben, and we had dinner served in the reception hall of its private quarters. Both Mother and I noticed how cold and distant my relatives were. Some of them left as soon as they had burned incense, without stopping to join us at dinner. Ever since Father had married a former entertainer my relatives had held an oddly hostile and disdainful attitude toward our family. And now, to make matters worse, I was engaged to marry the gardener's daughter: it was only to be expected that they would talk. Still, I hadn't thought they would treat us quite so brusquely. Mother carried it off with her usual aplomb; but Sawako, who had gone to great trouble to dress appropriately for the occasion, seemed so dejected that I had to feel sorry for her.

"I'm beginning to wonder how our wedding will turn out," I said to Mother. "Do you suppose those people will come?"

"Why should you worry? You're not getting married for *their* benefit—it's enough if you and I and Sawako are happy." Mother seemed unconcerned, but before long I discovered that the hostility of our relatives was even more bitter than I had imagined.

Okane, who had come from Nagahama for the service, stayed with us a few days before going home. On the morning of the day she left, she suggested we go for another walk through the shrine forest.

"Okane, do you have something to tell me?" I asked.

"Yes, I do."

"I think I know what it is. It's about my wedding, isn't it?"

"That's not the only thing."

"Then what is it?"

"Well . . . but you mustn't get angry, Tadasu."

"I won't. Go ahead and say it."

"Anyway, you're sure to hear about it from somebody, so I guess it ought to come from me." Then, little by little, she told me the following story.

Of course it was true that my relatives were opposed to my forthcoming marriage, but that wasn't the only reason why they disapproved of us. Mother and I were the objects of their criticism, more than the match with Kajikawa's daughter. To put it bluntly, they believed that we were committing incest. According to them, Okane said, Mother and I began carrying on that way while Father was still alive, and Father himself, once he knew he wouldn't recover, had tolerated it—even encouraged it. Some went so far as to ask whose baby had been smuggled out to Tamba, suggesting that Takeshi was my own child, not my father's.

I wondered how on earth these people, who had been avoiding us for years, could have heard anything that would make them spread such wild rumors. But Okane explained that everyone in our neighborhood had been gossiping this way about us for a long time. It seems they all knew that Mother and I spent many hours alone together in the Silk-Tree Pavilion, which is probably why the rumors began to circulate. My relatives thought that my dying father arranged for me to marry Sawako because only a girl with her disadvantages would accept such a match. Most scandalous of all, his reason for wanting me to keep up appearances by taking a wife was presumably to have me continue my immoral relationship with Mother. Kajikawa was well aware of these circumstances in giving his daughter, and Sawako was going to marry out of respect for her father's wishes —needless to say, they had their eyes on our property. And so my relatives were outraged first of all by my father's part in this, then by Mother's, by mine, by Kajikawa's, and by his daughter's, in that order.

"Tadasu, be careful!" Okane ended by warning me. "Everybody knows people will talk, but they can say terrible things!" And she gave me a strange look out of the corner of her eye.

"Let them say what they please," I answered. "Nasty rumors like that will soon be forgotten."

"Well, maybe they'll come to the wedding next month after all," she said doubtfully as we parted.

I have no interest in going into detail about later

events. But perhaps I should summarize the important ones.

Our wedding ceremony was held on an auspicious day in November of that year. To please Mother, I wore a crested black silk kimono of Father's instead of a morning coat. Hardly any of my relatives appeared for the wedding; even the ones on Mother's side stayed away. Those who came were chiefly persons related to the Kajikawa family. Dr. Kato and his wife were kind enough to act as go-between. The doctor had been taking lessons in the No drama for many years, and he was more than happy to oblige by chanting the usual lines from *Takasago*. But as I listened to his sonorous voice my thoughts were far away.

After our marriage, Sawako's attitude toward Mother and me showed no particular change. We spent a few days in Nara and Isé for our honeymoon, but I was always careful to take precautions against having a child —that was one thing I never neglected. On the surface, Mother appeared to get along with her newly wed son and daughter-in-law in perfect harmony. After Father's death, she had continued to sleep in the twelve-mat veranda room, and she stayed there even after Sawako came; Sawako and I slept in my little six-mat room. That was as it should be, we felt, since I was still going to school and was still a dependent. For the same reason, Mother was in charge of all the household accounts.

As for Mother's life in those days, anyone would have taken it to be enviably carefree and leisurely. She amused herself by practicing Konoé-style calligraphy, reading classical Japanese literature, playing the koto, or strolling in the garden; and whenever she felt tired, day or night, she would have one of us give her a massage. During the day she had her massages in the pavilion, but at night she always called Sawako to her bedroom. Occasionally the three of us would go out to the theater, or on an excursion; but Mother was inclined to be frugal and paid close attention to even trivial sums of money, warning us to do our best to avoid needless expense. She was especially strict with Sawako and caused her a good deal of worry over the food bills. Mother was looking fresher and more youthful than ever, and so plump that she was beginning to get a double chin. Indeed, she was almost too plump—as if now that Father was dead her worries were over.

Our life went on in that way while I finished two more years at the university. Then about eleven o'clock one night in late June, shortly after I had gone to bed, I found myself being shaken by Sawako and told to get up.

"It's your mother!" she exclaimed, hurrying me off toward the other bedroom. "Something dreadful has happened!"

"Mother!" I called. "What's wrong?" There was no reply. She was lying there face down, moaning weakly and clutching her pillow with both hands.

"I'll show you what did it!" Sawako said, picking up a round fan from the floor near the head of the bed to reveal a large crushed centipede. Sawako explained that Mother had wanted a massage, and she had been giving her one for almost an hour. Mother was lying on her back asleep, breathing evenly, as Sawako rubbed her legs all the way down to her ankles. Suddenly she gave a scream of pain, and her feet arched convulsively. When Sawako looked up in alarm she saw a centipede crawling across Mother's breast, near the heart. Startled into action, she snatched up a nearby fan and brushed the insect away, luckily flicking it to the floor, where she covered it with the fan and then crushed it.

"If I'd only paid more attention . . ." Sawako said, looking deadly pale. "I was so busy massaging her . . ."

Dr. Kato came over immediately and took emergency measures, giving one injection after another; but Mother's suffering seemed to increase by the moment. All her symptoms—her color, breathing, pulse, and the rest—showed that her condition was more serious than we had thought. Dr. Kato stayed by her side, doing his best to save her; but around dawn she took a turn for the worse, and died soon afterward.

"It must have been shock," Dr. Kato told us.

Sawako was weeping aloud. "I'm to blame, I'm to blame," she kept repeating.

I have no intention of trying to describe the feelings of horror, grief, despair, dejection, which swept over me then; nor do I think it reflects credit on myself to be suspicious of anyone without a shred of evidence. Yet I cannot escape certain nagging doubts. . . .

It was some forty years since my grandfather had built the house he called Heron's Nest, which was by then at its most beautiful, well seasoned, with the patina of age that suits a Japanese-style building of this kind. In Grandfather's day the wood must have been too new to have such character, and as it grows older it will doubtless lose its satiny luster. The one really old building at Heron's Nest was the teahouse that Grandfather had brought there; and during my childhood, as I have said, it was infested by centipedes. But after that centipedes began to be seen frequently both in the pavilion and in the main house. There was nothing strange about finding one of them in the veranda room, where Mother was sleeping. Probably she had often seen centipedes in her room before, and Sawako, who was always going in to massage her, must have had the same experience. And so I wonder if Mother's death was entirely accidental. Might not someone have had a scheme in mind for using a centipede, if one of them appeared? Perhaps it was only a rather nasty joke, with no thought that a mere insect bite could be fatal. But supposing that her weak heart had been taken into account, that the possibility had seemed attractive. . . . Even if the scheme failed, no one could prove that the centipede had been deliberately caught and placed there.

Maybe the centipede did crawl onto her by accident. But Mother was a person who fell asleep very easily: whenever we massaged her she relaxed and dropped off into a sound sleep. She disliked a hard massage, preferring to have us stroke her so lightly and gently that her sleep was not disturbed. It would have been quite possible for someone to put a small object on her body without immediately awakening her. When I ran into her room, she was lying face-down writhing with pain; but Sawako said that earlier she had been lying on her back. I found it hard to believe that Sawako, who was massaging her legs, saw the centipede on Mother's breast the moment she looked up. Mother wasn't lying there naked; she was wearing her night kimono. It was odd that Sawako happened to see the insect—surely it would have been crawling under the kimono, out of sight. Perhaps she knew it was there.

I wish to emphasize that this is purely my own assumption, nothing more. But because this notion has become so firmly lodged in my mind, has haunted me for so long, I have at last tried to set it down in writing. After all, I intend to keep this record secret as long as I live.

Three more years have passed since then.

When I finished school two years ago, I was given a job as a clerk at the bank of which Father had been a director; and last spring, for reasons of my own, I divorced Sawako. A number of difficult conditions were proposed by her family, and in the end I had to agree to their terms. The whole complicated affair was so unpleasant that I have no desire to write about it. At the same time that I took steps to be divorced I sold Heron's Nest, so full of memories for me, both happy and sad, and built a small house for myself near the Honen Temple. I had Takeshi come to live with me, insisting on bringing him back from Seriu in spite of his own reluctance as well as that of his foster parents. And I asked Okane, who was quietly living out her days at Nagahama, to come and look after him, at least for a few years. Fortunately, she is still in good health, at sixty-four, and still able to take care of children. "If that's what you want, I'll help out with the little boy," she said, and left her comfortable retirement to come and live with us. Takeshi is six. At first he refused to be won over by Okane and me, but now we have become very close. Next year he will begin going to school. What makes me happiest is that he looks exactly like Mother. Not only that, he seems to have inherited something of her calm, open, generous temperament. I have no wish to marry again: I simply want to go on living as long as possible with Takeshi, my one link with Mother. Because my real mother died when I was a child, and my father and stepmother when I was some years older, I want to live for Takeshi until he is grown. I want to spare him the loneliness I knew.

June 27, 1931 (the anniversary of Mother's death)

Otokuni Tadasu

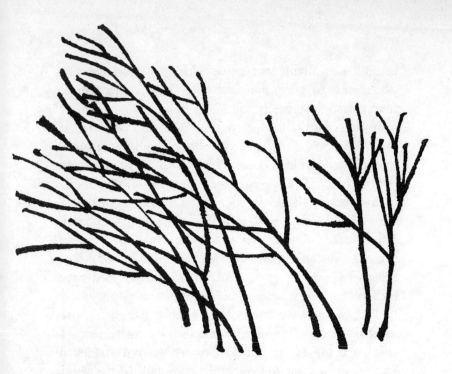

# THE TATTOOER

It was an age when men honored the noble virtue of frivolity, when life was not such a harsh struggle as it is today. It was a leisurely age, an age when professional wits could make an excellent livelihood by keeping rich or wellborn young gentlemen in a cloudless good humor and seeing to it that the laughter of Court ladies and geisha was never stilled. In the illustrated romantic novels of the day, in the Kabuki theater, where rough masculine heroes like Sadakuro and Jiraiya were transformed into women—everywhere beauty and strength were one. People did all they could to beautify themselves, some even having pigments injected into their precious skins. Gaudy patterns of line and color danced over men's bodies.

Visitors to the pleasure quarters of Edo preferred to hire palanquin bearers who were splendidly tattooed; courtesans of the Yoshiwara and the Tatsumi quarter fell in love with tattooed men. Among those so adorned were not only gamblers, firemen, and the like, but members of the merchant class and even samurai. Exhibitions were held from time to time; and the participants, stripped to show off their filigreed bodies, would pat themselves proudly, boast of their own novel designs, and criticize each other's merits.

There was an exceptionally skillful young tattooer named Seikichi. He was praised on all sides as a master the equal of Charibun or Yatsuhei, and the skins of dozens of men had been offered as the silk for his brush. Much of the work admired at the tattoo exhibitions was his. Others might be more noted for their shading, or their use of cinnabar, but Seikichi was famous for the unrivaled boldness and sensual charm of his art.

Seikichi had formerly earned his living as an ukiyoye painter of the school of Toyokuni and Kunisada, a background which, in spite of his decline to the status of a tattooer, was evident from his artistic conscience and sensitivity. No one whose skin or whose physique failed to interest him could buy his services. The clients he did accept had to leave the design and cost entirely to his discretion—and to endure for one or even two months the excruciating pain of his needles.

Deep in his heart the young tattooer concealed a secret

pleasure, and a secret desire. His pleasure lay in the agony men felt as he drove his needles into them, torturing their swollen, blood-red flesh; and the louder they groaned, the keener was Seikichi's strange delight. Shading and vermilioning—these are said to be especially painful—were the techniques he most enjoyed.

When a man had been pricked five or six hundred times in the course of an average day's treatment and had then soaked himself in a hot bath to bring out the colors, he would collapse at Seikichi's feet half dead. But Seikichi would look down at him coolly. "I dare say that hurts," he would remark with an air of satisfaction.

Whenever a spineless man howled in torment or clenched his teeth and twisted his mouth as if he were dying, Seikichi told him: "Don't act like a child. Pull yourself together—you have hardly begun to feel my needles!" And he would go on tattooing, as unperturbed as ever, with an occasional sidelong glance at the man's tearful face.

But sometimes a man of immense fortitude set his jaw and bore up stoically, not even allowing himself to frown. Then Seikichi would smile and say: "Ah, you are a stubborn one! But wait. Soon your body will begin to throb with pain. I doubt if you will be able to stand it. . . ."

For a long time Seikichi had cherished the desire to create a masterpiece on the skin of a beautiful woman. Such a woman had to meet various qualifications of character as well as appearance. A lovely face and a fine body were not enough to satisfy him. Though he inspected all the reigning beauties of the Edo gay quarters he found none who met his exacting demands. Several years had passed without success, and yet the face and figure of the perfect woman continued to obsess his thoughts. He refused to abandon hope.

One summer evening during the fourth year of his search Seikichi happened to be passing the Hirasei Restaurant in the Fukagawa district of Edo, not far from his own house, when he noticed a woman's bare milk-white foot peeping out beneath the curtains of a departing palanquin. To his sharp eye, a human foot was as expressive as a face. This one was sheer perfection. Exquisitely chiseled toes, nails like the iridescent shells along the shore at Enoshima, a pearl-like rounded heel, skin so lustrous that it seemed bathed in the limpid waters of a mountain spring—this, indeed, was a foot to be nourished by men's blood, a foot to trample on their bodies. Surely this was the foot of the unique woman who had so long eluded him. Eager to catch a glimpse of her face, Seikichi began to follow the palanquin. But after pursuing it down several lanes and alleys he lost sight of it altogether.

Seikichi's long-held desire turned into passionate love. One morning late the next spring he was standing on the bamboo-floored veranda of his home in Fukagawa, gazing at a pot of *omoto* lilies, when he heard someone at the garden gate. Around the corner of the inner fence appeared a young girl. She had come on an errand for a friend of his, a geisha of the nearby Tatsumi quarter.

"My mistress asked me to deliver this cloak, and she wondered if you would be so good as to decorate its lining," the girl said. She untied a saffron-colored cloth parcel and took out a woman's silk cloak (wrapped in a sheet of thick paper bearing a portrait of the actor Tojaku) and a letter.

The letter repeated his friend's request and went on to say that its bearer would soon begin a career as a geisha under her protection. She hoped that, while not forgetting old ties, he would also extend his patronage to this girl.

"I thought I had never seen you before," said Seikichi, scrutinizing her intently. She seemed only fifteen or sixteen, but her face had a strangely ripe beauty, a look of experience, as if she had already spent years in the gay quarter and had fascinated innumerable men. Her beauty mirrored the dreams of the generations of glamorous men and women who had lived and died in this vast capital, where the nation's sins and wealth were concentrated.

Seikichi had her sit on the veranda, and he studied her delicate feet, which were bare except for elegant straw sandals. "You left the Hirasei by palanquin one night last July, did you not?" he inquired.

"I suppose so," she replied, smiling at the odd question. "My father was still alive then, and he often took me there."

"I have waited five years for you. This is the first time I have seen your face, but I remember your foot. . . . Come in for a moment, I have something to show you."

She had risen to leave, but he took her by the hand
and led her upstairs to his studio overlooking the broad
river. Then he brought out two picture scrolls and un-
rolled one of them before her.

It was a painting of a Chinese princess, the favorite
of the cruel Emperor Chou of the Shang Dynasty. She
was leaning on a balustrade in a languorous pose, the
long skirt of her figured brocade robe trailing halfway
down a flight of stairs, her slender body barely able to
support the weight of her gold crown studded with
coral and lapis lazuli. In her right hand she held a large
wine cup, tilting it to her lips as she gazed down at a
man who was about to be tortured in the garden below.
He was chained hand and foot to a hollow copper pillar
in which a fire would be lighted. Both the princess and
her victim—his head bowed before her, his eyes closed,
ready to meet his fate—were portrayed with terrifying
vividness.

As the girl stared at this bizarre picture her lips trem-
bled and her eyes began to sparkle. Gradually her face
took on a curious resemblance to that of the princess. In
the picture she discovered her secret self.

"Your own feelings are revealed here," Seikichi told
her with pleasure as he watched her face.

"Why are you showing me this horrible thing?" the
girl asked, looking up at him. She had turned pale.

"The woman is yourself. Her blood flows in your
veins." Then he spread out the other scroll.

This was a painting called "The Victims." In the
middle of it a young woman stood leaning against the
trunk of a cherry tree: she was gloating over a heap of

men's corpses lying at her feet. Little birds fluttered about her, singing in triumph; her eyes radiated pride and joy. Was it a battlefield or a garden in spring? In this picture the girl felt that she had found something long hidden in the darkness of her own heart.

"This painting shows your future," Seikichi said, pointing to the woman under the cherry tree—the very image of the young girl. "All these men will ruin their lives for you."

"Please, I beg of you to put it away!" She turned her back as if to escape its tantalizing lure and prostrated herself before him, trembling. At last she spoke again. "Yes, I admit that you are right about me—I *am* like that woman. . . . So please, please take it away."

"Don't talk like a coward," Seikichi told her, with his malicious smile. "Look at it more closely. You won't be squeamish long."

But the girl refused to lift her head. Still prostrate, her face buried in her sleeves, she repeated over and over that she was afraid and wanted to leave.

"No, you must stay—I will make you a real beauty," he said, moving closer to her. Under his kimono was a vial of anesthetic which he had obtained some time ago from a Dutch physician.

The morning sun glittered on the river, setting the eight-mat studio ablaze with light. Rays reflected from the water sketched rippling golden waves on the paper sliding screens and on the face of the girl, who was fast asleep. Seikichi had closed the doors and taken up his tattooing instruments, but for a while he only sat there entranced, savoring to the full her uncanny beauty. He thought that he would never tire of contemplating her serene masklike face. Just as the ancient Egyptians had embellished their magnificent land with pyramids and sphinxes, he was about to embellish the pure skin of this girl.

Presently he raised the brush which was gripped between the thumb and last two fingers of his left hand, applied its tip to the girl's back, and, with the needle which he held in his right hand, began pricking out a design. He felt his spirit dissolve into the charcoal-black ink that stained her skin. Each drop of Ryukyu cinnabar that he mixed with alcohol and thrust in was a drop of his lifeblood. He saw in his pigments the hues of his own passions.

Soon it was afternoon, and then the tranquil spring day drew toward its close. But Seikichi never paused in his work, nor was the girl's sleep broken. When a servant came from the geisha house to inquire about her, Seikichi turned him away, saying that she had left long ago. And hours later, when the moon hung over the mansion across the river, bathing the houses along the bank in a dreamlike radiance, the tattoo was not yet half done. Seikichi worked on by candlelight.

Even to insert a single drop of color was no easy task. At every thrust of his needle Seikichi gave a heavy sigh and felt as if he had stabbed his own heart. Little by little the tattoo marks began to take on the form of a huge black-widow spider; and by the time the night sky was paling into dawn this weird, malevolent creature had stretched its eight legs to embrace the whole of the girl's back.

In the full light of the spring dawn boats were being rowed up and down the river, their oars creaking in the morning quiet; roof tiles glistened in the sun, and the haze began to thin out over white sails swelling in the early breeze. Finally Seikichi put down his brush and looked at the tattooed spider. This work of art had been the supreme effort of his life. Now that he had finished it his heart was drained of emotion.

The two figures remained still for some time. Then Seikichi's low, hoarse voice echoed quaveringly from the walls of the room:

"To make you truly beautiful I have poured my soul into this tattoo. Today there is no woman in Japan to compare with you. Your old fears are gone. All men will be your victims."

As if in response to these words a faint moan came from the girl's lips. Slowly she began to recover her senses. With each shuddering breath, the spider's legs stirred as if they were alive.

"You must be suffering. The spider has you in its clutches."

At this she opened her eyes slightly, in a dull stare. Her gaze steadily brightened, as the moon brightens in the evening, until it shone dazzlingly into his face.

"Let me see the tattoo," she said, speaking as if in a dream but with an edge of authority to her voice. "Giving me your soul must have made me very beautiful."

"First you must bathe to bring out the colors,"

whispered Seikichi compassionately. "I am afraid it will hurt, but be brave a little longer."

"I can bear anything for the sake of beauty." Despite the pain that was coursing through her body, she smiled.

"How the water stings! . . . Leave me alone—wait in the other room! I hate to have a man see me suffer like this!"

As she left the tub, too weak to dry herself, the girl pushed aside the sympathetic hand Seikichi offered her, and sank to the floor in agony, moaning as if in a nightmare. Her disheveled hair hung over her face in a wild tangle. The white soles of her feet were reflected in the mirror behind her.

Seikichi was amazed at the change that had come over the timid, yielding girl of yesterday, but he did as he was told and went to wait in his studio. About an hour later she came back, carefully dressed, her damp, sleekly combed hair hanging down over her shoulders. Leaning on the veranda rail, she looked up into the faintly hazy sky. Her eyes were brilliant; there was not a trace of pain in them.

"I wish to give you these pictures too," said Seikichi, placing the scrolls before her. "Take them and go."

"All my old fears have been swept away—and you are my first victim!" She darted a glance at him as bright as a sword. A song of triumph was ringing in her ears.

"Let me see your tattoo once more," Seikichi begged.

Silently the girl nodded and slipped the kimono off her shoulders. Just then her resplendently tattooed back caught a ray of sunlight and the spider was wreathed in flames.

# THE THIEF

It was years ago, at the school where I was preparing for Tokyo Imperial University.

My dormitory roommates and I used to spend a lot of time at what we called "candlelight study" (there was very little studying to it), and one night, long after lights-out, the four of us were doing just that, huddled around a candle talking on and on.

I recall that we were having one of our confused, heated arguments about love—a problem of great concern to us in those days. Then, by a natural course of development, the conversation turned to the subject of crime: we found ourselves talking about such things as swindling, theft, and murder.

"Of all crimes, the one we're most likely to commit is murder." It was Higuchi, the son of a well-known professor, who declared this. "But I don't believe I'd ever steal—I just couldn't do it. I think I could be friends with any other kind of person, but a thief seems to belong to a different species." A shadow of distaste darkened his handsome features. Somehow that frown emphasized his good looks.

"I hear there's been a rash of stealing in the dormitory lately." This time it was Hirata who spoke. "Isn't that so?" he asked, turning to Nakamura, our other roommate.

"Yes, and they say it's one of the students."

"How do they know?" I asked.

"Well, I haven't heard all the details—" Nakamura dropped his voice to a confidential whisper. "But it's happened so often it must be an inside job."

"Not only that," Higuchi put in, "one of the fellows in the north wing was just going into his room the other day when somebody pushed the door open from the inside, caught him with a hard slap in the face, and ran away down the hall. He chased after him, but by the time he got to the bottom of the stairs the other one was out of sight. Back in his room, he found his trunk and bookshelves in a mess, which proves it was the thief."

"Did he see his face?"

"No, it all happened too fast, but he says he looked

like one of us, the way he was dressed. Apparently he ran down the hall with his coat pulled up over his head— the one thing sure is that his coat had a wisteria crest."

"A wisteria crest?" said Hirata. "You can't prove anything by that." Maybe it was only my imagination, but I thought he flashed a suspicious look at me. At the same moment I felt that I instinctively made a wry face, since my own family crest is a wisteria design. It was only by chance that I wasn't wearing my crested coat that night.

"If he's one of us it won't be easy to catch him. Nobody wants to believe there's a thief among us." I was trying to get over my embarrassment because of that moment of weakness.

"No, they'll get him in a couple of days," Higuchi said emphatically. His eyes were sparkling. "This is a secret, but they say he usually steals things in the dressing room of the bathhouse, and for two or three days now the proctors have been keeping watch. They hide overhead and look down through a little hole."

"Oh? Who told you that?" Nakamura asked.

"One of the proctors. But don't go around talking about it."

"If *you* know so much, the thief probably knows it too!" said Hirata, looking disgusted.

Here I must explain that Hirata and I were not on very good terms. In fact, by that time we barely tolerated each other. I say "we," but it was Hirata who had taken a strong dislike to me. According to a friend of mine, he once remarked scornfully that I wasn't what everyone seemed to think I was, that he'd had a chance to see through me. And again: "I'm sick of him. He'll never be a friend of mine. It's only out of pity that I have anything to do with him."

He only said such things behind my back; I never heard them from him directly, though it was obvious that he loathed me. But it wasn't in my nature to demand an explanation. "If there's something wrong with me he ought to say so," I told myself. "If he doesn't have the kindness to tell me what it is, or if he thinks I'm not worth bothering with, then I won't think of *him* as a friend either." I felt a little lonely when I thought of his contempt for me, but I didn't really worry about it.

Hirata had an admirable physique and was the very type of masculinity that our school prides itself on, while I was skinny and pale and high-strung. There was something basically incompatible about us: I had to resign myself to the fact that we lived in separate worlds. Furthermore, Hirata was a judo expert of high rank, and displayed his muscles as if to say: "Watch out, or I'll give you a thrashing!" Perhaps it seemed cowardly of me to take such a meek attitude toward him, and no doubt I *was* afraid of his physical strength; but fortunately I was quite indifferent to matters of trivial pride or prestige. "I don't care how contemptuous the other fellow is; as long as I can go on believing in myself I don't need to feel bitter toward him." That was how I made up my mind, and so I was able to match Hirata's arrogance with my own cool magnanimity. I even told one of the other boys: "I can't help it if Hirata doesn't

understand me, but I appreciate his good points anyway."
And I actually believed it. I never considered myself a
coward. I was even rather conceited, thinking I must be
a person of noble character to be able to praise Hirata
from the bottom of my heart.

"A wisteria crest?" That night, when Hirata cast his
sudden glance at me, the malicious look in his eyes set my
nerves on edge. What could that look possibly mean?
Did he know that my family crest was wisteria? Or did I
take it that way simply because of my own private feelings? If Hirata suspected *me*, how was I to handle the
situation? Perhaps I should laugh good-naturedly and
say: "Then I'm under suspicion too, because I have the
same crest." If the others laughed along with me, I'd be
all right. But suppose one of them, say Hirata, only began
looking grimmer and grimmer—what then? When I
visualized that scene I couldn't very well speak out im-
pulsively.

It sounds foolish to worry about such a thing, but
during that brief silence all sorts of thoughts raced
through my mind. "In this kind of situation what difference is there, really, between an innocent man and an
actual criminal?" By then I felt that I was experiencing a
criminal's anxiety and isolation. Until a moment ago I had
been one of their friends, one of the elite of our famous
school. But now, if only in my own mind, I was an
outcast. It was absurd, but I suffered from my inability
to confide in them. I was uneasy about Hirata's slightest
mood—Hirata who was supposed to be my equal.

"A thief seems to belong to a different species."

Higuchi had probably said this casually enough, but now his words echoed ominously in my mind.

"A thief belongs to a different species. . . ." A thief! What a detestable name to be called! I suppose what makes a thief different from other men is not so much his criminal act itself as his effort to hide it at all costs, the strain of trying to put it out of his mind, the dark fears that he can never confess. And now I was becoming enshrouded by that darkness. I was trying not to believe that I was under suspicion; I was worrying about fears that I could not admit to my closest friend. Of course it must have been because Higuchi trusted me that he told us what he'd heard from the proctor. "Don't go around talking about it," he had said, and I was glad. But why should I feel glad? I thought. After all, Higuchi has never suspected me. Somehow I began to wonder about his motive for telling us.

It also struck me that if even the most virtuous person has criminal tendencies, maybe I wasn't the only one who imagined the possibility of being a thief. Maybe the others were experiencing a little of the same discomfort, the same elation. If so, then Higuchi, who had been singled out by the proctor to share his secret, must have felt very proud. Among the four of us it was he who was most trusted, he who was thought least likely to belong to that "other species." And if he won that trust because he came from a wealthy family and was the son of a famous professor, then I could hardly avoid envying him. Just as his social status improved his moral character, so my own background—I was acutely conscious of being a scholarship student, the son of a poor farmer—debased mine. For me to feel a kind of awe in his presence had nothing to do with whether or not I was a thief. We *did* belong to different species. I felt that the more he trusted me, with his frank, open attitude, the more the gulf between us deepened. The more friendly we tried to be, joking with each other in apparent intimacy, gossiping and laughing together, the more the distance between us increased. There was nothing I could do about it.

For a long time afterward I worried about whether or not I ought to wear that coat of mine with the "wisteria crest." Perhaps if I wore it around nonchalantly no one would pay any attention. But suppose they looked at me as much as to say: "Ah, he's wearing it!" Some would suspect me, or try to suppress their doubts of me, or feel sorry for me because I was under suspicion. If I became embarrassed and uneasy not only with Hirata and Higuchi but with all the students, and if I then felt obliged to put my coat away, that would seem even more sinister. What I dreaded was not the bare fact of being suspect, but all the unpleasant emotions that would be stirred up in others. If I were to cause doubt in other people's minds I would create a barrier between myself and those who had always been my friends. Even theft itself was not as ugly as the suspicions that would be aroused by it. No one would want to think of me as a thief: as long as it hadn't been proved, they'd want to go on associating with me as freely as ever, forcing themselves to trust me. Otherwise, what would friendship mean? Thief or not, I might be guilty of a worse sin than stealing from a friend: the sin of spoiling a friendship. Sowing seeds of doubt about myself was criminal. It *was* worse than stealing. If I were a prudent, clever thief—no, I mustn't put it that way—if I were a thief with the least bit of conscience and consideration for other people, I'd try to keep my friendships untarnished, try to be open with my friends, treat them with a sincerity and warmth that I need never be ashamed of, while carrying out my thefts in secrecy. Perhaps I'd be what people call "a brazen thief," but if you look at it from the thief's point of view, it's the most honest attitude to take. "It's true that I steal, but it's equally true that I value my friends," such a man would say. "That is typical of a thief, that's why he belongs to a different species." Anyhow, when I started thinking that way, I couldn't help becoming more and more aware of the distance between me and my friends. Before I knew it I felt like a full-fledged thief.

One day I mustered up my courage and wore the crested coat out on the school grounds. I happened to meet Nakamura, and we began walking along together.

"By the way," I remarked, "I hear they haven't caught the thief yet."

"That's right," Nakamura answered, looking away.

"Why not? Couldn't they trap him at the bathhouse?"

"He didn't show up there again, but you still hear about lots of things being stolen in other places. They say the proctors called Higuchi in the other day and gave him the devil for letting their plan leak out."

"Higuchi?" I felt the color drain from my face.

"Yes. . . ." He sighed painfully, and a tear rolled

down his cheek. "You've got to forgive me! I've kept it from you till now, but I think you ought to know the truth. You won't like this, but you're the one the proctors suspect. I hate to talk about it—I've never suspected you for a minute. I believe in you. And because I believe in you, I just had to tell you. I hope you won't hold it against me."

"Thanks for telling me. I'm grateful to you." I was almost in tears myself, but at the same time I thought: "It's come at last!" As much as I dreaded it, I'd been expecting this day to arrive.

"Let's drop the subject," said Nakamura, to comfort me. "I feel better now that I've told you."

"But we can't put it out of our minds just because we hate to talk about it. I appreciate your kindness, but I'm not the only one who's been humiliated—I've brought shame on you too, as my friend. The mere fact that I'm under suspicion makes me unworthy of friendship. Any way you look at it, my reputation is ruined. Isn't that so? I imagine you'll turn your back on me too."

"I swear I never will—and I don't think you've brought any shame on me." Nakamura seemed alarmed by my reproachful tone. "Neither does Higuchi. They say he did his best to defend you in front of the proctors. He told them he'd doubt himself before he doubted you."

"But they still suspect me, don't they? There's no use trying to spare my feelings. Tell me everything you know. I'd rather have it that way."

Then Nakamura hesitantly explained: "Well, it seems the proctors get all kinds of tips. Ever since Higuchi talked too much that night there haven't been any more thefts at the bathhouse, and that's why they suspect you."

"But I wasn't the only one who heard him!"—I didn't say this, but the thought occurred to me immediately. It made me feel even more lonely and wretched.

"But how did they know Higuchi told us? There were only the four of us that night, so if nobody else knew it, and if you and Higuchi trust me—"

"You'll have to draw your own conclusions," Nakamura said, with an imploring look. "You know who it is. He's misjudged you, but I don't want to criticize him."

A sudden chill came over me. I felt as if Hirata's eyes were glaring into mine.

"Did you talk to him about me?"

"Yes. . . . But I hope you realize that it isn't easy, since I'm his friend as well as yours. In fact, Higuchi and I had a long argument with him last night, and he says he's leaving the dormitory. So I have to lose one friend on account of another."

I took Nakamura's hand and gripped it hard. "I'm grateful for friends like you and Higuchi," I said, tears streaming from my eyes. Nakamura cried too. For the first time in my life I felt that I was really experiencing the warmth of human compassion. This was what I had been searching for while I was tormented by my sense of helpless isolation. No matter how vicious a thief I might be, I could never steal anything from Nakamura.

After a while I said: "To tell you the truth, I'm not worth the trouble I'm causing you. I can't stand by in silence and see you two lose such a good friend because of someone like me. Even though he doesn't trust me, I still respect him. He's a far better man than I am. I recognize his value as well as anyone. So why don't I move out instead, if it's come to that? Please—let *me* go, and you three can keep on living together. Even if I'm alone I'll feel better about it."

"But there's no reason for you to leave," said Nakamura, his voice charged with emotion. "I recognize his good points too, but you're the one that's being persecuted. I won't side with him when it's so unfair. If *you* leave, *we* ought to leave too. You know how stubborn he is—once he's made up his mind to go he's not apt to change it. Why not let him do as he pleases? We might as well wait for him to come to his senses and apologize. That shouldn't take very long anyway."

"But he'll never come back to apologize. He'll go on hating me forever."

Nakamura seemed to assume that I felt resentful toward Hirata. "Oh, I don't think so," he said quickly. "He'll stick to his word—that's both his strength and his weakness—but once he knows he's wrong he'll come and apologize, and make a clean breast of it. That's one of the likable things about him."

"It would be fine if he did . . . ," I said thoughtfully. "He may come back to you, but I don't believe he'll ever make friends with me again. . . . But you're right, he's really likable. I only wish he liked me too."

Nakamura put his hand on my shoulder as if to protect his poor friend, as we plodded listlessly along on the grass. It was evening and a light mist hung over the school grounds: we seemed to be on an island surrounded by endless gray seas. Now and then a few students walking the other way would glance at me and go on. They already know, I thought; they're ostracizing me. I felt an overwhelming loneliness.

That night Hirata seemed to have changed his mind; he showed no intention of moving. But he refused to speak to us—even to Higuchi and Nakamura. Yet for me to leave at this stage was impossible, I decided. Not only would I be disregarding the kindness of my friends, I would be making myself seem all the more guilty. I ought to wait a little longer.

"Don't worry," my two friends were forever telling me. "As soon as they catch him the whole business will clear up." But even after another week had gone by, the criminal was still at large and the thefts were as frequent as ever. At last even Nakamura and Higuchi lost some money and a few books.

"Well, you two finally got it, didn't you? But I have a feeling the rest of us won't be touched." I remember Hirata's taunting look as he made this sarcastic remark.

After supper Nakamura and Higuchi usually went to the library, and Hirata and I were left to confront each other. I found this so uncomfortable that I began spending my evenings away from the dormitory too, either going to the library or taking long walks. One night around nine-thirty I came back from a walk and looked into our study. Oddly enough, Hirata wasn't there, nor did the others seem to be back yet. I went to look in our bedroom, but it was empty too. Then I went back to the study and over to Hirata's desk. Quietly I opened his drawer and ferreted out the registered letter that had come to him from his home a few days ago. Inside the letter were three ten-yen money orders, one of which I leisurely removed and put in my pocket. I pushed the drawer shut again and sauntered out into the hall. Then I went down to the yard, cut across the tennis court, and headed for the dark weedy hollow where I always buried the things I stole. But at that moment someone yelled: "Thief!" and flew at me from behind, knocking me down with a blow to my head. It was Hirata.

"Come on, let's have it! Let's see what you stuck in your pocket!"

"All right, all right, you don't have to shout like that," I answered calmly, smiling at him. "I admit I stole your money order. If you ask for it I'll give it back to you, and if you tell me to come with you I'll go anywhere you say. So we understand each other, don't we? What more do you want?"

Hirata seemed to hesitate, but soon began furiously raining blows on my face. Somehow the pain was not wholly unpleasant. I felt suddenly relieved of the staggering burden I had been carrying.

"There's no use beating me up like this, when I fell right into your trap for you. I made that mistake because you were so sure of yourself—I thought: 'Why the devil can't I steal from *him*?' But now you've found me out, so that's all there is to it. Later on we'll laugh about it together."

I tried to shake Hirata's hand good-naturedly, but he grabbed me by the collar and dragged me off toward our room. That was the only time Hirata seemed contemptible in my eyes.

"Hey, you fellows, I've caught the thief! You can't say I was taken in by him!" Hirata swaggered into our room and shoved me down in front of Nakamura and Higuchi, who were back from the library. Hearing the commotion, the other boys in the dormitory came swarming around our doorway.

"Hirata's right!" I told my two friends, picking myself up from the floor. "I'm the thief." I tried to speak in my normal tone, as casually as ever, but I realized that my face had gone pale.

"I suppose you hate me," I said to them. "Or else you're ashamed of me. . . . You're both honest, but you're certainly gullible. Haven't I been telling you the truth over and over again? I even said: 'I'm not the person you think I am. Hirata's the man to trust. He'll never be taken in.' But you didn't understand. I told you: 'Even if you become friendly with Hirata again, he'll never make friends with *me*!' I went as far as to say: 'I know better than anyone what a fine fellow Hirata is!' Isn't that so? I've never lied to you, have I? You may ask why I didn't come out and tell you the whole truth. You probably think I was deceiving you after all. But try looking at it from my position. I'm sorry, but stealing is one thing I can't control. Still, I didn't like to deceive you, so I told you the truth in a roundabout way. I couldn't be any more honest than that—it's your fault for not taking my hints. Maybe you think I'm just being perverse, but I've never been more serious. You'll probably ask why I don't quit stealing, if I'm so anxious to be honest. But that's not a fair question. You see, I was born a thief. I tried to be as sincere as I could with you under the circumstances. There was nothing else I could do. Even then my conscience bothered me—didn't I ask you to let *me* move out, instead of Hirata? I wasn't trying to fool you, I really wanted to do it for your sake. It's true that I stole from you, but it's also true that I'm your friend. I appeal to your friendship: I want you to understand that even a thief has feelings."

Nakamura and Higuchi stood there in silence, blinking with astonishment.

"Well, I can see you think I've got a lot of nerve. You just don't understand me. I guess it can't be helped, since you're of a different species." I smiled to conceal my bitterness, and added: "But since I'm your friend I'll warn you that this isn't the last time a thing like this will happen. So be on your guard! You two made friends with a thief because of your gullibility. You're likely to run into trouble when you go out in the world. Maybe you get better grades in school, but Hirata is a better man. You can't fool Hirata!"

When I singled him out for praise, Hirata made a wry face and looked away. At that moment he seemed strangely ill at ease.

Many years have passed since then. I became a professional thief and have been often behind bars; yet I cannot forget those memories—especially my memories of Hirata. Whenever I am about to commit a crime I see his face before me. I see him swaggering about as haughtily as ever, sneering at me: "Just as I suspected!" Yes, he was a man of character with great promise. But the world is mysterious. My prediction that the naïve Higuchi would "run into trouble" was wrong: partly through his father's influence, he has had a brilliant career—traveling abroad, earning a doctoral degree, and today holding a high position in the Ministry of Railways. Meanwhile nobody knows what has become of Hirata. It's no wonder we think life is unpredictable.

I assure my reader that this account is true. I have not written a single dishonest word here. And, as I hoped Nakamura and Higuchi would, I hope you will believe that delicate moral scruples can exist in the heart of a thief like me.

But perhaps you won't believe me either. Unless of course (if I may be pardoned for suggesting it) you happen to belong to my own species.

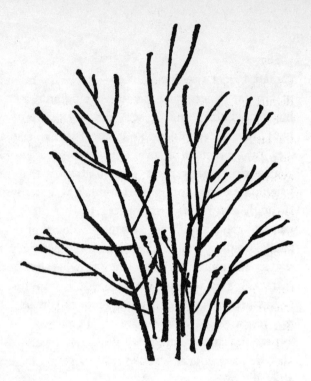

# AGURI

*"Getting a bit thinner, aren't you? Is anything wrong? You're not looking well these days. . . ."*

That was what his friend T. had said in passing when they happened to meet him along the Ginza a little while ago. It reminded Okada that he had spent last night with Aguri too, and he felt more fatigued than ever. Of course T. could scarcely have been teasing him about *that*—his relations with Aguri were too well known, there was nothing unusual about being seen strolling on the Ginza in downtown Tokyo with her. But to Okada, with his taut-stretched nerves and his vanity, T.'s remark was disturbing. Everyone he met said he was "getting thinner" —he had worried about it himself for over a year. In the last six months you could almost see the change from one day to the next, as his fine rich flesh slowly melted away. He'd got into the habit of furtively examining his body in the mirror whenever he took a bath, to see how emaciated it was becoming, but by now he was afraid to look. In the past (until a year or two ago, at least) people said he had a feminine sort of figure. He had rather prided himself on it. "The way I'm built makes you think of a woman, doesn't it?" he used to say archly to his friends at the bathhouse. "Don't get any funny ideas!" But now . . .

It was from the waist down that his body had seemed most feminine. He remembered often standing before a mirror entranced by his own reflection, running his hand lovingly over his plump white buttocks, as well rounded as a young girl's. His thighs and calves were almost *too* bulging, but it had delighted him to see how fat they looked—the legs of a chophouse waitress—alongside Aguri's slim ones. She was only fourteen then, and her legs were as slender and straight as those of any Western girl: stretched out beside his in the bath, they looked more beautiful than ever, which pleased him as much as it did Aguri. She was a tomboy, and used to push him over on his back and sit on him, or walk over him, or trample on his thighs as if she were flattening a lump of dough. . . . But now what miserable skinny legs he had! His knees and ankles had been nicely dimpled, but for some time now the bones had stuck out pathetically, you could see them moving under the skin. The exposed blood vessels looked like earthworms. His buttocks were flattening out too: when he sat on something hard it felt as if a pair of boards had been clapped together. Yet it was only lately that his ribs began to show: one by one they had come into sharp relief, from the bottom up, till now you could see the whole skeleton of his chest so distinctly that it made a somewhat grim anatomy lesson. He was such a heavy eater that his little round belly had seemed safe enough, but even *that* was gradually shriveling—at this rate, you'd soon be able to make out his inner organs! Next to his legs, he had prided himself on his smooth "feminine" arms; at the slightest excuse he rolled up his sleeves to show them off. Women admired and envied them, and he used to joke with his girl friends about it. Now, even to the fondest eye, they didn't look at all feminine—or masculine either for that matter. They weren't so much human arms as two sticks of wood. Two pencils hanging down beside his body. All the little hollows between one bone and the next were deepening, the flesh dwindling away. How much longer can I go on losing weight like this? he asked himself. It's amazing that I can still get around at all, when I'm so horribly emaciated! He felt grateful to be alive, but also a little terrified. . . .

These thoughts were so unnerving that Okada had a sudden attack of giddiness. There was a heavy, numbing sensation in the back of his head; he felt as if his knees were shaking and his legs buckling under him, as if he were being knocked over backward. No doubt the state of his nerves had something to do with it, but he knew very well that it came from long overindulgence, sexual and otherwise—as did his diabetes, which caused some of his symptoms. There was no use feeling sorry now, but he *did* regret having to pay for it so soon, and pay, moreover, by the deterioration of his good looks, his proudest possession. I'm still in my thirties, he thought. I don't see why my health has to fail so badly. . . . He wanted to cry and stamp his feet in rage.

"Wait a minute—look at that ring! An aquamarine, isn't it? I wonder how it would look on me."

Aguri had stopped short and tugged at his sleeve; she was peering into a Ginza show window. As she spoke she waved the back of her hand under Okada's nose, flexing and extending her fingers. Her long slender fingers—so soft they seemed made only for pleasure—gleamed in the bright May afternoon sunlight with an especially seductive charm. Once in Nanking he had looked at a singsong girl's fingers resting gracefully on the table like the petals of some exquisite hothouse flower, and thought there could be no more delicate beauty than a Chinese woman's hands. But Aguri's hands were only a little larger, only a little more like those of an ordinary human being. If the singsong girl's hands were hothouse flowers, hers were fresh young wildflowers: the fact that they were not so artificial only made them more appealing. How pretty a bouquet of flowers with petals like these would be. . . .

"What do you think? Would it look nice?" She poised

her fingertips on the railing in front of the window, pressed them back in the half-moon curve of a dancer's gesture, and stared at them as if she had lost all interest in the ring.

Okada mumbled something in reply but forgot it immediately. He was staring at her hands too, at the beautiful hands he knew so well. . . . Several years had passed since he began playing with those delicious morsels of flesh: squeezing them in his palms like clay, putting them inside his clothes like a pocket warmer, or in his mouth, under his arm, under his chin. But while he was steadily aging, her mysterious hands looked younger every year. When Aguri was only fourteen they seemed yellow and dry, with tiny wrinkles, but now at seventeen the skin was white and smooth, and yet even on the coldest day so sleek you'd think the oil would cloud the gold band of her ring. Childish little hands, as tender as a baby's and as voluptuous as a whore's—how fresh and youthful they were, always restlessly seeking pleasure! . . . But why had his health failed like this? Just to look at her hands made him think of all they had provoked him to, all that went on in those secret rooms where they met; and his head ached from the potent stimulus. . . . As he kept his eyes fixed on them, he began to think of the rest of her body. Here in broad daylight on the crowded Ginza he saw her naked shoulders . . . her breasts . . . her belly . . . buttocks . . . legs . . . one by one all the parts of her body came floating up before his eyes with frightening clarity in queer, undulating shapes. And he felt crushed under the solid weight of her hundred and fifteen or twenty pounds. . . . For a moment Okada thought he was going to faint—his head was reeling, he seemed on the verge of falling. . . . Idiot! Suddenly he drove away his fantasies, steadied his tottering legs. . . .

"Well, are we going shopping?"

"All right."

They began walking toward Shimbashi Station. . . . Now they were off to Yokohama.

Today Aguri must be happy, he thought, I'll be buying her a whole new outfit. You'll find the right things for yourself in the foreign shops of Yokohama, he had told her; in Arthur Bond's and Lane Crawford, and that Indian jeweler, and the Chinese dressmaker. . . . You're the exotic type of beauty; Japanese kimonos cost more than they're worth, and they're not becoming to you. Notice the Western and the Chinese ladies: they know how to set off their faces and figures to advantage, and without spending too much money at it. You ought to do the same from now on. . . . And so Aguri had been looking forward to today. As she walks along, breathing a little heavily in the early-summer heat, her white skin damp with sweat under the heavy flannel kimono that hampers her long, youthful limbs, she imagines herself shedding these "unbecoming" clothes, fixing jewels on her ears, hanging a necklace around her throat, slipping into a near-transparent blouse of rustling silk or cambric, swaying elegantly on tiptoes in fragile high-heeled shoes. . . . She sees herself looking like the Western ladies who pass them on the street. Whenever one of them comes along Aguri studies her from head to toe, following her with her eyes and badgering him with questions about how he likes that hat, or that necklace, or whatever.

But Okada shared her preoccupation. All the smart young foreign ladies made him think of an Aguri transfigured by Western clothes. . . . I'd like to buy that for you, he thought; and this too. . . . Yet why couldn't he be a little more cheerful? Later on they would play their enchanting game together. It was a clear day with a refreshing breeze, a fine May afternoon for any kind of outing . . . for dressing her up in airy new garments, grooming her like a beloved pet, and then taking her on the train in search of a delightful hiding place. Somewhere with a balcony overlooking the blue sea, or a room at a hot-spring resort where the young leaves of the forest glisten beyond glass doors, or else a gloomy, out-of-the-way hotel in the foreign quarter. And there the game would begin, the enchanting game that he was always dreaming of, that gave him his only reason for living. . . . Then she would stretch herself out like a leopard. A leopard in necklace and earrings. A leopard brought up as a house pet, knowing exactly how to please its master, but one whose occasional flashes of ferocity made its master cringe. Frisking, scratching, striking, pouncing on him—finally ripping and tearing him to shreds, and trying to suck the marrow out of his bones. . . . A deadly game! The mere thought of it had an ecstatic lure for him. He found himself trembling with excitement. Once again his head was swimming, he thought he was going to faint. . . . He wondered if he might be dying, now at last, aged thirty-four, collapsing here in the street. . . .

"Oh, are you dead? How tiresome!" Aguri glances absent-mindedly at the corpse lying at her feet. The two-o'clock sun beats down on it, casting dark shadows in the hollows of its sunken cheeks. . . . If he *had* to die he might have waited half a day longer, till we finished our shopping. . . . Aguri clicks her tongue in annoyance. I don't want to get mixed up in this if I can help it, she thinks, but I suppose I can't just leave him here. And there are hundreds of yen in his pocket. That money was *mine*—he might at least have willed it to me before he died. The poor fool was so crazy about me he couldn't possibly resent it if I take the money and buy anything I please, or flirt with any man I please. He knew I was fickle—he even seemed to enjoy it, sometimes. . . . As she makes excuses to herself Aguri extracts the money from his pocket. If he tries to haunt me I won't be afraid of *him*—he'll listen to me whether he's alive or dead. I'll have my way. . . .

"Look, Mr. Ghost! I bought this wonderful ring with your money. I bought this beautiful lace-trimmed skirt. And see!" (She pulls up her skirt to show her legs.) "See these legs you're so fond of, these gorgeous legs? I bought a pair of white silk stockings, and pink garters too—all with your money! Don't you think I have good taste? Don't you think I look angelic? Although you're dead I'm wearing the right clothes for me, just the way you wanted, and I'm having a marvelous time! I'm so happy, really happy! You must be happy too, for having given me all this. Your dreams have come true in me, now that I'm so beautiful, so full of life! Well, Mr. Ghost, my poor love-struck Mr. Ghost who can't rest in peace—how about a smile?"

Then I'll hug that cold corpse as hard as I can, hug it till his bones crack, and he screams: "Stop! I can't bear any more!" If he doesn't give in, I'll find a way to seduce him. I'll love him till his withered skin is torn to shreds, till his last drop of blood is squeezed out, till his dry bones fall apart. Then even a ghost ought to feel satisfied. . . .

"What's the matter? Is something on your mind?"

"Uh-h . . ." Okada began mumbling under his breath.

They looked as if they were having a pleasant walk together—it ought to have been extremely pleasant—and yet he couldn't share her gaiety. One sad thought after another welled up, and he felt exhausted even before they began their game. It's only nerves, he had told himself; nothing serious, I'll get over it as soon as I go outside. That was how he had talked himself into coming, but he'd been wrong. It wasn't nerves alone: his arms and legs were so tired they were ready to drop off, and his joints creaked as he walked. Sometimes being tired was a mild, rather enjoyable sensation, but when it got this bad it might be a dangerous symptom. At this very moment, all unknown to him, wasn't his system being invaded by some grave disease? Wasn't he staggering along letting the disease take its own course till it overwhelmed him? Better to collapse right away than be so ghastly tired! He'd like to sink down into a soft bed. Maybe his health had demanded it long ago. Any doctor would be alarmed and say: "Why in heaven's name are you out walking in *your* condition? You belong in bed —it's no wonder you're dizzy!"

The thought left Okada feeling more exhausted than ever; walking became an even greater effort. On the Ginza sidewalk—that dry, stony surface he so much enjoyed striding over when he was well—every step sent a shock of pain vibrating up from his heel to the top of his head. First of all, his feet were cramped by these tan box-calf shoes that compressed them in a narrow mold. Western clothes were intended for healthy, robust men: to anyone in a weakened condition they were quite insupportable. Around the waist, over the shoulders, under the arms, around the neck—every part of the body was pressed and squeezed by clasps and buttons and rubber and leather, layer over layer, as if you were strapped to a cross. And of course you had to put on stockings before the shoes, stretching them carefully up on your legs by garters. Then you put on a shirt, and then trousers, cinching them in with a buckle at the back till they cut into your waist and hanging them from your shoulders with suspenders. Your neck was choked in a close-fitting collar, over which you fastened a noose-like necktie, and stuck a pin in it. If a man is well filled out, the tighter you squeeze him, the more vigorous and bursting with vitality he seems; but a man who is only skin and bones can't stand that. The thought that he was wearing such appalling garments made Okada gasp for breath, made his arms and legs even wearier. It was only because these Western clothes held him together that he was able to keep on walking at all—but to think of stiffening a limp, helpless body, shackling it hand and foot, and driving it ahead with shouts of "Keep going! Don't you dare collapse!" It was enough to make a man want to cry. . . .

Suddenly Okada imagined his self-control giving way, imagined himself breaking down and sobbing. . . . This sprucely dressed middle-aged gentleman who was strolling along the Ginza until a moment ago, apparently out to enjoy the fine weather with the young lady at his side, a gentleman who looks as if he might be the young lady's uncle—all at once screws up his face into a dreadful shape and begins to bawl like a child! He stops there in the street and pesters her to carry him. "*Please*, Aguri! I can't go another step! Carry me piggyback!"

"What's wrong with you?" says Aguri sharply, glaring at him like a stern auntie. "Stop acting like that! Everybody's looking at you!" . . . Probably she doesn't notice that he has gone mad: it's not unusual for her to see him in tears. This is the first time it's happened on the street, but when they're alone together he always cries like this. . . . How silly of him! she must be thinking. There's nothing for him to cry about in public—if he wants to cry I'll let him cry his heart out later! "Shh! Be quiet! You're embarrassing me!"

But Okada won't stop crying. At last he begins to kick and struggle, tearing off his necktie and collar and throwing them down. And then, dog-tired, panting for breath, he falls flat on the pavement. "I can't walk any more. . . . I'm sick . . . ," he mutters, half delirious. "Get me out of these clothes and put me in something soft! Make a bed for me here, I don't care if it *is* in the street!"

Aguri is at her wit's end, so embarrassed her face is as red as fire. There is no escape—a huge crowd of people has swarmed around them under the blazing sun. A policeman turns up. . . . He questions Aguri in front of everyone. ("Who do you suppose she is?" people begin whispering to one another. "Some rich man's daughter?" "No, I don't think so." "An actress?") "What's the matter there?" the policeman asks Okada, not unkindly. He regards him as a lunatic. "How about getting up now, instead of sleeping in a place like this?"

"I won't! I won't! I'm sick, I tell you! How can I ever get up?" Still sobbing weakly, Okada shakes his head. . . .

He could see the spectacle vividly before his eyes. He felt as if he were actually sobbing. . . .

"Papa . . ." A faint voice is calling—a sweet little voice, not Aguri's. It is the voice of a chubby four-year-old girl in a printed muslin kimono, who beckons to him with her tiny hand. Behind her stands a woman whose hair is done up in a chignon; she looks like the child's mother. . . . "Teruko! Teruko! Here I am! . . . Ah, Osaki! Are you there too?" And then he sees his own mother, who died several years ago. She is gesturing eagerly and trying hard to tell him something, but she is too far away, a veil of mist hangs between them. . . . Yet he realizes that tears of loneliness and sorrow are streaming down her cheeks. . . .

I'm going to stop thinking sad thoughts like that, Okada

told himself; thoughts about Mother, about Osaki and the child, about death. . . . Why did they weigh so heavily on him? No doubt because of his poor health. Two or three years ago when he was well they wouldn't have seemed so overpowering, but now they combined with physical exhaustion to thicken and clog all his veins. And when he was sexually excited the clogging became more and more oppressive. . . . As he walked along in the bright May sunshine he felt himself isolated from the world around him: his sight was dimmed, his hearing faded, his mind turned darkly, obstinately in upon itself.

"If you have enough money left," Aguri was saying, "how about buying me a wrist watch?" They had just come to Shimbashi Station; perhaps she thought of it when she saw the big clock.

"They have good watches in Shanghai. I should have bought you one when I was there."

For a moment Okada's fancies flew off to China. . . . At Soochow, aboard a beautiful pleasure boat, being poled along a serene canal toward the soaring Tiger Hill Pagoda . . . Inside the boat two young lovers sit blissfully side by side like turtledoves. . . . He and Aguri transformed into a Chinese gentleman and a singsong girl. . . .

Was he in love with Aguri? If anyone asked, of course he would answer "Yes." But at the thought of Aguri his mind became a pitch-dark room hung with black velvet curtains—a room like a conjurer's stage set—in the center of which stood the marble statue of a nude woman. Was that really Aguri? Surely the Aguri he loved was the living, breathing counterpart of that marble figure. This girl walking beside him now through the foreign shopping quarter of Yokohama—he could see the lines of her body through the loose flannel clothing that enveloped it, could picture to himself the statue of the "woman" under her kimono. He recalled each elegant trace of the chisel. Today he would adorn the statue with jewels and silks. He would strip off that shapeless, unbecoming kimono, reveal that naked "woman" for an instant, and then dress her in Western clothes: he would accentuate every curve and hollow, give her body a brilliant surface and lively flowing lines; he would fashion swelling contours, make her wrists, ankles, neck, all strikingly slender and graceful. Really. shopping to enhance the beauty of the woman you love ought to be like a dream come true.

A dream . . . There was indeed something dreamlike about walking along this quiet, almost deserted street lined with massive Western-style buildings, looking into show windows here and there. It wasn't garish, like the Ginza; even in daytime a hush lay over it. Could anyone be alive in these silent buildings, with their thick gray walls where the window glass glittered like fish eyes, reflecting the blue sky? It seemed more like a museum gallery than a street. And the merchandise displayed behind the glass on both sides was bright and colorful, with the fascinating, mysterious luster of a garden at the bottom of the sea.

A curio-shop sign in English caught his eye: ALL KINDS OF JAPANESE FINE ARTS: PAINTINGS, PORCELAINS, BRONZE STATUES. . . . And one that must have been for a Chinese tailor: MAN CHANG DRESS MAKER FOR LADIES AND GENTLE-

MEN. . . . And also: JAMES BERGMAN JEWELLERY . . .
RINGS, EARRINGS, NECKLACES. . . . E & B CO. FOREIGN DRY
GOODS AND GROCERIES . . . LADY'S UNDERWEARS . . . DRA-
PERIES, TAPESTRIES, EMBROIDERIES. . . . Somehow the
very ring of these words in his ear had the heavy, solemn
beauty of the sound of a piano. . . . Only an hour by
streetcar from Tokyo, yet you felt as if you had arrived
at some far-off place. And you hesitated to go inside these
shops when you saw how lifeless they looked, their doors
firmly shut. In these show windows—perhaps because
they were meant for foreigners—goods were set out on
display in a cold, formal arrangement well behind the
glass, quite unlike the ingratiating clutter of the windows
along the Ginza. There seemed to be no clerks or shop-
boys at work; all kinds of luxuries were on display, but
these dimly lit rooms were as gloomy as a Buddhist shrine.
. . . Still, that made the goods within seem all the more
curiously enticing.

Okada and Aguri went up and down the street several
times: past a shoeshop, a milliner's shop, a jeweler, a
furrier, a textile merchant. . . . If he handed over a
little of his money, any of the things in these shops would
cling fast to her white skin, coil around her lithe, graceful
arms and legs, become a part of her. . . . European
women's clothes weren't "things to wear"—they were
a second layer of skin. They weren't merely wrapped
over and around the body but dyed into its very surface
like a kind of tattooed decoration. When he looked again,
all the goods in the show windows seemed to be so many
layers of Aguri's skin, flecked with color, with drops of

blood. She ought to choose what she likes and make it part of herself. If you buy jade earrings, he wanted to tell her, think of yourself with beautiful green pendants growing from your earlobes. If you put on that squirrel coat, the one in the furrier's window, think of yourself as an animal with a velvety sleek coat of hair. If you buy the celadon-colored stockings hanging over there, the moment you pull them on, your legs will have a silken skin, warmed by your own coursing blood. If you slip into patent-leather shoes, the soft flesh of your heels will turn into glittering lacquer. My darling Aguri! All these were molded to the statue of woman which is you: blue, purple, crimson skins—all were formed to your body. It's *you* they are selling there, your outer skin is waiting to come to life. Why, when you have such superb things of your own, do you wrap yourself up in clothes like that baggy, shapeless kimono?

"Yes, sir. For the young lady? . . . Just what does she have in mind?"

A Japanese clerk had emerged out of the dark back room of the shop and was eying Aguri suspiciously. They had gone into a modest little dress shop because it seemed least forbidding: not a very attractive one, to be sure, but there were glass-covered cases along both sides of the narrow room, and the cases were full of dresses. Blouses and skirts—women's breasts and hips—dangled overhead. There were low glass cases in the middle of the room, too, displaying petticoats, chemises, hosiery, corsets, and all manner of little lacy things. Nothing but cool, slippery, soft fabrics, literally softer than a woman's skin:

delicately crinkled silk crepe, glossy white silk, fine satin. When Aguri realized that she would soon be clothed in these fabrics, like a mannequin, she seemed ashamed at being eyed by the clerk and shrank back shyly, losing all her usual vivaciousness. But her eyes were sparkling as if to say: "I want this, and that, and that. . . ."

"I don't really know what I'd like. . . ." She seemed puzzled and embarrassed. "What do *you* think?" she whispered to Okada, hiding behind him to avoid the clerk's gaze.

"Let me see now," the clerk spoke up briskly. "I imagine any of these would look good on you." He spread out a white linen-like dress for her inspection. "How about this one? Just hold it up to yourself and look at it—you'll find a mirror over there."

Aguri went before the mirror and tucked the white garment under her chin, letting it hang down loosely. Eyes upturned, she stared at it with the glum look of a fretful child.

"How do you like it?" Okada asked.

"Mmm. Not bad."

"It doesn't seem to be linen, though. What's the material?"

"That's cotton voile, sir. It's a fresh, crisp kind of fabric, very pleasant to the touch."

"And the price?"

"Let's see. . . . Now this one . . ." The clerk turned toward the back room and called in a startlingly loud voice: "Say, how much is this cotton voile—forty-five yen?"

"It'll have to be altered," Okada said. "Can you do it today?"

"Today? Are you sailing tomorrow?"

"No, but we *are* rather in a hurry."

"Hey, how about it?" The clerk turned and shouted toward the back room again. "He says he wants it today —can you manage it? See if you can, will you?" Though a little rough-spoken, he seemed kind and good-natured. "We'll start right now, but it'll take at least two hours."

"That will be fine. We still need to buy shoes and a hat and the rest, and she'll want to change into the new things here. But what is she supposed to wear underneath? It's the first time she's ever had Western clothes."

"Don't worry, we have all those too—here's what you start with." He slipped a silk brassière out of a glass case. "Then you put this on over it, and then step into this and this, below. They come in a different style too, but there's no opening, so you have to take it off if you want to go to the toilet. That's why Westerners hold their water as long as they can. Now, this kind is more convenient: it has a button here, you see? Just unbutton it and you'll have no trouble! . . . The chemise is eight yen, the petticoat is about six yen—they're cheap compared with kimonos, but see what beautiful white silk they're made of! Please step over here and I'll take your measurements."

Through the flannel cloth the dimensions of the hidden form were measured; around her legs, under her arms, the leather tape was wound to investigate the bulk and shape of her body.

"How much is this woman worth?" Was that what the clerk was calculating? It seemed to Okada that he was having a price set on Aguri, that he was putting her on sale in a slave market.

About six o'clock that evening they came back to the dress shop with their other purchases: shoes, a hat, a pearl necklace, a pair of amethyst earrings. . . .

"Well, come in! Did you find some nice things?" The clerk greeted them in a breezy, familiar tone. "It's all ready! The fitting room is over here—just go in and change your clothes!"

Okada followed Aguri behind the screen, gently holding over one arm the soft, snowy garments. They came to a full-length mirror, and Aguri, still looking glum, slowly began to undo her sash. . . .

The statue of woman in Okada's mind stood naked before him. The fine silk snagged on his fingers as he helped apply it to her skin, going round and round the white figure, tying ribbons, fastening buttons and hooks. . . . Suddenly Aguri's face lit up with a radiant smile. Okada felt his head begin to swim. . . .

# A BLIND MAN'S TALE

*The following narrative is in the words of an old man—
a blind masseur and, in the medieval Japanese tradition,
a kind of minstrel—who is reminiscing to an indulgent
client over saké at one of the inns where travelers rested
on the long journey between Edo and Kyoto. All of
the major events described have a basis in historical fact.
Among the characters are Oda Nobunaga and his successor, Hideyoshi: the two great predatory generals,
otherwise so different, who subdued their many rivals
in the anarchic civil wars of sixteenth-century Japan.*

*The tale is being told only a few years after the fall of Osaka Castle (1615), when Tokugawa Ieyasu, the successor to Hideyoshi, crushed the last of the opposition to his new dynasty of Shoguns.* —TRANS. NOTE

I was born in the province of Omi, not far from Naga-hama, in the twenty-first year of the Tembun Period. That was 1552, the Year of the Rat—so how old does that make me? About sixty-five? . . . Yes, they tell me I lost my sight when I was three. At first I could still see things dimly, enough to know what I was looking at: even now I remember how the blue water of Lake Biwa shone in my eyes on a fine day. But within a few months I was blind as a bat—none of our prayers and offerings did any good. My parents were farmers; but my father died when I was nine years old, and my mother when I was twelve. After that I had to depend on the kindness of our neighbors. I learned how to massage people, and managed to make a living at it.

Later on, when I was seventeen or eighteen, I was lucky enough to perform my services at Odani Castle, and eventually, thanks to the kind gentleman who recommended me, I went there to join its regular staff. I'm sure you know that Odani Castle belonged to Lord Asai Nagamasa, a fine young man who had already made a name for himself as a general. His father, old Lord Hisamasa, was still alive, but there were rumors that they didn't get along very well. People said that his father was to blame. Most of the samurai, even the chief retainers, seemed to take sides with Nagamasa.

According to what I heard, it all started when Lord Nagamasa was fourteen. His coming of age was celebrated early in 1559—that was when he received his title—and he married the daughter of the senior vassal of the Sasaki family, who held southern Omi. But they say that this marriage wasn't to Nagamasa's liking, that he had been forced into it against his will. Apparently Lord Hisamasa decided that, considering the long history of warfare between northern and southern Omi, you could never tell when the present calm might be shattered by another battle. A marriage alliance with the south would be a sign of reconciliation, likely to keep the Asai lands out of danger in the years to come. But Nagamasa didn't relish the thought of being the son-in-law of one of Sasaki's vassals. Still, it was his father's order, and he had to obey. He went through with the marriage. Later, though, when he was told to go pay his respects to his new father-in-law, Lord Nagamasa was furious.

"This is too much!" he said to himself. "It's already humiliating to have married into that family just because of my father. But to go there and make a vow of filial piety! I was born a samurai—why shouldn't I act like one? I must watch for my chance to lead an army into the field so that I can take over the country someday. That is the ambition of a true warrior."

Finally he sent his bride back to her home, without even consulting Lord Hisamasa. Now, that was being a little highhanded no doubt; it's natural that his father got angry. But all the retainers admired Nagamasa immensely: how extraordinary for a young gentleman

of only fourteen to have such strength of mind! He must
have the spirit of a great hero, they thought, of a man
like their former master Lord Sukemasa, who had raised
the House of Asai to its high position. Under such a
master the house would have a brilliant future, he was a
truly splendid young man! Soon there was no one left
who would take orders from Hisamasa, and he had no
choice but to turn all responsibility over to his son. They
say he retired to the island of Chikubu, in the northern
part of Lake Biwa, along with his wife, Lady Inokuchi.

But all this happened before I went into service at
Odani. By then the father and son were on better terms,
and Hisamasa and his wife had come back from the
island and were living at the castle compound. I think
Nagamasa was about twenty-four. In the meantime he
had taken a second wife—none other than Lady Oichi,
the younger sister of the powerful Lord Oda Nobunaga!
The way the marriage came about was that Nobunaga,
in passing through Omi from his home province of
Mino to the capital, learned that Asai Nagamasa was a
dashing young commander and would make a strong
ally. So Nobunaga asked him to become his brother-in-
law, and told him that if he accepted, the Asai and Oda
could join forces to crush the Sasaki family. Then they
could go on to Kyoto and, together, take over control
of the entire country. Nagamasa could have Mino, if
he wanted it; and Nobunaga said he would sign a pledge
giving him a free hand throughout Echizen: certainly,
in view of the close ties which the Asakura family of
Echizen had with the Asai, he would never take it upon

himself to launch an attack on them. All this was put so courteously that Nagamasa agreed, and the matter was settled. You see, the fact that he had refused to subordinate himself to Sasaki after marrying the daughter of his vassal was what made Lord Nobunaga, who was already the absolute master of a great many provinces, so eager to have him as a relative. Of course, Nagamasa was also an outstanding general, and he had the kind of grand ambition a man ought to have.

I don't know anything about his former wife, the one he divorced so promptly, but Lady Oichi was famous for her beauty even before she married him. This time it was an extremely happy marriage, and a fruitful one, with a child born almost every year. I believe they had two or three by the time I came to the castle. The eldest daughter, who was called Ochacha, was still only a sweet little girl—to think that she would become the Lady of Yodo, the favorite of the Regent Hideyoshi and the mother of his heir Lord Hideyori! Really, there's no telling what the future will bring. But even then people said that Ochacha was beautiful, the perfect twin of her mother in mouth and eyes, the shape of her nose, in all her features. Blind as I was, I felt somehow aware of the resemblance.

How on earth could a lowly person like me have had the good luck to serve such noble ladies? Oh yes, I forgot to mention it earlier, but at first my job was to massage the samurai. When they were bored they'd say: "Come on, give us a tune on your samisen!" Rumors that I was singing and playing the latest popular songs must have reached the ladies, for one day a messenger arrived from them asking to have a look at the servant who was supposed to be a good singer, and so amusing. After that I was called to attend them several more times. That was how it began. Of course a huge castle like that had all sorts of people in service, besides the samurai. Why, they even had a troupe of actors—they didn't need *me* to entertain them. But I suppose that to persons of exalted rank ordinary popular songs were a novelty. And then too, in those days the three-stringed samisen wasn't nearly as well known as it is now; it was just beginning to be taken up by a few curiosity seekers. Maybe its exotic twang appealed to them.

The fact is, I never had a lesson on the samisen in my life. I've always been fond of music: no sooner would I hear a tune than I'd pick it up and begin singing and playing it, as naturally as breathing. I began playing the samisen that way, just for amusement, and before long I had a fair degree of skill at it. Of course, I was only an amateur, scarcely qualified to play for an audience, and yet—maybe because my awkwardness had a certain appealing charm—my performances were extravagantly praised. Whenever I played for the ladies I was given wonderful presents. Now, in those days the whole country was at war, there was always a battle going on somewhere. But it had its pleasant side too: when the lords were far away on a campaign, their ladies would have nothing to do but try to forget their worries, by playing the koto, for instance; and in time of siege there were often gay, boisterous parties through-

out the castle to keep our spirits up. It wasn't always as
bad as people nowadays seem to think.

Lady Oichi's favorite diversion was the koto, which
she played expertly. Once while she was playing I took
up my samisen and accompanied her, following whatever melody she chose. She seemed delighted and said I
was very clever. From that time on I served in the ladies'
quarters. Little Ochacha would call me too, wanting me
as her constant playmate. "Sing me the gourd song!"
she would say in her childish voice. Yes, I remember
that song even now:

> *Deep under the eaves*
> *Let us plant gourd vines,*
> *Plant them and let them flourish*
> *So that they can sway freely, freely,*
> *As freely as they please.*

I knew all sorts of other songs too, but even if I remember the tunes I forget the words. Well, that's the
way it is when you're as old as I am.

Meanwhile Nobunaga and Nagamasa had a falling
out, and there was fighting between the two families.
Now when did that happen? Wasn't the Battle of
Anegawa in 1570, the first year of the Genki Period?
I'm sure a gentleman like you, who can read, knows
far better than I do about such things. Anyway, not
long after I went into service the trouble began, and
the reason was that Lord Nobunaga, without giving my
master a word of notice, invaded the territory of Lord
Asakura of Echizen. Ever since Nagamasa's grandfather

had founded the family fortunes with the help of the Asakura, the House of Asai had owed them a debt of gratitude. That is why our lord, at the time when his marital alliance with the Oda family was being arranged, got a binding pledge from Nobunaga that he would never touch the province of Echizen.

The first one to lose his temper was old Lord Hisamasa. "You can't trust that damned Nobunaga!" he exclaimed. "In less than three years he treats his pledge like a scrap of paper and goes into Echizen. It's outrageous!" And he went to Nagamasa's quarters, summoned everyone down to the last samurai, and declared fiercely: "Nobunaga is going to conquer Echizen and attack our castle! We've got to join forces with Asakura and smash him while Echizen is still safe."

For a while Lord Nagamasa and his retainers kept their silence. You see, as wrong as it was of Nobunaga to break his word, the truth is that Lord Asakura had taken advantage of that pledge by behaving contemptuously toward the Oda family. Worst of all, he had refused Nobunaga's invitations to confer on affairs of state at the capital, which was insulting to the Emperor too, as far as that goes. And so our retainers suggested that we get out of the situation by sending a token force of a thousand men to Echizen to help the Asakura, and still try to keep on reasonably good terms with the Oda family. After all, they argued, once you make an enemy of Nobunaga you might as well give up any hope of victory, whoever your allies are.

That made Hisamasa angrier than ever. "What are you

miserable cowards talking about?" he cried. "Even if Nobunaga is a living demon, how can you think of deserting the Asakura family when it's in trouble? Do you forget everything you've owed to it since my father's time? You'd disgrace yourselves as warriors and bring everlasting shame on the House of Asai! If I have to stand alone, I'll not act like such an ungrateful wretch!" And he glared haughtily at the assembled company.

The older retainers clustered around him, trying to calm him down. They urged him to think the question over carefully, not to be so hasty. But he only gritted his teeth in rage, his whole body trembling, and said: "You all think I'm in the way, and you want to make me cut open my old belly."

Most old men are touchy about matters of honor, so it seemed natural enough to hear him talk like that. But the feeling had long rankled in his mind that his retainers had made a fool of him, and he held a grudge against Nagamasa for having married Lady Oichi, scorning the wife that he himself had gone to so much trouble to provide. He wanted to let Nagamasa understand a little of his own feelings. "You see what's happened," he wanted to say. "You've got into this situation because you disobeyed your father. Now that it has come to this, why should you go on being polite to that liar Nobunaga? It looks as if you've swallowed his insults all this time because you're so fond of your darling wife that you can't draw your bow against the Oda!"

Lord Nagamasa listened in silence to the argument

between his father and his retainers, sighed, and then declared firmly: "My father is right. Even though I am Nobunaga's brother-in-law I cannot fail to repay our long-standing debt of gratitude to the Asakura. Tomorrow I will send a messenger to Nobunaga to return his pledge. He may pride himself on having the strength of wolves and tigers, but if we join our forces with those of Echizen in a battle to the death, we will surely defeat him!"

And so everyone had to make up his mind to it.

But later, whenever there was a council of war, Nagamasa and his father held different opinions and got along very badly. Since Nagamasa was a brilliant general, a man of bold, high-spirited temperament, he felt that once having antagonized Nobunaga, who was quick to act, you could hardly afford to deliberate. It was best to take the offensive and engage him in battle. But his father had an old man's tendency to be cautious, and was actually inviting disaster.

When Nobunaga withdrew from Echizen to Kyoto, Lord Nagamasa reasoned out his own strategy this way: "Suppose I join forces with Asakura, drive into Mino, and storm Nobunaga's home castle at Gifu. Then he will come hurrying back, but he'll have trouble getting past the Sasaki south of the lake. In the meantime I'll return from Gifu, ambush him on the way, and take his head." And he sent a messenger to propose this plan to the Asakura.

But they too were reluctant to act. No one liked his plan, least of all Lord Asakura: it would be dangerous to go all the way to Mino, they said, and have enemies both in front and in the rear. Their reply was: "We think it better to wait for Nobunaga to advance on Odani Castle, as he is sooner or later sure to do. Then we will bring up the forces of our whole province to support you." And so, unfortunately, Nagamasa's strategy was never adopted.

It seems that when he heard this reply Lord Nagamasa became pensive. "So Asakura is being cautious too! Now I know what he is really like—with that kind of sluggishness we have no chance of defeating anyone as quick-witted as Nobunaga. Our fate is sealed. I listened to my father, and now I have a worthless ally." After that he was resigned to the thought that neither he nor his family would survive much longer.

After that came the battles of Anegawa and Sakamoto, and then there were negotiations for peace. But the truce was broken and the Asai domains were still being whittled away steadily by the Oda forces. Our bold general had not been mistaken: there was good cause to remember his advice. In two or three short years all our minor strongholds had fallen, and the main castle of Odani stood naked and unprotected, with the enemy pressing up to its very walls. An attacking force of over sixty thousand mounted warriors ringed the castle round as tightly as a coiled snake. Lord Nobunaga himself was in command, and he was aided by renowned heroes such as Shibata Katsuie. Lord Hideyoshi, who was then a minor commander known simply as Tokichiro, had built a small fortress on a hill only a thousand yards from our castle and kept us under close surveillance. There were splendid warriors among the Asai vassals too, but even some of those you would have relied on to the death had a change of heart and began slipping out one by one to surrender to the Oda, so that every day our strength weakened a little.

At first our morale had been very high; and there were more people than usual at Odani, what with women and children who were being held as hostages, and samurai who had escaped and fled to us from the smaller castles. Day and night we vied with each other in our bravery, singing songs like this:

> *Sadness lasts but a moment,*
> *And once you awaken*
> *Happiness was only a dream.*

But soon the two Asai housemen who were in charge of the middle ring of fortifications—between the outworks held by Hisamasa and the central stronghold held by Nagamasa—secretly got in touch with Hideyoshi and led the enemy into their part of the vast castle grounds. Suddenly all the castle's defenders lost heart.

At this point Nobunaga sent an envoy to say that his quarrel with us had been started because of Asakura, but now that he had killed him and conquered Echizen he felt no enmity toward us, nor did we ourselves, surely, owe any further duty to the Asakura cause. If we would give up the castle and withdraw elsewhere, he for his part, in view of the intimate relations between our two families, would be perfectly satisfied; and if we would henceforth follow the banner of the Oda family and serve it loyally, he was prepared to grant us the province of Yamato. It was a most courteous message.

In the castle, some were delighted and said that everything would be settled just in the nick of time; but others said: "No, you can't trust him—he probably means to save his sister and then make our lord commit suicide." There were all shades of opinion about it; but Nagamasa, when he finally received the envoy, gave him a flat refusal. He was grateful for Lord Nobunaga's kindness, he said, but having sunk so low he had nothing left to live for and wished only to die honorably in battle.

Nobunaga sent another envoy to assure Nagamasa, since he seemed doubtful, that the offer was sincere, and to urge him not to seek death in battle but to withdraw quietly from the castle in confidence of being well treated. Nagamasa refused to listen, saying that he had made his mind up once and for all.

So, on the evening of the twenty-sixth day of September in the year 1573, Lord Nagamasa adopted a posthumous Buddhist name and had it carved on a tombstone. Then, during the early morning hours of the twenty-seventh, well before sunrise, Lord Nagamasa gathered together all the samurai who were under siege with him and prepared to hold his own last rites, with the abbot Yuzan of the Bodai Temple officiating. Taking a seat beside his tombstone, he asked his retainers to burn incense and pray for his spirit. Naturally they declined at first, but he was so insistent that they had to go through with the ceremony. Later the stone tablet was secretly taken outside the castle walls and sunk in the depths of Lake Biwa, about a thousand yards east of the island of Chikubu. Every man at the castle knew of this, and resolved to fight to the death.

Lady Oichi had given birth to the young lord in June of that year and had spent more than a month in bed recuperating. I was constantly in attendance on her, sometimes massaging her back and shoulders, sometimes gossiping with her to try to amuse her. Yes, and Lord Nagamasa, for all that he was such a bold warrior, was extremely kind and gentle. All day long he would risk his life in savage fighting, but when he came to the inner apartments he drank saké in the best of humor and did everything he could to entertain her. He even joked with her ladies in waiting, and with me, as if he'd completely forgotten that thousands and thousands of enemy troops were ringed all around the castle. Of course, even those who are closest to a great lord and his lady can't expect to know how they feel toward each other. Still, it seemed to me that my mistress suffered grievously from the pain of being torn between her elder brother and her husband, and that Lord Nagamasa felt deeply sorry for her and did his best to cheer her up, so that she would be spared any sense of humiliation.

Once, when I was waiting on them, Lord Nagamasa called out to me: "Never mind the samisen—can't we have something livelier to drink to? How about doing that 'Laundry dance'?"

I performed my clumsy dance to amuse them, as I sang:

*"Sweet sixteen,*
*Taking clothes from the laundry pole—*
*How lovely!*
*Drawing them in hand over hand—*
*How lovely!*
*But putting* your *arm around her slim waist—*
*How much more lovely!"*

It was a comic dance that I had invented; my queer, groping gestures as I pantomimed "putting *your* arm around her slim waist" left everyone weak from laughter. When I heard Lady Oichi's voice in the midst of the noisy gaiety, I was delighted to think that she seemed a little more cheerful. How rewarded I felt! But, to my sorrow, as the days went by I never heard more than a faint laugh from her, no matter what I did. Before long she seldom responded even that much.

One day my mistress complained that her shoulders were stiff, so I took up my position behind her and began massaging them. She was sitting on her bed, leaning against an armrest; soon I began to think she was dozing. But she wasn't—now and then I heard her sigh. In the past I had always chatted with her as I worked, but these days she hardly spoke to me. So I kept a respectful silence and went ahead with my treatment, though the feeling of constraint became almost more than I could bear. Of course, blind people develop a sharp intuition. And I was all the more sensitive to her moods since it was my duty to attend her day or night: I knew her body so well that even her innermost secrets seemed to be communicated to me through my fingertips. Thus, as I was silently massaging her, unhappy thoughts filled my heart.

By that time Lady Oichi was past twenty and already the mother of five children. Yet she was such a natural beauty, and had always led such a sheltered life, a life protected from every care, every gust of rough wind, that the feel of her soft rich flesh under my fingers—if I may be excused for speaking of it—was like nothing I had experienced with other women. To be sure, she had recently given birth for the fifth time and was not quite so plump as usual, but her very slenderness only increased my astonishment at the beauty of her exquisite body. I have spent all my life at this profession, and I've massaged any number of young ladies, but never, to this day, have I touched a more lithe, beautiful body. And then the smoothness and fine texture of her skin, the flowerlike freshness of her sleek arms and legs —surely that is what is meant by "a dewy skin." Her hair, which she told me had thinned out noticeably since her confinements, flowed in wonderful abundance down to her feet: so thick it seemed almost oppressive, yet every strand as straight and perfect as if silk threads had been laid out one by one. It spread out over her back so profusely that it was hard for me to massage her shoulders.

But what would become of this noble lady if the castle fell? Would that dewy skin, that long, luxuriant hair, that soft flesh covering the delicate bones—would all that go up in smoke with the castle towers? Though the taking of human life is only to be expected in time of war, how could it be right to kill such a frail, beautiful lady? Perhaps Lord Nobunaga himself was planning at that very moment to save his sister. Oh, it was useless for a person like me to worry, but fate had brought me into her service—my blindness had allowed me the privilege of touching such a lady, of massaging her morning and night, and that task alone had made life precious to me. Now, when I wondered how much longer I would be able to serve her, the future seemed black. All at once my chest throbbed with pain.

Then Lady Oichi sighed again, and spoke my name. The others at the castle had various nicknames for me, or called me by saying: "You, there!" But she insisted that I have a proper name of my own and gave me the name of Yaichi.

"Yaichi," she repeated, "what is wrong?" I mumbled something nervously, and she said: "You seem to have lost your strength today. Rub a little harder, won't you?"

"I am very sorry, madam," I apologized, wondering if my futile worries had made my hands falter. I set to work in earnest, massaging her briskly. But that day her shoulders were especially stiff; it wasn't easy to smooth away the tensions that had so painfully tightened the muscles at the nape of her neck. Yes, I told myself, it must be torture for my lady. She must have suffered great anxiety and spent many sleepless nights. I felt a surge of sympathy for her.

Just then she spoke again. "Yaichi," she asked, "how long do you intend to stay in the castle?"

"My own wish," I answered, "is to serve you always. I know I am clumsy and of no use to you, but I'll be grateful if you will take pity on me and let me stay."

"Oh?" she said, rather sadly. She was silent for a moment. "Still, as you know, our men have been slipping away from the castle, till there are very few of us left now. When even warriors abandon their lord and flee, why should anyone who isn't a samurai stand on ceremony? And you can't see, either—if you wait too long you're sure to get hurt!"

"It is very kind of you to think of me," I said, "but there are those who prefer to desert the castle and those who prefer to stay. Probably I could leave under cover of darkness if I had my sight; as it is, though, with the castle surrounded like this, even if you dismissed me I'd have no way to escape. I know I'm only a worthless blind servant, but I don't want to let myself fall into the hands of the enemy."

Lady Oichi made no reply. She seemed to be wiping away a tear—I heard the rustle of paper handkerchiefs as she took a packet of them from her bosom. My deepest concern was not for myself, but for her. What would she do? At heart, I was desperately anxious to know whether she would stay with her husband to the end, or whether, out of pity for her five children, she might possibly have some other intention. But I could hardly be so impertinent as to ask a question of that kind, and she said no more. I had to let it go at that and keep my thoughts to myself.

That was two days before the memorial service in

front of Lord Nagamasa's tombstone. At about dawn on the morning of the twenty-seventh of September, after he had had the samurai burn incense for him, Lord Nagamasa summoned his wife, his children, the ladies in waiting, and even servants like me to the same place, and said: "I want all of you to pray for me too." But the women were overwhelmed with grief. Alas, they thought, can it be true that the fate of the castle has been decided, and that our lord is going to kill himself? Not one of them made the slightest move toward the altar.

For the past two or three days the enemy troops had been attacking more violently than ever; the battle had gone on day and night without interruption. That morning, however, the enemy seemed to have tired at last. The attack eased off and a hush fell over the castle, inside and out. The great hall was deathly still. It was just before sunrise in mid-autumn, there on a windswept mountaintop in northern Omi. As I sat in my humble place at the back of the hall I felt chilled by the piercing wind and I could hear crickets shrilling away endlessly in the garden. One of the women sitting in a corner began sobbing quietly; and then other women, who had managed to control themselves until that moment, burst out weeping, and even the children began to wail. But my mistress remained perfectly calm. "Now, now, don't cry," she scolded Ochacha firmly. "You're the oldest, you know. Remember what I have always told you about being brave." And she called little Lord Mampukumaru's nurse, and said to her: "Let us go

ahead. My son should be the first to offer incense."
When Mampukumaru had finished taking part in the
ceremony, and had been followed by the baby born
that year, she said: "Ochacha, it is your turn."

But Lord Nagamasa spoke up sternly. "Why do you
not precede your daughter?"

Lady Oichi murmured something, as if agreeing, but
she remained in her place. At this, Lord Nagamasa, who
had always been so gentle to her, spoke with deliberate
harshness. "I have talked to you about this often enough.
Are you going to disobey me now?"

Still she was unflinching, and refused to get up. "I
am sorry," she said, "though I respect your intentions."

Then Lord Nagamasa roared out at her. "So you've
forgotten your duty, have you? A true wife should pray
for me after my death and care for my children. If you
can't agree to that, I shall never think of us as husband
and wife again!" He railed at her so fiercely that his
voice reverberated through the great hall. Everyone
gasped, wondering what would happen. For a few moments there was not a sound. At last I heard the whisper
of a gown trailing over the straw-matted floor—it was
Lady Oichi going, most reluctantly, to make her offering
of funeral incense. She was followed by Ochacha, her
eldest daughter, by Ohatsu, her second, and by Kogo,
her third, each burning incense and saying a prayer in
turn. Finally all the others went through with the ceremony too.

As I've said before, the stone tablet was taken from
the castle and sunk in the bottom of the lake. They say

Lady Oichi spent the whole of that night pleading with her husband, arguing that although she had consented to take part in the last rites for him, having been pressed to do so before all the others, she felt that she could not go on living after he committed suicide. She couldn't bear to have people point at her contemptuously behind her back, and say: "That's Nagamasa's widow!" And so she begged him to let her accompany him in death, but he showed not the least sign of agreeing to what she asked.

Then on the next day, the twenty-eighth, at about ten o'clock in the morning, Nobunaga's envoy came for the third time and delivered a message asking if Nagamasa might not care to reconsider, and give himself up. To which Lord Nagamasa replied: "I can never forget the many kindnesses of Lord Nobunaga, but I have resolved to commit hara-kiri in this castle. However, since my wife and daughters are his close relatives, I wish to send them to him immediately. I shall be very grateful if he will mercifully spare their lives, and grant them his protection in the years to come." After sending the envoy back with this polite request, he seems to have spent a long time arguing with Lady Oichi again.

Of course, the two had always been so happy together that he could hardly take offense at her for wanting to die with him. When you think of it, their married life had lasted less than six years, and during those years the world had been in turmoil: sometimes Nagamasa was far away in the capital or on campaigns in southern Omi; he had never been able to enjoy a full day of ease and relaxation. It's no wonder that my mistress wanted to die with him, to be eternally by his side on a lotus flower in Paradise. But Nagamasa had the compassion of a real man of valor. To kill his young wife in cold blood would have been unbearably painful to him—he must have wanted to do everything he could to save her. And he must have worried about the future of his children.

Well, it seems that he did his best to persuade her to leave, using all the arguments he could think of, and at last she consented. It was agreed that she would go home to her parents and take their daughters along with her. Though the two boys were still very young, Lord Nagamasa said it would be dangerous to let them fall into the hands of the enemy; and so, late on the night of the twenty-eighth, little Mampukumaru was smuggled out of the castle in the care of a page named Kimura Kinainosuke, to be taken to the home of a trusted friend in Echizen. The youngest child, only a tiny infant, was to be placed in the charge of the nearby Fukuden Temple; he was smuggled out the same night, attended by his nurse and two samurai. I heard later that they had to draw their boat in among the reeds along the lake shore and stay in hiding for several hours before they reached the temple.

Throughout the night of the twenty-eighth Lady Oichi and Lord Nagamasa exchanged farewell cups of saké, but as they talked on and on of their inexhaustible grief at parting, the long autumn night came to an end. Dawn was glowing in the eastern sky when, after a final word of farewell, my mistress got into her palanquin at the castle gate. Her three daughters, together with their nurses, got into the palanquins which were to follow. The party was guarded by men under the command of a samurai who had been in Lady Oichi's service ever since he came with her from the Oda family at the time of her marriage. In addition, some twenty or thirty ladies in waiting accompanied her as she left Odani.

Lord Nagamasa came out to the palanquin to see her off. They say he was already dressed in his last costume: a suit of black-braided armor, draped over with a surplice of gold brocade. When the palanquin was lifted up, he called to her: "Now everything is in your hands —I wish you well!" His voice was clear and strong and full of courage.

Of course, my mistress kept her feelings under control, never shedding a tear. "You need not worry," she replied in a steady voice. "Give a good account of yourself!" The two younger daughters had no idea what was going on, and lay calmly in their nurses' arms. But Ochacha looked back at her father again and again, wailing bitterly all the while; and she kept on crying in spite of attempts to soothe her. It was this that the attendants found hardest to bear. Who could have imagined that all three daughters were destined to rise to such heights—Ochacha to become the Lady of Yodo, the favorite of Lord Hideyoshi; Ohatsu the wife of Lord Kyogoku Takatsugu; and Kogo, the youngest of all, nothing less than the wife of the present Shogun? Truly, there is no way of telling what the future holds!

Lord Nobunaga welcomed Lady Oichi and his nieces with genuine delight. "I am very glad that you have had the good sense to come here," he said cordially. "Nagamasa appears to be a splendid warrior, and a man of honor—as much as I urged him to surrender, he wouldn't listen to me. I am sorry that he must die, but my own honor as a warrior is at stake. I hope you can forgive me. No doubt the long siege caused you a great deal of suffering." Since they were blood relatives they felt a special affection for each other, and they had a long, intimate talk together. Then my mistress was put under the care of her brother Nobukane, who was told to do everything he could for her.

The fighting had been halted since the morning of the twenty-seventh, but Lord Nobunaga, now that his sister had been brought to him, decided that there was no reason to wait any longer; it was time to crush the castle with a single blow and make Hisamasa and his son kill themselves. Nobunaga himself mounted a nearby height and gave the order for his whole army to storm the castle. Responding with an ear-splitting battle cry, his troops rushed forward. At that time there were about eight hundred men still holding fast in the outer circle of fortifications under the command of the old master, Lord Hisamasa; but the attackers were numberless, and their commander, Shibata Katsuie, scaled the wall swiftly at their head. Hisamasa, realizing that all was lost, ordered the enemy held off long enough for him to commit hara-kiri. It was Lord Fukujuan who seconded him by administering the final stroke, cutting off his lord's head as soon as the old man had disemboweled himself. An entertainer called Kakusho-dayu was also present; it seems he told Hisamasa that, having always served as his companion in the past, he hoped to have the privilege of accompanying him this time as well. After drinking a cup of saké with him and witnessing his death, he acted as second for Fukujuan and then, retiring to a corner of the room, committed suicide. Four other retainers killed themselves too. It was a sad fate for an old gentleman like Lord Hisamasa; but if you stop to think of it, the whole thing was really his own fault. He should have listened to his son long ago, and abandoned the Asakura before he got into this predicament. Yet he insisted on carrying out his foolish notion of duty, not having the vision to see that Nobunaga's star was rising. Who is to be blamed because he came to such an end?

Not only that, he was always spoiling Lord Nagamasa's plans by meddling—even in battle tactics—instead of keeping in the background as a retired master should have. Time after time he made Nagamasa stand helplessly by and miss his chance, letting a victory slip through his fingers. No matter what demoniacal power Nobunaga had, things would never have turned out so disastrously if Nagamasa had been free to take full command. So the House of Asai, even though its founder and his grandson were both brilliant generals, came to ruin simply because Hisamasa, of the second generation, was a blunderer who lacked good judgment. I felt terribly sorry for Lord Nagamasa. He could have ruled the country in place of Nobunaga, if he'd had the chance. To think that he cut short his own life by obeying his father's orders! How my mistress Oichi must have felt! But defeat was inevitable because of Nagamasa's filial piety.

It was noon on the twenty-ninth when the outer ring of fortifications fell; after that, the enemy troops surged toward the inner citadel. Lord Nagamasa with about five hundred of his trusted young samurai cut his way into their ranks, harassing them mercilessly, and then abruptly withdrew; whereupon the attackers released a cloud of black smoke and hurled themselves forward once again. But all those who tried to scale the wall were thrust down, sent flying head over heels—not a single enemy soldier was allowed to pass. And so that night the assault was given up, only to be resumed the next morning.

It was then that Lord Nagamasa learned of his father's death: at last the news reached him that the old master had committed suicide the day before. "I never dreamed of it!" he exclaimed. "Now there is nothing more to live for—I have only to avenge his spirit in battle and then follow his example honorably."

At ten o'clock that morning he led some two hundred men straight into the enemy lines, cutting down the swarming attackers one after another. But the forces of Katsuie and Hideyoshi hemmed him in so tightly that, when he had only fifty or sixty of his own troops left, he tried to rush back to the inner citadel, driving his way through the surrounding soldiers. Meanwhile, though, the enemy had overrun the main stronghold and blocked the gate from within. So Nagamasa took refuge in a house near the gate, and there he committed hara-kiri.

His second immediately followed him in death, and half a dozen other retainers chose to die with him too. They say the enemy, under orders from Nobunaga, did its best to capture him alive. But when a great and fearless general is determined to die, he leaves no such opening. All they could do was to break into the house afterward and take his head.

As for those who were captured alive, three warriors —Lord Mimasaka and his son Shimbei, and Lord Iwami —suffered the shame of being bound like common criminals and brought into the presence of Nobunaga. "You there!" he greeted them. "You got your master Nagamasa to turn against me, and gave me all these years of trouble, didn't you?"

Lord Iwami, a strong-willed man, replied: "My master was not a two-faced general like you, My Lord."

This so enraged Nobunaga that he cried out: "Fool! What would a samurai stupid enough to be taken alive know about it?" And he rapped him over the head with the butt end of his spear.

But Lord Iwami never flinched. "Does it soothe Your Lordship's feelings to beat a person who is bound hand and foot?" he asked scornfully. "That is certainly a curious attitude for a great general to take." Nobunaga executed him on the spot.

Lord Mimasaka behaved very quietly and submissively. "Why did you yield?" he was asked. "You have been a hero ever since you were young—they say you're a lion in battle!"

"I am now an old man," he replied. "That is why I

have come to this." But although Nobunaga promised to spare his life and take him into his service, Lord Mimasaka only begged to be allowed to go away. "I have no further wish," he said.

"In that case, I'll look after your son Shimbei," Nobunaga declared.

"No!" cried Lord Mimasaka, turning to his son. "You must refuse! Don't be tricked into playing the coward!"

Nobunaga burst into a roar of laughter. "You don't trust me, do you, you foolish old man?" he said. "Do I look like such a liar to you?" After that, he actually did take Shimbei into his service.

As soon as Lady Oichi heard of her husband's suicide she shut herself up in her room and spent all her time praying for him. One day Lord Nobunaga, who had come to express his sympathy, told her: "I understand that you have a son. If the child has surivived, I'd like to take care of him and bring him up as Nagamasa's heir."

At first, my mistress felt uncertain of her brother's intentions. "I don't know what has become of him," she said.

But Nobunaga persisted. "Your husband was my enemy," he went on, "but the child is blameless. I am asking about him out of pity, because he is my nephew." She began to feel reassured, since he seemed so concerned, and finally revealed the exact location of little Mampukumaru's hiding place.

At once a messenger was dispatched to Echizen with orders for Kimura Kinainosuke to bring the young lord back. But Kinainosuke was cautious, and told the messenger that he had taken it upon himself to execute the boy. However, that was not the end of the matter. Again and again messengers came to him, and Lady Oichi strongly urged him to bring the child as soon as possible. They must not risk offending her brother, she said, especially since he had shown such great sympathy; and she too was eager to see her dear child before her, safe and sound. Still doubtful whether he should agree to this, Kinainosuke reflected that in any case the secret of the boy's hiding place was out; and so, on the third of October, he brought Mampukumaru to Kinomoto in Omi. Then Hideyoshi, who had come to meet them, received the young lord and went to report to Nobunaga.

"Kill the child and put its head on view," he was told.

This distressed even Hideyoshi. "Is it necessary to—?" he began. But he was reprimanded harshly, and had to carry out the order.

The heads of Nagamasa and Asakura, too, were exposed on spikes until they were bare of flesh, and then lacquered with vermilion. At the following New Year the skulls were placed on a square tray as a table decoration to show the other lords who came to pay their respects. I suppose Nobunaga felt a profound hatred for Nagamasa, having so often been in danger from him; but the truth is, it all happened because he himself had broken his word. If he had had any consideration for his sister's grief, he would surely not have done a thing like that to the remains of a gentleman who, after all, was so closely related to him. Worse yet, it was horribly cruel of him to play on the feelings of his sister, pretending brotherly sympathy, in order to put her innocent child to the spike. His own murder in 1582 must have resulted from the long-smoldering resentment of the many he had wronged—not just from Mitsuhide's treachery. Such acts as Nobunaga was guilty of have fearful consequences.

It was about this time that Lord Hideyoshi, later the all-powerful Regent, began to rise in the world. Though Shibata Katsuie and the others who had taken part in the siege of Odani had tried to surpass each other in valor, it was Hideyoshi who had distinguished himself most in battle. Nobunaga was so delighted with him that he made him Lord of northern Omi, giving him Odani Castle together with all the Asai territories. But Hideyoshi said that Odani was difficult to guard with a small force, and made his headquarters at Nagahama, my own former home.

Now, when was it that he began to fall in love with my mistress Oichi? Just before leaving the castle she had graciously said to me: "I wish I could take you along, but you can count on my help as soon as you have escaped from here." I had already decided I was as good as dead, which only made life seem all the more precious to me, so I stole out of the castle behind her palanquin and spent the next day or two hiding in the town, waiting for the battle to end. Then, eager to be with her again, I went to her brother Nobukane's camp, where she was staying; and since she told him I was her favorite servant I luckily escaped being punished and found myself back in her service once more. That is why I often happened to be waiting in the next room when Lord Hideyoshi came to call on her.

The first time he came to see my mistress he prostrated himself before her and respectfully announced his name. Lady Oichi responded to his greeting with propriety. Then Lord Hideyoshi said: "Although I scarcely distinguished myself during the campaign, I have been rewarded by being given the Asai domains— it is an undeserved honor for me, as a soldier, to become the successor to Lord Nagamasa. All I hope to do is to govern Omi exactly as it has been governed in the past, and to model myself on the splendid example of the late general." And he added: "I am sure Your Ladyship has been greatly inconvenienced by the difficulties of wartime. If there is anything whatever which you may need, please do not hesitate to call on me." He was really very polite—an extremely amiable gentleman!

And he was particularly charming with the little girls: he did everything he could to please them. "Is Your Ladyship the oldest?" he asked Ochacha. "Come! Let me hold you." He put her on his lap and began stroking her hair, asking her how old she was and what her name was.

But Ochacha fidgeted in his arms and wouldn't answer. Then—maybe because she realized that this was the hateful man who captured her father's castle—she suddenly stared into his face and said: "You *do* look like a monkey!"

Hideyoshi seemed a little taken aback. No one had ever dared to comment to him on this resemblance. "Yes, of course!" he said, laughing to cover his embarrassment. "I look like a monkey, but Your Ladyship is the very image of your mother!"

After that he paid regular calls on my mistress, and

brought her and the children all sorts of gifts. He showed such extraordinary devotion that Lady Oichi herself said: "Hideyoshi is a man you can rely on." She became much more at ease with him. When I think of it now, I wonder if he wasn't already in love with her. Perhaps he had been enchanted by her beauty from the very first. Of course, she was the sister of his master, Nobunaga, a flower on a mountain peak far too high for him to pluck, and so he may have had no specific intentions toward her at that time. Still, he was Lord Hideyoshi, a cunning man, and one with an eye for women. As for the difference in rank between them, ceaseless change is the way of the world—and changes in fortune are especially drastic in time of war. It is not for me to say whether he might or might not have felt a secret desire for her during those long months, and thought he'd have her sooner or later. Who can tell what goes on in the mind of a great man? But I don't think I'm just being suspicious.

Furthermore, they say that Hideyoshi was in a terrible dilemma when he received the order to kill Mampuku-maru. He did his best to save the child's life. "What harm could come from sparing an infant like that?" he asked Nobunaga. "Would it not be better for the peace of the country, as well as for your own peace of mind, to earn his gratitude by making him Asai's heir?" When his master refused to listen to him, he carried his opposition to unheard-of lengths. "In that case," he said, "I beg to be relieved of the mission."

That made Nobunaga furious. "You've become very proud of yourself since your recent exploits, haven't you?" he rebuked him sharply. "Who are you to give me advice I don't want, and even disobey my orders?"

It seems that after this outburst Hideyoshi left with a heavy heart, and executed the young lord. You can imagine how bitter it must have been for him to kill Mampukumaru, at the risk of becoming the object of my mistress Oichi's lifelong hatred. And this was not just an ordinary killing—he had to put the child's head on a spike and expose it to public view! To say the least, it was ironic that Lord Hideyoshi, of all men, was given this role to play. Years later he vied with Shibata Katsuie for the favors of my mistress, and lost out. He was beaten in love, but he finally destroyed both of them, becoming their eternal enemy. Perhaps that fate was decided by the child's murder.

At the time, Lord Nobunaga was anxious that nothing be said to Lady Oichi about her son's death, so it is unlikely that anyone told her. But since the head was exposed for all to see, she may have heard some gossip about it; whether she did or whether it was only her intuition, she seems to have realized what had happened. Clearly something was weighing on her mind. From then on Hideyoshi's visits only seemed to make her more unhappy.

One day she said to him: "I'm worried—I've had no news at all from Echizen, and I've been having bad dreams, too. I wonder if something has happened to my son."

"I'm afraid I don't know any more than Your Ladyship," he replied innocently. "Perhaps you should send another messenger. . . ."

"But I understand that you went to get him," she said, her voice quiet but with an edge to it. Just then, according to her attendants, she turned pale and fixed an angry look on him. After that incident his relations with her were strained, and eventually he stayed away altogether.

Now, Lord Nobunaga had lately extended his sway over a number of new provinces, had issued the necessary orders to reward his men and dispose of the enemy prisoners, and by the ninth of October was already back at his castle in Gifu celebrating the Chrysanthemum Festival. Every year there was a huge banquet, but people said that this time the spectacle was astonishing in its magnificence: all the lords, great and small, had done their utmost to equip themselves splendidly to come to pay their homage to Nobunaga.

Lady Oichi had let it be known that she was not feeling well and remained for a time in seclusion in Omi, refusing to see any visitors. But on about the tenth of that month she finally set out, accompanied by her ladies and me, to her old home of Kiyosu, Nobunaga's castle in the province of Owari. At that time Nobunaga was making his headquarters at Gifu, and so my mistress preferred to be at the quiet, peaceful castle of Kiyosu. But since she said she wanted to visit the temple on Chikubu Island on her way, we took a boat at Nagahama. At that season Mount Ibuki was already covered with snow, and a cold wind blew over the lake. But it was a crisp, clear morning: I imagine you could see the mountains far into the distance. All her attendants were clinging to the gunwales, distressed at being off the familiar solid ground; they wept to hear the cries of the wild geese overhead and the beating of the gulls' wings, and felt saddened even by the sound of reeds rustling in the wind and the shadows of fish darting through the water.

When the boat reached a point off Chikubu Island, Lady Oichi said: "Stop here for a moment." We all wondered uneasily what she meant to do; but then she had a little prayer table brought to the bow, and joining her hands reverently, fingertips pointed toward the surface of the water, she began to pray. We were probably at the place where the tombstone had been sunk to the bottom of the lake, and we realized that this was what she must have had in mind when she said she wanted to visit the island. While the boat drifted there, rocked gently by the waves, my mistress burned incense, closed her eyes in fervent concentration, and called her husband's posthumous name. She sat there for such a long time that, as I was told later, those around her grasped the hem of her gown, fearing that she might throw herself overboard to make her own watery grave in the depths of the lake. But all I was aware of was the murmur of the prayer beads in my lady's hands, and the exquisite fragrance of the incense.

After that, Lady Oichi went ashore on the island and spent the night at the temple. The next day she went to Sawayama, where she again rested overnight. Finally, after an uneventful journey, she arrived safely at Kiyosu

Castle. Her family had built a handsome residence for her, and provided her with everything she wanted. However, apart from the pleasure of watching her daughters grow up, she had nothing to do but spend her days reading the sutras. Since she had no visitors, she led as sad and lonely a life as if she had actually become a recluse. Formerly, she always had a great many people around her and enjoyed all sorts of diversions, but now she spent the whole day shut away in a dark room. Time hung heavily on her hands—even the short winter days must have seemed long to her. Naturally the image of her late husband would float up before her eyes and she would become despondent, recalling memory after memory and yearning for the past that was gone forever. Having come from a military family, she had borne her troubles with fortitude—she rarely gave way to tears. But by then her strength of will seemed to have ebbed away. She abandoned herself to her sorrow: if you happened to go down the corridor past her lonely inner room you could hear the soft muffled sobbing. Whatever her memories were, they caused her many days of weeping.

Thus one year went by, and then another, as if in a dream. In the meantime we kept urging her to go on various outings, whether to see the cherry blossoms in spring or the scarlet leaves in autumn; but she always said: "I'd rather not. Why don't the rest of you go?" She lived entirely cut off from the world—her one consolation was to be in the company of her daughters. That was the only time when you heard her laugh. Happily, all three of her children were in excellent health, growing so fast that they seemed taller every day. Even little Kogo was already toddling about and beginning to prattle. But that was another source of grief. Looking on, Lady Oichi would say to herself: "If her father could see her now . . ." What hurt her most of all, as a mother, was the memory of Lord Mampukumaru's death. She could not forget it. Out of sheer thoughtlessness she had turned her own child over to the enemy, to meet that horrible end. Full of hatred toward the one who had deceived her—and chagrin for having been deceived— she was quite unable to resign herself to what had happened. Besides, though she never mentioned it, she must have worried constantly about her youngest son, who had been hidden at the Fukuden Temple. How was he getting along? Luckily, he was safe for the time being, since Nobunaga was not aware of his existence. But she had heard nothing whatever of him after being separated from him when he was only an infant at the breast. As a result, she idolized her daughters all the more, giving them the love and affection that she could no longer give her sons.

I believe that Lord Kyogoku Takatsugu was about twelve or thirteen at that time. Later he served under Nobunaga; but he was supposed to stay at Kiyosu until he came of age, and sometimes he visited Lady Oichi. Takatsugu was the heir of Lord Takahide, whose family had once ruled northern Omi with the Asai family as their vassals. For that reason, he ought by rights to have become master of half of Omi. However, at the time that his ancestor Takakiyo took religious orders and retired to live in seclusion at the foot of Mount Ibuki, all these lands were seized by the Asai, and the family reduced to poverty. So after the fall of Odani, Nobunaga singled the boy out to become one of his own samurai, with a view to establishing him as a grateful ally in northern Omi. Later, in June of 1582, Takatsugu joined in the rebellion against Nobunaga and was one of those who attacked the castle at Nagahama; and in 1600, while the Battle of Sekigahara was being fought, he betrayed Lord Hideyoshi's heir and shut himself up in his own castle at Otsu, holding off fifteen thousand attackers with only three thousand men. But when he was still a young boy at Kiyosu he showed no sign of turning out to be so perverse.

Takatsugu was just at the age when you might expect him to be at his naughtiest, and yet, because of the obscurity in which he had been brought up, there was a rather melancholy air about him. Even when he came to see my mistress he talked so little and behaved so meekly that I hardly knew he was present. Now, since his mother had been Asai Nagamasa's sister, Lady Oichi was his aunt by marriage and her daughters were his cousins. So, partly out of longing for Mampukumaru, she lavished affection on him. "Think of me as your mother," she would say, "and come to see me whenever you have the time." She was extremely kind to him, and praised him warmly. "The boy is quiet, but there's something fine and strong in him. I am sure he's very intelligent too." Yes, it was much later—seven or eight years, I think—

that he married Ohatsu; in those days Lady Oichi's daughters were too young for talk of a match with him. Still, I wonder if he didn't secretly prefer Ochacha to Ohatsu, and if his visits weren't really for the purpose of stealing a glimpse of her. No one else paid any attention to it, but I'm sure he had *some* reason for sitting there respectfully with my mistress hour after hour, scarcely talking, as calm and self-possessed as any adult. Otherwise, why did he come so often to a place where there was nothing to amuse him, and sit there quietly being bored? But I was the only one who had an inkling of what was going on. When I whispered to the other servants: "That child seems to be making eyes at Ochacha!" they all laughed and said I thought so because I was blind. None of them took me seriously.

Well, my mistress Oichi stayed at Kiyosu from the autumn of 1573—that was when Odani Castle fell—till about autumn of the year Nobunaga died. So it was nine full years in all. Indeed, time flies like an arrow, as people say; once it's gone and you look back, you can see how true that is. But still, nine years seems awfully long to a person living in isolation from the disturbances all around, not even knowing what battles have taken place. And so, without quite realizing it, Lady Oichi began to forget her sorrows—she got to taking out her koto again and diverting herself with music. I followed her example and began to spend my leisure hours practicing the samisen and singing, not only because I enjoyed it but because I wanted to help cheer her up. I worked hard, so that I would be able to please her.

That was about the time when the little songs named after Ryutatsu were becoming popular. One of them went this way:

> *Can you really be frost or the virgin snow?*
> *You seem to melt into my arms*
> *Tonight as I hold you close.*

I often entertained the ladies with them. Nowadays Ryutatsu songs are out of date, but for a while they were all the rage—everyone, high and low, sang them. Once when the Regent Hideyoshi was watching No plays at his Fushimi Castle he summoned Ryutatsu and had him sing them on the stage, with Lord Yusai accompanying him on the small drum. But they were only beginning to be popular while I was at Kiyosu; at first all I did was teach them to the maidservants, beating time with my fan and singing in a low voice so that no one else would hear. They liked the suggestive ones, such as the song about the "virgin snow," and whenever I sang for them they went into gales of laughter. Before long, Lady Oichi heard us and said: "Please sing that for me, too!"

I tried to refuse, explaining that it wasn't the sort of thing for a great lady to hear. But she insisted, and after that I often sang for her. She was especially fond of the song that goes "Sweet spring showers, don't scatter the cherry blossoms!" and always asked for it. On the whole, she seemed to like the sad, sentimental ones, songs like this:

*The cold winter rains and the snow*
*Only fall now and then—*
*But because of you, my tears*
*Are falling constantly.*

Or this:

*Even though you love,*
*Do not let your love be known.*
*But do not forget*
*While you pretend you do not love!*

Maybe the words of these songs touched some hidden feelings of mine. . . . Anyway, whenever I sang them, pouring out my heart, I felt a mysterious strength within me and found myself elaborating on the melody, singing in a warmer, more passionate tone of voice. Those who listened to me were moved, as I was myself—my cares vanished into thin air.

Also, I gave a good deal of thought to the samisen accompaniment and improvised pleasing interludes between the vocal phrases, which made the songs all the more effective. It sounds boastful of me to say such a thing, I suppose, but it's a fact that I was the first one to add a samisen accompaniment to songs of that kind. In those days most people simply beat out the rhythm for them on the small drum.

I seem to go on talking about music, but I've always thought that no one is more fortunate than a person who has a naturally beautiful voice and who knows how to sing. Ryutatsu himself was only a druggist in Sakai at first, but because he was a good singer he received the honor of a lifetime: performing before the Regent, and being accompanied by Lord Yusai. Of course, he was a master who invented a new style; compared with him, I am utterly insignificant. But it was because of my own humble accomplishments that I enjoyed such extraordinary favor with Lady Oichi: during those nine years at Kiyosu I was constantly at her side, her companion in every pleasure. People have all sorts of desires, you can't say what is likely to appeal to them; so perhaps some would feel sorry for a man like me. But those nine years were the happiest of my life. Because of them, I don't have the slightest envy of Ryutatsu. After all, I played the samisen to my heart's content in accompanying my mistress, I soothed her troubled feelings by singing her favorite songs, time and again I was showered with praise by her—I was far happier than I would have been at entertaining Lord Hideyoshi! Since I could not have known such pleasure except for being blind, I have never to this day regretted my handicap.

There is a proverb: "The ant's wish is heard in Heaven." Even a poor blind musician can be loyal, and I gave myself up wholly to serving Lady Oichi, trying to ease her cares a little, to do all I could to brighten her mood. Maybe because of my prayers to the gods—not that that was the only reason—she slowly began blossoming out again, after having been very thin. When she first came home to Kiyosu there was a hollow between her shoulder blades, and it gradually deepened—all over her body the flesh shrank away alarmingly. Tears came to my eyes whenever I massaged her. But, happily, from about the third year she began gaining weight; after seven or eight years she was even more beautiful, more alluring than she had been at Odani—you could hardly believe she had given birth to five children!

According to her attendants, Lady Oichi's round face became thin and drawn for a time, but then her cheeks filled out again adorably. She was so lovely, they said, with a few loose strands of hair across her cheek, that even women were enchanted by her. She had always had a milk-white skin, to be sure, but those long years spent shut away in a sunless inner room, like a still drift of snow, had made it almost transparent: they say that the whiteness of her face, if you happened to see her sitting pensively in the shadows at dusk, was enough to make your hair stand on end. Of course, a sensitive blind person can distinguish such things by touch; I didn't need to be told how white her skin was. And fair skins are not all alike—that of a lady of high rank is quite out of the ordinary. Indeed, Lady Oichi was nearly thirty, and with each year her beauty had grown more striking. Her skin was even smoother than it had been in her youth. Her face was lovelier than ever, her black hair all but dripping with dew; she looked as fresh as a lotus flower. The fine silks she wore seemed to flow over her like water, such was the bewitching grace of her delicate, softly rounded body. To think that she was widowed early, her dazzling beauty hidden away, and that she was left to spend all her nights sleeping pitifully alone! They say a flower hidden in the mountains has a richer perfume than a garden flower: had anyone been able to catch a glimpse of her behind her curtains—there where only the nightingale sang to her in spring and only the slanting moonlight came to her in autumn—he would surely have burned with passionate devotion, just as Hideyoshi once did. But fate decided otherwise.

So life went on in that way, and Lady Oichi seemed to be eagerly awaiting the arrival of another spring. But apparently she was still haunted by the old pain and bitterness. One day while I was massaging her and chatting with her as usual, she must have felt a sudden impulse to open her heart, for she spoke to me with such amazing frankness as she never did before or since. At first she seemed in remarkably good spirits: she talked about old memories—memories of her life at Odani, and of Lord Nagamasa—in the course of which she recalled the first meeting between Nobunaga and Nagamasa, at the castle of Sawayama. And she told me the whole story.

It seems that the meeting took place soon after her marriage. At that time Sawayama was part of the Asai domains; so Nobunaga came there from Mino, and Nagamasa went as far as the Surihari Pass to meet him. After escorting his guest back to the castle and exchanging formal greetings, Nagamasa gave a magnificent banquet. Now, the following day Lord Nobunaga made this proposal: "Allow me to borrow your castle instead of entertaining you in mine. I wish to be your host and return the honor you have paid me, but the situation is so critical throughout the country just now that I doubt whether it is safe to waste time traveling." Thus he invited Lord Nagamasa and the old master to a banquet in this very same castle; and his presents to them included a sword made by Muneyoshi, along with a fortune in gold and silver, with some for each of the retainers as well. In return, Nagamasa gave him a sword by Kanemitsu, long a family heirloom, a collection of poems on famous places in Omi composed by Fujiwara Teika, a cream-colored charger, Omi cotton, and many other splendid gifts. He gave new swords and daggers to all the members of Nobunaga's party too.

When Lady Oichi arrived there from Odani to see her brother once again after long separation, Nobunaga was almost beside himself with joy. He summoned the chief Asai retainers and addressed them in these words: "Listen to me, all of you! Now that your master is my brother-in-law, the whole of Japan will soon come under the banners of our two houses. If you will give us your full support, your last ounce of strength, you can be sure that I'll make every one of you a great lord!" The banqueting went on all day, and that night the brothers-in-law went to Lady Oichi's room, where the three of them had a long, intimate talk. Nobunaga stayed on at the castle more than ten days. During that time he was feasted on fresh-water fish such as carp and crucian, of which large numbers were netted from Lake Biwa in the inlet at the foot of the mountain. These delicacies pleased him so much that he asked to take some of them home with him, since they were not to be had in Mino. Finally he left in the best of humor, the day after a last farewell banquet.

After telling me all this Lady Oichi said: "At that time my brother and my late husband were always smiling together, as if they were really close to each other. You can imagine how happy it made me." And she added: "I see now that those ten days were the happiest of my life. I suppose happiness isn't something you find often in a lifetime."

In those days neither my mistress nor the retainers dreamed that the two families would have a falling out; everyone celebrated the coming victories. Later, though, it seems there were some who criticized Lord Nagamasa for giving away the Kanemitsu sword. According to their argument, he should never have parted with such a treasure, for the sword had been the favorite weapon of his grandfather Lord Sukemasa. To have given it to another family, whatever the occasion, they said, was an omen that the House of Asai would be destroyed by the Oda.

But it's easy enough to blame other people. I'm sure Lord Nagamasa gave such a precious object because of his extraordinary regard for his wife and brother-in-law. To grumble about bringing on the destruction of the family—isn't that the kind of talk you hear from know-it-alls, after they see how things have turned out? When I said as much to Lady Oichi she nodded approval. "You are perfectly right," she said. "No one should marry into a family and still let his mind dwell on thoughts of destroying it, or being destroyed. After all, it wasn't easy for my brother to make that long journey from Mino with only a small number of men, crossing through what might well be hostile territory as far as he knew. I think it was quite natural for a man like my husband to be so generous under the circumstances."

She paused a moment. "But we had a few bad men among our retainers, too. Endo Kiemon came galloping up after us as soon as we were back at Odani. 'Nobunaga is going to spend the night at Kashiwabara,' he whispered to my husband, trying not to let me hear. 'It's a good chance to finish him off!' My husband merely laughed and said: 'What an idiotic notion!' "

It seems that Nagamasa had accompanied Nobunaga as far as the Surihari Pass, where he took his leave, ordering Endo Kiemon and two of his other samurai to escort the party further. When Nobunaga arrived at Kashiwabara he went to the Jobodai Monastery to stay overnight. Remarking that since this was part of Nagamasa's territory there was nothing to fear, he kept with him only his own pages and the usual night watch: all his other samurai were allowed to spend the night in town. Endo, seeing how matters stood, immediately turned and galloped back to Odani, lashing his horse all the way. What he said to Nagamasa in private was something like this: "I have been watching Lord Nobunaga carefully—his mind is as quick as lightning, and he's as sharp-eyed as a monkey leaping from limb to limb. You can't expect to keep on good terms forever with such a formidable general. But tonight he seems very much at ease, and has stationed a mere fourteen or fifteen men around him; I think it might be best to act immediately. If you seize this chance and send a large force to kill him, and then attack Gifu Castle, both Mino and Owari will fall into your hands. And if you go on to defeat the Sasaki in southern Omi, carry the war to the capital, and put down the Miyoshi family, the whole country will be yours in the twinkling of an eye!"

This suggestion was argued most persuasively, but Lord Nagamasa would have nothing to do with it. "There are certain rules of conduct for a general," he replied. "It's all right to ambush an enemy, but it's cowardly to trick a man who has come to you because he trusts you. Nobunaga has confidence in me and is going to spend tonight in my domains. If I take advantage of this by attacking him when he is off guard, I may win a momentary victory, but in the end Heaven will punish me for it. If I wanted to kill him I could have done it while we were at Sawayama. I detest the very thought of such a dishonorable act."

So Endo gave up trying to influence him. "Then there is nothing to be done," he said, "but the time will come when you'll be sorry." And he went back to Kashiwabara, where he joined the feasting as if nothing had happened. The following day he escorted Nobunaga safely to Sekigahara.

After giving me a detailed account of these events, my mistress commented: "When I look back on it today, I have to admit that there was truth in what Endo said." As she spoke, her voice quivered strangely. It startled me somehow, and disturbed me. But she went on at once, as if talking to herself. "No matter how honorably one side behaves, it's useless if the other side won't do the same. Must you really be such a beast to rule the country?" Then she fell silent—she seemed on the verge of tears.

I stopped massaging her, and threw myself at her feet. "Forgive me!" I burst out. "I must tell you how much I sympathize with you!"

At this, Lady Oichi, quite composed again, thanked me for my services and dismissed me.

I hurried out to the next room, but soon I could hear her faint sobbing through the sliding doors. I was still puzzled by her change of mood. She had been cheerful enough until a little while ago—what made her talk to me as she did just now? Had she begun by simply reminiscing about the past, and then gradually warmed to her subject and found herself remembering things she had tried to forget? She was not the sort of person to confide her thoughts and feelings to a servant—maybe the memories she had kept locked up in her heart all these years had suddenly, when she least expected it, forced their way out. To think that even now, almost ten years later, she still felt so bitter about what had happened at Odani—above all, that she felt such hatred for her brother Nobunaga! For the first time I realized what it meant to be a woman robbed of her husband and her sons. I couldn't help trembling with pity and horror.

I have a great many other memories of the days when my mistress Oichi was at Kiyosu, but I'd especially like to tell you how Lord Nobunaga's unexpected death led to her second marriage. Of course I needn't remind you how Nobunaga was assassinated. Mitsuhide's night attack took place on the second of July in 1582, the Year of the Horse. Who could have foreseen his treachery? And when it was learned that Nobunaga's eldest son had died too, committing suicide under attack by other rebel troops, the whole country seethed with excitement. Just then Nobunaga's second and third sons were in distant provinces; and Hideyoshi, Shibata Katsuie, and the other chief Oda retainers were all campaigning far away. They say Mitsuhide reached Azuchi Castle by the fifth, occupied it without any difficulty, and plundered it of all its treasures. Those of us at Kiyosu were terrified lest we too would soon be overwhelmed. In the midst of the confusion the wife and child of Nobunaga's eldest son arrived at our castle. The child, who was called Samboshi, was barely two years old. His father had feared for the safety of the boy and his mother at Gifu, and before committing suicide had asked one of his men to help them escape to Kiyosu.

Meanwhile, Mitsuhide's forces had taken the castles of Sawayama and Nagahama, overrun the province of Omi, and besieged Hino Castle. But then Nobunaga's third son, Nobutaka, attacked the rebel troops at Osaka and killed Mitsuhide's son-in-law. When he heard this, Mitsuhide left the siege of Hino in other hands and returned to his headquarters at Sakamoto, arriving there on the tenth. The Battle of Yamazaki, in which Hideyoshi crushed the revolt with one swift blow, took place on the thirteenth; by the next day Hideyoshi had already moved on to another camp, after rejoining Mitsuhide's severed head to his body and crucifying him in the capital.

Well, that was another great victory for Lord Hideyoshi, and made him even more famous. Of course, others had added their troops to his for the battle; but what was most remarkable was his speed in finishing up his western campaign and driving back toward Kyoto— truly a master stroke! They say that Mitsuhide at first knew nothing of Hideyoshi's movements, and took up a position at Yamazaki; Hideyoshi's forced march caught him by surprise, making him scramble to redeploy his men. As things turned out, Hideyoshi naturally was the commander of the loyal armies; and he won the victory so rapidly that overnight his power became supreme.

Reports of the battle began to reach Kiyosu from the capital, and we were all delighted and relieved that things had gone so well. One after another the various lords who had been vassals of Nobunaga, great or small, hastened to our castle. By that time the remnants of Mitsuhide's forces had burned Azuchi, there was no one left at Gifu, and Kiyosu, which was formerly the main castle of the Oda family, had become the residence of little Lord Samboshi, Nobunaga's grandson and presumable heir; so that all those who were loyal to the Oda family felt obliged to visit Kiyosu to pay their respects. Foremost among them was Lord Shibata Katsuie, who, as soon as he learned of Nobunaga's assassination, had cut short his campaign in the North and rushed toward the capital to avenge his master—and then, hearing that Mitsuhide was dead, had decided to come directly to Kiyosu. In addition, Nobunaga's second and third sons, Nobukatsu and Nobutaka, had gathered here by about the sixteenth or seventeenth; Hideyoshi himself soon arrived, after receiving the ashes of his master at Kyoto and stopping briefly at his own castle in Nagahama.

Since Nobunaga had long ago changed his headquarters from Kiyosu to Gifu, and then to Azuchi, very seldom returning to this lonely place, it had been many, many years since the leading vassals were assembled here at Kiyosu. Moreover, Katsuie and the other senior retainers who had shared in Nobunaga's struggles were all by now masters of at least a castle and a province of their own—some of them had even become great lords ruling over several provinces. One by one their splendid processions arrived, and the castle town was suddenly thronged with people. Even under the shadow of mourning, everyone felt new hope and confidence.

Now, beginning on the eighteenth the lords gathered to confer in the main hall of the castle. Of course, I don't know exactly what went on among them, but it seems they discussed such matters as the choice of a successor to Nobunaga and the disposition of his provinces. Day after day they met together and always argued far into the night, since their opinions were hopelessly divided. Sometimes they even quarreled angrily. No doubt the problems were thorny ones—for example, there were those who said that, while Lord Samboshi was technically the next in line, he was still so young that his uncle Lord Nobukatsu, Nobunaga's second son, ought to replace him for the time being. But although the right to succession was finally settled on Samboshi, it seems that Katsuie and Hideyoshi had been at odds from the very beginning, and had fought over every point. That was supposed to be because Hideyoshi had carried out the most brilliant exploits of the recent campaign, attracting a great deal of secret support; while Katsuie, since he was the chief retainer of the family, outranked everyone except Nobunaga's brothers, and wanted to impose his will on the assembled lords. People said that what deepened the rift between them was Katsuie's highhanded action in taking from Hideyoshi—in an unequal exchange —the vast estates of Nagahama, which had been Hideyoshi's home territory. But I wonder if that wasn't just on the surface. Maybe the real reason for their quarrel was that both of them were in love with Lady Oichi, and both of them wanted her.

Earlier, as soon as he arrived at Kiyosu, Lord Katsuie had called on my mistress and greeted her most courteously. After that he seems to have approached Lord Nobutaka, Nobunaga's third son, for the latter came to Lady Oichi's mansion one day and urged her to marry Katsuie. Now when all is said and done, my mistress had depended entirely on her brother Nobunaga; and for that reason, as much as she had hated him while he was alive, she found herself mourning his death. All the old resentment was forgotten, and she devoted herself to praying for his soul. Just at this time, too, she must have been desperately worried about the future, not for herself but for her three daughters. Who would stand by them? And so when she heard of Katsuie's love for her she may have been rather glad—at least, she was not displeased! But she hadn't yet made up her mind. For one thing, she wanted to remain faithful to the memory of her husband; also, she was concerned about the propriety of marrying a vassal of her brother, who had been her husband's enemy.

Soon, though, she received the same kind of overtures from Lord Hideyoshi. I'm not sure, but I think the go-between must have been Lord Nobukatsu. Anyhow, Nobukatsu and Nobutaka were only half-brothers, and got along very badly: since one of them sided with Katsuie, the other would have pushed Hideyoshi's claim. Of course, I couldn't be too inquisitive, but I managed to catch a little of what the ladies whispered among themselves, and it occurred to me that I'd been right. So Hideyoshi really did fall in love with her at Odani, I thought; it wasn't just my imagination! And yet for the past ten years he had gone from one battle to another, seizing fortresses and destroying castles. . . . Had Lady Oichi's lovely face remained before him in the midst of all that fighting? Once there was a great difference in rank between them, but he had avenged his master's death at Yamazaki, and could, if all went well, expect to take over the whole country. Apparently that had emboldened him to reveal his love. But I had never even imagined that Katsuie, who seemed to be a warrior first and last, harbored tender thoughts of love in his breast. Maybe it wasn't only love—maybe Nobutaka and Katsuie were in collusion, and having guessed Hideyoshi's feelings long ago, were purposely trying to thwart him. I wouldn't be surprised if they were.

However that may be, marriage to Hideyoshi was out

of the question. When Lady Oichi received his proposal she was outraged. "Does he intend to make me his concubine?" she asked. True enough, a certain Lady Asahi had long been part of his household, so that to marry him—even if the formalities were carefully observed—would in effect be to become a concubine. And now that Nobunaga was dead she seemed to have transferred all her old enmity to Hideyoshi. After all, it was he who had actually committed those hateful deeds: it was he who struck the heaviest blows in the siege of Odani, and who took over the Asai lands; it was he who murdered little Mampukumaru and put his head on a spike. Furthermore, how could she allow herself—a daughter of the House of Oda—to become the concubine of a man who, in spite of his sudden new power, was a mere upstart of the most obscure birth and lineage? It was quite natural that if she ever married again she would choose Katsuie over Hideyoshi.

Thus, although my mistress had not yet made any clear decision, everyone at the castle had an inkling of how she felt; and so the discord between the two rival lords became even worse. Katsuie, as the senior retainer, was the one who ought to have avenged his dead master, and he resented having been robbed of that triumph; Hideyoshi, on the other hand, was not only jealous as a lover but full of bitterness at the loss of his lands. Matters had come to such a pass that they showed open resentment toward each other, even at the formal conferences. Whenever one of the two made a statement, the other glared and said: "That will never do!" All the lords, from Nobunaga's brothers on down, were divided into two factions: the supporters of Katsuie and those of Hideyoshi.

They say that for this reason Katsuie's adopted son Katsumasa quietly drew his father aside during the height of the conference, and whispered: "Kill Hideyoshi now and get it over with! If you let him live he'll make trouble for you."

But Lord Katsuie, like the samurai he was, wouldn't hear of it. "This is a time when we ought to be helping the young lord," he said. "We'll all be ridiculed if we fight among ourselves."

Maybe Hideyoshi too suspected a plot of that sort, and was on his guard. They say that one night, when he got up to relieve himself, Niwa Gorozaemon stopped him in the corridor and made the same kind of suggestion: "If you want to rule the country, kill Katsuie!"

But Hideyoshi didn't consent either. "Why should I consider him my enemy?" he asked. Still, he must have decided that there was no point in staying too long. As soon as the conference was over he took his departure from Kiyosu secretly, at midnight. So the whole thing ended peacefully, for the time being.

After that all the other lords exchanged firm pledges of loyalty and returned to their own provinces. My mistress Oichi's second marriage was decided on at the end of that autumn. Since it was Nobutaka who had arranged the match, Lady Oichi came from Kiyosu and Lord Katsuie from Echizen to be married at Gifu Castle. After the ceremony they left together for the North, taking the three daughters along with them. There were all sorts of rumors about it; but I went along to Echizen as part of their retinue, so I have a good idea of what really happened.

One rumor had it that as soon as Hideyoshi heard of the marriage he swore he would never let Katsuie return to Echizen, and brought his troops to Nagahama, intending to ambush the procession. But some said that he had been persuaded to give it up; others, that the whole story was without a shred of truth. The fact is, Hideyoshi sent his adopted son Hidekatsu to Gifu to offer congratulations on his behalf. "My father regrets that he is unable to be present on this occasion," said Hidekatsu, "He will await Lord Katsuie's trip home to Echizen, and hopes to have the privilege of entertaining him on the way and drinking a cup of saké with him as a token of his pleasure at this joyful event." For his part, Katsuie welcomed the invitation, and promised to accept Lord Hideyoshi's hospitality. Just then a large body of troops from Echizen came galloping down to meet us. After what seemed to be a very serious discussion, a messenger was sent to Hidekatsu to say that the invitation would be declined. That night we set out hastily for the North. Whatever Hideyoshi may have actually had in mind, that is all I know of the matter.

But how did my mistress Oichi feel when she left on that long journey? No matter how splendid the ceremony, there is a tinge of sadness to a second marriage. When Lady Oichi married into the Asai family, the ceremony must have been magnificent in every way;

but now she was a woman past thirty who had suffered greatly, leaving with three children on a journey into the deep snows of the North. By some trick of fate, the very route we were to travel led through Omi along the same road that she had taken before: she would have to go by Odani Castle, with all its memories. I understand that she first went to Odani in the spring of 1568, the Year of the Dragon; now, fifteen more years had passed, and though it was still autumn the northern provinces seemed to be in the grip of winter. Besides, the departure was a hurried one by night; there was nothing gay or colorful about it. Some of her ladies were even panicky because of a rumor that Hideyoshi planned to abduct her on the way.

Furthermore, the trip itself was extremely difficult. It was just the season when the wind blew down fiercely from Mount Ibuki, and the farther we went, the more intense was the cold. Around Yanagase rain mixed with sleet began to fall, as the men and horses, their breath freezing, struggled along the steep mountain roads. I could well imagine how the ladies in the party must have despaired. Traveling was always hard for me, I suppose I suffered even more than the others; but what bothered me most of all was worrying about what lay in store for my mistress, who had to cross mountain after mountain under this wintry sky, going toward a place she had never seen. I prayed that her marriage would be a happy one, that this time she and her husband could stay together all the rest of their lives, and that their family would prosper forever.

Fortunately, Lord Katsuie was a far kinder and gentler man than I had expected. Not only did he always treat her with the consideration due a sister of his late master, but the fact that he had won her away from a rival made him cherish her all the more. From the day she arrived at his Kitanosho Castle, my mistress began to throw off her gloom—she basked gratefully in the warmth of her husband's love. Thus life went on quite pleasantly: cold as it was outside, it seemed like spring in the ladies' quarters of the castle. All of her attendants felt relieved too, after ten long years of anxiety, and exclaimed at how well the marriage was turning out. But that was only for a little while. Before the year ended, war had begun.

At first Lord Katsuie wanted to have a reconciliation with Hideyoshi. Shortly after the wedding he sent a group of emissaries to him with this message: "Since it would be an inexcusable affront to the spirit of our dead master for comrades like us to quarrel, I hope to remain on the most cordial terms with you."

Lord Hideyoshi was very pleased at this, and replied with his usual tact. "I share your feelings completely, and I am grateful for this kind expression of friendship. Since you were the chief vassal of Lord Nobunaga, how could I turn against you? I hope that you will henceforth give me whatever instructions you think best." Then he entertained the messengers lavishly, and sent them home.

All of us—even a lowly servant like myself—breathed a sigh of relief at the news of the reconciliation of the two houses, thinking that now there would be nothing to worry about and that Lady Oichi would be safe. But within a month Hideyoshi led an army of fifty thousand horsemen into Omi and threw a loose ring around Nagahama Castle, which he had earlier relinquished to one of Katsuie's sons. Some said that there seemed to be good reason for it, that Hideyoshi had forestalled the Kitanosho strategy. According to their explanation, Katsuie only wanted a temporary peace, because during the winter the northern snows were too deep to permit sending out a military force. He had laid plans of his own, they said, in collusion with Nobutaka of Gifu, for a thrust south toward the capital as soon as the spring thaw came. I don't know if that was true or not; anyway, Katsuie's son, who had a long-standing grievance against his father, soon reached an understanding with Hideyoshi and turned Nagahama Castle over to him. Then Hideyoshi's forces swept into Mino like the tide, and rushed on toward Gifu Castle.

Reports of the invasion began arriving at Kitanosho one after another; but since it was just then the coldest season of the year and a heavy blanket of snow covered the ground, all Lord Katsuie could do was glare angrily at the winter sky and exclaim: "That monkey-faced rascal has tricked me! Except for this snow, I'd have smashed his army as easily as you break an egg!" Then he would grit his teeth and stamp through the snow in the garden so furiously that my mistress would tremble, and her servants would be terrified. Meanwhile, Hideyoshi's troops had subdued nearly all of Mino with crushing force: in two weeks Gifu Castle was isolated, and Lord Nobutaka had to surrender. Since he was Nobunaga's son, he was spared by Hideyoshi, who agreed to accept his aged mother as a hostage instead. Hideyoshi took the old woman to Azuchi Castle, and then withdrew to the South amid shouts of triumph.

In the meantime, the year 1582 had drawn to a close and we were well into the next year. But it was still bitterly cold in the North; there was not the least sign of a thaw. Lord Katsuie was always irritated, sometimes railing at "that insolent monkey," and sometimes at his other enemy: "That damned snow!" Naturally, the New Year festivities had been a mere formality, you would hardly have thought we were celebrating the holidays. It seems that Hideyoshi intended to conquer all our allies before the snows were gone: with the coming of the new year we began to get reports that he had led another huge army into the field, invaded Isé and taken the lands of one of our supporters, and was going on from battle to battle. So, even though our province was quiet at the moment, we knew for certain there would be a struggle with him as soon as the spring thaw came. The whole castle was busy with preparations for war, everyone was in a turmoil.

I was useless at a time like that, so I spent the days crouching alone by the fireside, feeling depressed. But it was my mistress that I worried about from morning till night. Alas, I thought, as things are now she probably never even has a chance for a quiet talk with her husband—maybe she should have stayed at Kiyosu if this is what marriage means for her. Of course, I hoped that our side would win, but might not this castle become another scene of bloodshed and suffer the same fate as Odani? I wasn't the only one who had such thoughts: the ladies in waiting talked of nothing else. "Don't be afraid!" they would say, trying to comfort each other. "Surely our lord won't be defeated! There's no use worrying about the future!"

One day, just as we were all so distraught, Lord Kyogoku Takatsugu came to Kitanosho to seek Lady Oichi's protection. Earlier, at Kiyosu, he was only a boy; but since then he had grown up into a splendid young man, one who in the ordinary course of events would by now have been a full-fledged general. However, because he had betrayed Lord Nobunaga and gone over to the side of the rebel Mitsuhide, he was a hunted criminal. Pursued relentlessly by Hideyoshi, he had been in hiding first in one place and then another, all over Omi. Finally, with the spreading warfare in that region, he must have become desperate and decided to throw himself on the mercy of his aunt Oichi. Fleeing across the snowy mountains in a peasant's straw raincoat, he reached Kitanosho so haggard and emaciated that he could scarcely be recognized. When he was brought before Lady Oichi, he humbly appealed to her: "I beg you to give shelter to this poor fugitive. Whether I am to live or die depends entirely on my aunt."

Lady Oichi fixed her eyes on him for a moment. All she said was: "I am ashamed of you!" Then she sat there quietly weeping.

Later, she must have made an eloquent plea on his

behalf, for Lord Katsuie allowed him to remain at the castle. But perhaps our master forgave him because he took pity on anyone—even a traitor—who was being hunted down by Hideyoshi.

Not long after, Takatsugu and Ohatsu were quietly engaged to be married. I heard something interesting about that from one of the maidservants: according to her, Takatsugu really wanted to marry Ochacha, but she refused him, saying: "I don't like outcasts," and so he reluctantly decided on Ohatsu. Now, from the time she was a little girl Ochacha had had a great deal of pride; also, having been brought up in the sole care of her mother, she was badly spoiled. I wouldn't be surprised if she *did* say such a thing—and I'm sure Takatsugu would have resented being scorned as an "outcast." Was it because the insult still rankled that years later, at the time of the Battle of Sekigahara, he turned traitor once more and went over to Ieyasu's side? Maybe I'm being suspicious again, but I have a notion that the real reason why he came to hide at Kitanosho was that he was longing to see Ochacha, the girl he fell in love with at first sight when he was at Kiyosu. Otherwise, why come all the way to Echizen, when his own sister was the wife of the powerful Lord Takeda? My mistress was only his aunt by her first marriage. It was absurd for a rebel like him to seek the protection of Lord Katsuie: one slip, and he might have ended with his head stuck on a pike. So I imagine it was because of Ochacha that he came fleeing to us through the snow, risking his life. It seems a great shame that such an ardent desire should come to nothing. Of course, this was still only a pledge of betrothal—a simple exchange of cups within the family circle—but I wonder if he turned to Ohatsu on the spur of the moment, rather than from any long-standing intention.

It was around the end of February or the beginning of March when this happy event took place, in the midst of so much trouble and confusion. Already Sakuma Gemba had set out at the head of more than twenty thousand horsemen as Lord Katsuie's advance force, driving into northern Omi through the melting snow-drifts.

Hideyoshi hurried up to Nagahama from his camp at Isé; and early the next morning, disguising himself as an ordinary foot soldier, climbed to the top of a mountain along with a few of his most trusted retainers and carefully studied Gemba's various outposts. "They look as if they won't be easy to take," he said. "All we can do is fortify our own positions as strongly as possible, and then settle down to a long siege." Intensifying his preparations, he made no attempt to go on the attack immediately.

So another month went by, as the two armies confronted each other. Finally, in May, Lord Katsuie set out toward Nagahama. The cherry blossoms had fallen, even in the North: it was the time of year when one regrets the passing of spring. As this was her husband's first campaign since their marriage, Lady Oichi gave a farewell celebration for him in the main hall, ordering all sorts of auspicious delicacies. Lord Katsuie drank his saké cheerfully, and declared: "I'll destroy the enemy in a single battle and put Hideyoshi's head on display in the capital within the month. You'll have good news soon!" Then he got up to leave, and my mistress went to see him off at the inner gate. But they say that just as he was mounting his horse, using his bow as a staff to help himself up, the horse gave a sudden ominous neigh, and Lady Oichi blanched.

However, it seems that this time Lord Nobutaka at Gifu had a secret agreement with us, and would once more turn against Hideyoshi's forces, and that another ally of the enemy would come over to our side in a few days. Besides, though Hideyoshi was a shrewd, resourceful general, Lord Katsuie was unsurpassed for his bravery and fighting ability. Above all, as the chief retainer of the Oda family he had the allegiance of a number of powerful men. Who could have imagined he would suffer such a stunning defeat?

The battles of Yanagase and Shizugatake are so familiar that there's really nothing more to say about them, but I still can't get over Gemba's reckless insubordination. If he had listened to Lord Katsuie's orders, withdrawn immediately, and gone on the defensive, our Mino allies would have struck the enemy from the rear. Of course, no one knows how the battle would have turned out even so. But the fact is, Gemba called his uncle Katsuie a senile old man and paid no attention to his orders—for all the repeated warnings dispatched to him by high-ranking samurai. That is why his large army was routed. Still, the distance between Lord

Katsuie's headquarters and Gemba's fortress was only a few miles, not more than fifteen or sixteen even by a roundabout way. They say that Lord Katsuie flew into a terrible rage, but why, in that case, didn't he rush over there himself and drag Gemba back with him? It wasn't like him to be so slow to act. Even if you couldn't say he was in his dotage, wasn't he a little slack, after all, now that he had a beautiful wife? I hate to say such a thing about him, but I'm afraid he was partly to blame for what happened.

News reached Kitanosho on the twentieth of May that Gemba had taken an enemy fortress and cut off the head of one of Hideyoshi's allies. Everyone rejoiced at this, and considered it a very good omen. But that night enemy torches flared on the road from Mino and on all the hills and mountains along the way: they reddened the sky, outshining the waning moon, and gradually their number increased till the whole country-side looked like an enormous lantern festival. Hideyoshi must have galloped back from Ogaki all through the night; for we were told that fighting broke out on the other side of Lake Yogo around dawn, and that Gemba's camp was in danger. It was mid-afternoon when a courier arrived with that news, and before long little bands of fleeing soldiers came running back to the castle. They said that our forces had suffered total defeat and that Lord Katsuie himself seemed to be in a hopeless situation. All of us were shocked and horrified, and wondered how it could be possible. That evening Lord Katsuie returned, looking miserable. Summoning his most trusted leaders, he said to them: "I have come to grief because Gemba disobeyed my orders, and the accomplishments of my whole life have been in vain. I suppose this is retribution for some past misdeed." He seemed resigned to his fate, with all the calm one would expect of such a great warrior.

No one knew whether or not his son Gonroku had survived the heavy fighting; Lord Katsuie himself was going to fight to the death at Yanagase, but Kekke Katsunosuke had strongly urged him to withdraw. "At least, go back to the castle and commit suicide in peace!" he pleaded. "I will take charge here."

So Lord Katsuie entrusted his golden battle-standard to Katsunosuke and galloped off toward Kitanosho. On his way he stopped to have a bowl of rice at Maeda Toshiie's castle at Fuchu. It seems that Toshiie left the castle with him, saying he wanted to be at his side to the end; but Lord Katsuie insisted that he turn back, and told him: "Unlike myself, you have always had good relations with Hideyoshi. Since you have already fulfilled your pledge to me, you should now make peace with him in order to keep your lands safe. I am very grateful for all that you have done in this campaign." And he parted from him most amicably.

That was on the evening of the twenty-first, and the next day the initial wave of the southern forces swept in to assault Kitanosho. Soon Hideyoshi arrived and established his command post on Mount Atago. The castle was surrounded.

By this time everyone in the castle was prepared to

die, so there was no panic even at the sight of the ring of enemy soldiers. On the night before, Lord Katsuie had summoned all his retainers and declared to them: "I intend to engage the enemy here, fight one last battle, and then kill myself. Those who want to stay on with me are welcome, but some of you must have parents still living or wives and children; the sooner such men return to their homes the better. I do not wish to see any innocent people suffer."

Since he let anyone go who wanted to, even hostages, those warriors who remained at the castle, while few in number, were all men who valued honor more than life itself. I need scarcely mention such illustrious samurai as Lord Wakasa, but think of his only son, Shingoro. Too sick to walk, Shingoro rushed to the castle by palanquin and posted this declaration on the great front gate: "I, Shingoro, seventeen years of age, son of Lord Wakasa, was prevented by illness from going to fight at Yanagase. I now take my place in the castle, and will do all I can to fulfill my obligations."

An even younger gentleman was Sakuma Juzo, who was fourteen. Since he was already the son-in-law of Maeda Toshiie, and still so very young, his retainers advised him to leave. "There is no reason why you should feel obliged to stand this siege," they said. "Lord Toshiie will take you in—leave here and go to Fuchu!"

But he refused, explaining: "For one thing, I am deeply indebted to Lord Katsuie, who has looked after me since my childhood and even bestowed a large estate on me. Perhaps I should try to escape in order to care for my mother, but I think it would be cowardly to prolong my life by clinging to my father-in-law's protection. Furthermore, if I stain our family name I will have disgraced my ancestors. For these reasons I intend to stay in the castle." And he was prepared to die in battle.

Again, Murakami Rokuzaemon took his place in the castle wearing a shroud. When he was ordered to escort Lord Katsuie's sister Suemori and her daughter away, he asked that the mission be given to someone else. But Lord Katsuie said: "No, I want you to do it. This is how you can best show your loyalty to me." And so, reluctant as he was, Rokuzaemon fled with the two ladies to a nearby village. But at four o'clock on the afternoon of the twenty-second they looked back and saw smoke rising from the castle tower; whereupon all three committed suicide.

Well, this is about as much as I remember, but I am sure that you have heard of these gentlemen before, since their names were on everyone's lips at the time. Indeed, there were some splendid men among them.

I suppose you wonder how I escaped. Of course, I couldn't pretend to be helping in the defense, but I stayed on at the castle anyway. My life had been spared once, during the siege of Odani; and now I was ready to die without regret. To tell the truth, though, I intended to wait and see what became of Lady Oichi before giving up all thought of my own survival. That may sound cowardly of me, but I had no idea what she would do. Her married life at Odani lasted for six years, and yet because of her children she allowed herself to be parted from Nagamasa: it seemed quite possible that she would leave this time too. How could Lord Katsuie let her stay? They were man and wife, to be sure, but they had been married less than a year. After releasing even the enemy hostages, was he going to take the sister and nieces of his former master along with him in death? Or was he determined, out of stubborn pride, not to turn his beloved wife over to Hideyoshi? But surely he would urge her to leave before much longer—a man like that would hardly behave selfishly at such a moment. . . . So my thoughts ran. It wasn't just because I wanted to save my own life. I had decided to share my mistress's fate.

On the morning of the twenty-second, at about cock-crow, the attackers began to close in. I was told that they had set fire to all the towns along the road, and that a vast cloud of smoke filled the sky, darkening the sun: the castle appeared to be surrounded by a sea of fog. It seems that under cover of this darkness the southern forces began stealing up to the castle as quietly as possible, with only whispered commands, each soldier carrying an arrow shield of bamboo, or whatever he could find to protect himself. As it grew lighter outside they could be seen clinging to the edge of the moat, crawling up like so many ants. But a constant rain of musket fire from the castle walls killed all the enemy soldiers who came that far, and each wave of fresh troops pressed forward only to be beaten back. The defenders were holding out very strongly. As things were going, it seemed that the castle would not easily be taken.

So the day ended with both sides withdrawing after suffering heavy casualties. But at dawn the next day, the twenty-third, a hush fell over the enemy camp as the drums signaling its attack were silenced. No sooner had we noticed this and wondered what it meant than five or six mounted warriors made an appearance beyond the moat, and shouted as loudly as they could to us: "We regret to inform you that last night we captured Lord Katsuie's son, Gonroku." At this news, all of us lost heart. After that we left our gates almost unguarded; even our musket fire slackened off.

Actually, I expected to hear of a message from Hideyoshi soon. If he still loves my mistress, I thought, he will send someone to offer us peace terms. I kept hoping he would, and sure enough an envoy appeared. The message he delivered was this: "By an unavoidable destiny Lord Hideyoshi has been at war with Lord Katsuie since last year, and he has been fortunate enough to carry his attack this far. However, in view of their long association as comrades in the service of their late master, he does not wish to demand his friend's life. Although it was Lord Katsuie who was attacked, will he not remember that victory and defeat are the lot of the warrior, according to the whim of fate, and be willing to let bygones be bygones, hand over the castle, and retire to the foothills of Mount Koya? If so, he will be offered a large domain and a secure income for the rest of his life."

But was Hideyoshi really being sincere about this?

No one took him at his word; even in the enemy camp there seems to have been a rumor that he issued his proposal as a last resort, out of his desire to capture Lady Oichi alive.

Of course, Lord Katsuie was furious. "The insolence of telling me to surrender!" he exclaimed to the envoy, at white heat. "It goes without saying that victory or defeat depends on a turn of fate—does he think he has to teach me that? If luck had been with me, I'd be chasing down that monkey-faced Hideyoshi now, and I'd see that *he* was the one who cut open his belly! But Gemba was beaten at Shizugatake because he disobeyed my orders, and so I've had to suffer humiliation at the hands of that damned monkey. All I can do now is set fire to the castle tower and commit suicide. Let the way I meet my end be an example to later generations! One thing more: this castle has a stock of gunpowder built up for over ten years—once the fire reaches it, a great many lives will be lost. Go back, and be sure to tell Hideyoshi to withdraw his troops well to the rear. I say this because I don't want any useless killing." And he left the room abruptly. The envoy fled from the castle, his mission a complete failure.

When I heard what had happened, my one hope was dashed and I gave myself up to misery and despair. But then I began to reflect that Lady Oichi's pitiful life would soon end, and I would accompany her across the River of Death, to remain always at her side. I wanted only to be born into the next life able to see, able to gaze on her beauty—for me, that indeed would be the great awakening. My mind was made up, and it gave me a profound sense of calm and well-being. Now death itself seemed to hold more happiness than life.

After that Lord Katsuie said: "As bitter as it is to be driven to this extremity, there is no use regretting our fate. Let us spend our last night drinking together cheerfully, and disappear with the clouds of dawn." He ordered various preparations for the banquet, told the servants to bring out all the remaining casks of the best saké, and had bundles of dry grass heaped up in the castle tower and the other strategic points, ready to be set afire at a moment's notice. It was evening before these tasks were finished. Meanwhile the enemy troops —maybe they realized how determined the men in the castle were—gradually drew farther and farther back, loosening the siege lines. "You see, their watch fires aren't so near," remarked Lord Katsuie calmly. "Hideyoshi knows that I mean what I say." His voice sounded more noble than ever.

It must have been about seven o'clock when the banquet began. Casks of saké had gone to all the watch-towers as well as to the main hall, and the cooks had prepared the finest dishes they could. Many marvelous delicacies were produced; soon everyone throughout the castle was eating and drinking to his heart's content. Of course, the most splendid feast was in the main hall: there, on a fur-covered dais, sat Lord Katsuie, with Lady Oichi beside him and her daughters next to her; sitting just below them were such famous warriors as Bunkasai and Lord Wakasa. Lord Katsuie offered the first cup of saké to his wife. Since he had graciously told all the personal servants to join the party, even I was sitting not far away. I heard that all the ladies and gentlemen were turned out in brilliant fashion, since this was to be their last night. Lord Katsuie and his retainers wore dazzling, many-colored robes and armor; they vied with each other in the splendor of their weapons and their dress, and bore themselves with immense dignity. Even the ladies in waiting, determined not to be outdone on this last occasion, were dressed in their finest apparel. Yet Lady Oichi, they say, far outshone the others. Her rouge and powder were applied a bit more heavily than usual; her milk-white skin was set off by a luxurious gown of white figured silk with a sash of thick gold-flecked brocade, over which she wore a Chinese brocade outer robe with a pattern embroidered in gold and silver and a variety of colors.

As soon as the first round of saké was over, Lord Katsuie declared: "We can't just sit here drinking in silence! The enemy will scorn us for being so gloomy at the prospect of saying farewell to the world. I want to astonish them by spending this whole night in elegant amusements."

Just then the beat of a small drum resounded from a distant watchtower, and we could hear someone singing a lively song, which seemed to be accompanied by dancing. "There!" Lord Katsuie cried. "Those fellows have the right spirit! Let's join them!" And he launched into the song of Atsumori:

*"Our brief span of fifty years . . ."*

This song had been greatly loved by Nobunaga; they say he sang it at Okehazama, where he won such a decisive battle, and so it has always been auspicious for the House of Oda. But this time it made everyone feel sad to hear Lord Katsuie singing it in his strong, resonant voice:

> *"Our brief span of fifty years*
> *Is like an empty dream.*
> *Who of us can hope to live forever?"*

They found themselves remembering the days when their former lord was alive, and they grieved to think of the endless changes of this uncertain world. All those brave armor-clad warriors were moved to sudden tears.

After that Bunkasai and Ichirosai each sang a passage from a No play, and Wakadayu danced. But many of the others present were also highly accomplished; and as the saké cups were filled and refilled they all wanted to display their artistic talents—to dance one last dance, to sing one last song before they died. It was a wonderfully gay party, and the longer it went on, the gayer and livelier it became. There was no telling when it would end.

At last, in a voice so beautiful that the rest of the company fell silent, a man began to sing these lines:

> *"As lovely as pear blossoms wet with rain,*
> *Pear blossoms wet with rain . . ."*

The singer was a warrior-priest called Choroken. This gentleman was skillful at all the arts, and played the biwa and the samisen extremely well. That was how I happened to know him, and I had long admired his singing, too. But a strange feeling came over me as I listened closely to the words of his song, recognizing it as a song in praise of the Emperor Hsuan-tsung's favorite, Lady Yang Kuei-fei:

> ". . . *Pear blossoms wet with rain,*
> *Eyebrows like the green willow in the Palace garden,*
> *Lips like the crimson lotus in the Imperial pond.*
> *Truly, the painted beauties of the Inner Palace*
> *Seem wan and pale beside her.*"

Perhaps Choroken had no such thing in mind, but to me, as I listened, he seemed to be praising Lady Oichi's beauty. Alas, I thought, is such a lovely flower to be soon destroyed? At that moment I felt another sharp pang of regret.

Then Choroken said: "Listen! The blind one over there can play the samisen! Let's have him sing something for us, with Lady Oichi's permission!"

"Go ahead, Yaichi!" Lord Katsuie called out at once.

I couldn't refuse—indeed, it was just what I'd been hoping for. Quickly I took up my samisen and began singing one of the little songs she liked so well:

> "*The cold winter rains and the snow*
> *Only fall now and then—*
> *But because of you, my tears*
> *Are falling constantly.*"

"Ah," cried Choroken, "he's as good as ever! Now let me try one." Borrowing my samisen, he began to accompany himself as he sang about the moon shining on the Bay of Shiga. I listened carefully, paying special attention to the long instrumental passages which he inserted here and there. Choroken played these passages with the most exquisite tone, but I noticed that certain queer phrases, twice repeated, were mingled with them. Now, there is a secret code that all of us blind samisen players know very well. Since each string of a samisen has sixteen stops, the three strings together have forty-eight: when you teach a beginner how to play the instrument you help him memorize these stops by marking them with the forty-eight characters of the *i ro ha* alphabet. Everyone who studies the samisen learns this system; but we blind musicians, since we can't see the characters, have to learn it by heart—we associate each note with its proper letter quite automatically, as soon as we hear it. So when blind musicians want to communicate secretly they can do it by playing on the samisen, using this system as a code. Well, when I listened to those "queer phrases" of Choroken's the notes seemed to be telling me something like this:

> *"A reward is waiting.*
> *Is there no way to save your mistress?"*

I must be deluded, I thought. How could one of our men be saying such a thing? Even supposing I'd heard correctly, the syllables must have formed that sequence purely by accident. But while these thoughts were running round and round in my brain, Choroken once more began to sing:

> "*What can I do?*
> *The path to my love is barred*
> *And the gatekeeper won't let me pass!*"

Although his samisen accompaniment was entirely different from that of the earlier song, he still inserted those strange phrases here and there.

Suddenly my heart began to pound. Ah, I thought, so Choroken is a spy for the other side, or else he's turned traitor! In any case he is following Hideyoshi's orders, and trying to deliver Lady Oichi to the enemy. Help had come when I least expected it—but I was amazed to think how strong Hideyoshi's love must be, since he still refused to give her up!

Then Choroken returned the samisen to me. "Come on, Yaichi," he said. "Give us another song!"

I wondered why he was relying so heavily on a poor blind minstrel like me. Had he seen what was in my guilty heart and realized that I would go through fire and water for my mistress? To be sure, I had the advantage of being the only manservant who was allowed in the ladies' quarters. Then too, I knew every nook and corner of the castle, all its many rooms and passageways, better than anyone with sight; in an emergency I could scamper through them as freely as the mice! The more I thought of it, the more it seemed to me that Choroken had done well to put his confidence in me. It was because I wanted to perform just such a service that I had allowed my worthless life to drag on this long. Now I would do my utmost to save Lady Oichi—if I failed, I had only to die in the flames with her! In that instant I formed my plan. Without hesitating, I took up my samisen and began to sing:

> *"If I could only tell you*
> *What is in my heart*
> *And show you my tear-drenched sleeves . . ."*

As I pressed the strings with trembling fingers, pretending to improvise new interludes of my own, I used the secret code to give Choroken this answer:

> *"When you see smoke,*
> *Come to the foot of the tower."*

Of course, none of the others who were listening so attentively had any notion that we were exchanging these messages. Meanwhile, I had devised a scheme for saving Lady Oichi's life. You see, she and Lord Katsuie were to climb to the top of the castle tower at dawn and commit suicide there, after which the dry grass that had been heaped up would be put to the torch. So it had occurred to me that by careful timing I could set the fire just before they were to kill themselves. In the midst of all the confusion I could lead in Choroken and his confederates; and perhaps, by force of numbers, my mistress could be separated from her husband.

Now, I have to admit that I'm a born coward, and I'm no good at all at deceiving people. I couldn't help being horrified at my own plan to set fire to the castle and then abduct my mistress in collusion with an enemy spy. But what made me decide to go through with it was the thought that it would be an act of loyalty, after all, since I was doing it solely out of my desire to save her life.

And so the party went on, but all too soon the brief night of early summer was ending. Already the sound of distant temple bells came echoing to our ears, and we could hear thrushes singing in the garden. At this, Lady Oichi asked for paper, and wrote a poem in the classical style:

> *Even before we sleep*
> *On this summer night*
> *The voice of the thrush reminds us*
> *To bid it a last farewell.*

Next, Lord Katsuie wrote one:

> *The dreams of a summer night*
> *Are fleeting—*
> *Mountain thrush, soar to the sky*
> *With the name we leave behind.*

Bunkasai read both of these aloud to us, and said: "I, too, will write a poem." This was what he composed:

> *Bound by earthly ties*
> *I will accompany you*
> *On the road to Paradise*
> *And serve you in the life to come.*

I could only admire how elegantly nonchalant they were, even on such a painful occasion.

After that everyone retired to his appointed place, to prepare for suicide. The ladies in waiting and I attended our master and mistress as they went at last to the castle tower. However, we were ordered to stop at the fourth level—only Bunkasai and the three young daughters went along to the top. Deciding that this was the critical moment, I crept stealthily halfway up the stairs to the fifth level, where I listened, holding my breath, and heard everything that went on overhead.

First of all, Lord Katsuie had Bunkasai open the windows on all four sides. As the morning wind swept through the room, he remarked how refreshing it felt. Sitting down, he said with formal dignity: "Let us drink a last cup of saké among ourselves in farewell." He had Bunkasai serve it, and exchanged cups once again with Lady Oichi and her daughters.

When they had finished, he addressed his wife in these words: "The unfailing love which you have shown me has made me very happy. Had I realized what the future held in store, I would not have married you last autumn—but there is no use talking about that now. My one desire was for us to be together always, as husband and wife; but after long and careful thought I have come to believe that because you are the sister of my late master, and furthermore because these little girls are the children left behind by Lord Nagamasa, my real duty is to save you. A warrior who is going to die is not obliged to take his wife and children along with him. If I were to kill you here, people might say I did it in a burst of pride, forgetting both duty and compassion. Please try to understand, and leave the castle.

I am afraid this is all very sudden for you, but it is something to which I have given a great deal of thought."

His words took me completely by surprise. He must have been in inner turmoil as he spoke, but there was not a trace of it in his quiet, steady voice. As I heard him I thought: Ah, how splendid! Just as they say, a true warrior has a tender heart—it was my own contemptible nature that made me harbor a grudge against him, not realizing what a fine gentleman he was! Shedding unexpected tears of gratitude, I clasped my hands reverently and bowed in the direction of his voice.

But the next moment I heard Lady Oichi reply: "After coming this far, what you ask of me is more than I can endure—" She broke off, weeping. Then she said: "Even while Lord Nobunaga was alive I considered myself a member of the family I had married into—not of the Oda family. And now today, when I no longer have my brother to depend on, where would I go if you abandon me? I know from bitter experience that to escape death would mean to leave myself open to humiliation worse than death. That is why, from the day I married you, I have been determined that this time I would never let myself be separated from my husband. Our married life has been short, but if we can die together as husband and wife, half a year of marriage is as much a lifetime as a hundred years. It is cruel of you to tell me to leave. Please don't ask that of me!" Her voice came to me in broken, uneven phrases, as if she had buried her face in her sleeves.

"But have you no pity for your daughters?" Lord

Katsuie objected. "If they die the Asai line comes to an end. Will you not have failed in your duty to your dead husband?"

"You are very generous to the Asai!" she exclaimed, and began weeping harder than ever. "I want to stay with you; but I will take advantage of your kindness to save the children so that they will be able to pray for the spirit of their father, and for mine too after I die."

But this time Ochacha cried: "No, no, Mama! I want to stay too!"

"So do I! So do I!" cried Ohatsu and Kogo, clinging to their mother from both sides. All four of them sobbed together.

At Odani, her daughters had been only infants, unaware of the tragedy they were living through; but now, when even little Kogo was almost ten, there was no way to soothe them. Lady Oichi herself, with all her fortitude, was so moved by the tears of her beloved children that she could not control her weeping. In all these years I had never known her to be so distressed. But time was running out—how would it end?

My thoughts were interrupted by the sound of Bunkasai's voice scolding the children: "Now, now, don't behave like that!" He seemed to be forcing himself between Lady Oichi and her daughters, trying to separate them from her. "Come along, you're making it hard for your mother to carry out her duty."

When I heard these words I knew I couldn't afford to wait another moment. Pulling out a bundle of the dried grass that had been stuffed under the stairway, I set fire to it with the flame of a lamp. At that time, the only other people on the fourth floor of the tower were the ladies in waiting, all of whom, dressed in ceremonial white ready to die, were fortunately too busy intoning loud prayers to the Buddha to notice what I was doing. Hastily I went around touching off heaps of dried grass everywhere and scattering firebrands against all the paper doors and windows. Then, choking from the smoke, I began shouting: "Fire! Fire!"

Since the top windows were open, a strong draft of wind blew up through the tower, spreading the flames quickly through the tinder-dry grass. Soon the crackle of burning wood became a terrifying roar; and the moans and shrieks of women in panic, not knowing how to escape, were mingled in my ears with the fierce hissing of the flames. Then a large group of men came running upstairs through the smoke, shouting: "Our lord is in danger!" and "Watch out for traitors!" After that, I was caught in confused fighting: fighting between the castle's defenders and Choroken's men, who seemed to be trying to force their way up the narrow stairs. As I was buffeted about, shoved from one side to the other, a hot wind scattered stinging showers of sparks against me, and it became harder and harder to breathe. As long as I have to die in the heart of this inferno, I thought, I want to be with my mistress when the fire consumes us. But just as I began to grope my way up the steps, some-one—I don't know who it was—called out to me: "Yaichi! Take this lady down!" And he lifted a young girl to my back.

"Lady Ochacha!" I cried, realizing at once who I was carrying. "What has happened to your mother?" I called Ochacha's name over and over again, but she seemed to have lost consciousness in the swirling smoke. But why would a samurai entrust her to a blind man like me, instead of carrying her to safety himself? No doubt he had loyally made up his mind to die here with his master. And I too felt I should stay to see my mistress through to the end, instead of running away. Yet if I didn't save her child, she would hate me. Suppose she took me to task for it in the next world, saying: "Yaichi! Where did you abandon my precious daughter?" Such a deed would be unpardonable. I was convinced that Ochacha had been given to me because I was the one destined to save her.

But to tell the truth there was something else, an even stronger feeling, that made me want to rescue her. The instant that Ochacha settled heavily against my back and I put my arms behind me and clasped her firmly around the buttocks—in that instant I had an odd, sweet sense of familiarity. Her youthful voluptuousness reminded me all too keenly of how her mother's body had felt under my hands years ago. How could a notion like that have come into my head, at a moment when any delay or hesitation meant the risk of being burned alive? A man has the strangest thoughts at the strangest times! I'm ashamed to admit it, but I suddenly recalled that when I went into service at the castle and was summoned to massage Lady Oichi for the first time, her arms and legs had had just that same resilient young flesh—yes, beautiful as my mistress was, the years had stolen up on her. Memories of happy days at Odani began coming back to me, one linked to another. Not only that, when I felt the soft pressure of Ochacha's body it seemed to me that somehow I too had returned to my youth of ten years before. It was disgusting of me, but my desire to live flared up again at the thought that serving this young lady would be just like serving Lady Oichi.

All this sounds as if I hesitated a long time; but the fact is, the whole thing flashed through my mind with incredible swiftness. And no sooner had I made my decision than I began running through the smoke, dodging the others as best I could. "I'm carrying one of the young ladies!" I shouted at the top of my voice. "Clear a path for us!" Being blind, I had to force my way ruthlessly, pushing people aside or trampling over them as I dashed headlong down the stairs.

I wasn't the only one trying to escape. People were streaming out of the castle under a rain of fiery sparks; I hurried along with them, thrust ahead by the weight of the surging crowd. As I crossed the bridge over the moat there was a long, horrible rumbling noise.

"Was that the tower?" I cried out.

"Yes," said a man next to me. "There's a pillar of flame straight up into the sky—the fire must have reached the gunpowder!"

"What's become of Lady Oichi and her other daughters?" I asked him.

"The children are safe," he answered, "but it's too bad about Her Ladyship."

Later I heard more of the details of what had happened; but the man beside me told me that Choroken was the first to reach the top of the tower, and that Bunkasai, who saw through his plot at once, shouted: "Traitor! What are you here for?" and cut him down in a twinkling and kicked his body back down the steps. Then Choroken's men faltered, and more and more of the defenders came rushing up, so that not only was it impossible to abduct Lady Oichi but most of the attackers were either felled by the sword or burned to death. At that time, the three daughters were still clinging to their mother; but Bunkasai, trying to get them out as quickly as he could, thrust them into the midst of a swarm of warriors and cried: "The men who rescue these ladies and take them to the enemy camp will be the most loyal of all!" Each of the nearest samurai took one of the girls in his arms and fled.

"I expect Lord Katsuie and his wife committed suicide in the fire," the man added. "I didn't stay around long enough to see!"

"Then where are the other two daughters?" I asked.

"Our men must have gone ahead with them," he said. "The one you're carrying was the stubbornest of all; she hung on to her mother's sleeve till the very last, and wouldn't let go. But she was finally pried loose and given to the fellow who handed her over to you and then ran back into the flames. You have to admire a samurai like that, even if he wasn't one of our own men."

I wondered what he meant by "our own men"—and then it dawned on me that Hideyoshi's troops had penetrated the inner walls and crept up to the very base of the tower, ready to go in after Lady Oichi at a signal from Choroken, and that the men I was escaping with were either traitors or enemy soldiers! "Anyway," he went on, "even though Lord Hideyoshi worked so hard to win his battle it didn't get him the lady he wanted. He can't be very pleased about the way Choroken bungled it! It's just as well Choroken isn't alive now." He paused a moment, and added: "But you'll get some credit for saving this young lady, so I think I'll stick close to you."

With his arm to lean on, I kept going as fast as I could, though I was panting hard and had long since begun to feel exhausted. Luckily the commander of the enemy foot soldiers had come to look for us, bringing a litter, into which he immediately transferred Ochacha. "You, the blind one," he said to me. "Did you carry her all the way here?"

"Yes, sir, I did," I answered, and I told him the whole story.

"Very well," he said. "Come along with the litter!" So I went with them, past camp after camp, till we reached the enemy headquarters.

Ochacha seemed to have revived completely by then, but she rested for a while and was attended by the servants. Lord Hideyoshi asked to see her as soon as she was ready, and summoned her sisters along with her. That was understandable, of course, but he even asked for me. As I prostrated myself in the anteroom, I heard him call out: "Yaichi! Do you remember my voice?"

"Yes, My Lord," I replied. "I remember it perfectly."

"Do you?" he said. "It's been a long time since I saw you last. . . . For a blind man, what you did today was amazing. I'll give you any reward you like—tell me what you want!"

It was like a dream: everything had turned out better than I could have hoped. "I am very grateful for your kindness," I answered; "but why should you reward a coward who shamelessly abandoned his mistress after enjoying her favor so many years? My heart aches when I think of what happened to Lady Oichi this morning. All I can wish for now is to be allowed to go on serving her daughters, as I have in the past. That would be my greatest happiness."

Lord Hideyoshi agreed at once. "A reasonable request," he said. "I shall grant it and make you one of their servants." Then: "I very much regret the death of Lady Oichi, and from now on I intend to look after these children in her place. But see how big they have all grown! I'm sure it was Ochacha who used to play on my knee!" As he said it, he laughed good-naturedly.

That is how I was lucky enough to remain in the service of the young ladies, instead of being left to wander about on my own. But to tell the truth my life ended on that day—the twenty-fourth of May in 1583, the day Lady Oichi died. Never again was I to be as happy as I had been at Odani and Kiyosu. You see, the young ladies seemed to have heard that I set fire to the castle tower and let the traitors in, and they began to treat me more and more coldly. In particular, Lady Ochacha would sometimes declare, within my hearing: "This blind fellow rescued me against my will and turned me over to my mortal enemy!" To be with them was like sitting on needles. Better to have died when I had the chance—that was how I felt about my wretched lot. Of course, I deserved my punishment: there was no one to blame but myself. Yet having once failed to die at the proper time, I dared not follow Lady Oichi into the next world and present myself before her; and so I lived on in shame and dishonor, shunned by everyone. Before long, other servants were called in to massage the young ladies, or to accompany them when they played the koto. At last I found myself with nothing to do.

By that time Ochacha and her sisters had gone to live at Azuchi Castle, and it was only on the orders of Lord Hideyoshi that they allowed me to remain in their service at all. Knowing how they felt, I found it acutely painful to go on being tolerated, clinging to Hideyoshi's favor. Finally I could bear it no longer. One day, without a word of farewell to anyone, I stole quietly out of the castle and set off down the road—I had no idea where.

Well, that was when I was thirty-one. Of course, if I had gone to Kyoto, asked for an audience with the Regent Hideyoshi, and explained everything to him, I suppose I could have had a stipend large enough to support me for the rest of my life. But I had made my mind up to atone for my sin by living in poverty, as you see me. From that day to this I have wandered from one post town to another, massaging weary gentlemen or trying to distract them by my crude talents at music. . . . For over thirty years now I've lived this way, through the many changes we've had, and still it seems to be my fate to go on living.

Ochacha, for all her hatred of Hideyoshi, her "mortal enemy" as she called him, soon yielded herself to that enemy and went to live at his Yodo Castle. I'd expected that to happen sooner or later. They said Hideyoshi was furious at the failure to abduct Lady Oichi, but when he summoned me into his presence, far from showing any anger, he actually praised me! That was because seeing Ochacha had changed his attitude. In short, he must have had the same feeling that came to me in the midst of the flames—maybe even great heroes, in their innermost hearts, are no different from us ordinary men. But because of a single mistake I had to be separated from her for the rest of my life; while the Regent—the man who destroyed her father and mother and even skewered her brother's head on a pike—soon made her his own, satisfying a desire that had been transferred from mother to daughter, a desire that had lurked in his heart since the far-off days at Odani.

By what quirk of fate was Hideyoshi so susceptible to ladies of the same blood as Nobunaga? They say he also wanted Gamo Ujisato's wife—she was Nobunaga's daughter, and looked like her aunt Oichi. No doubt that explained his interest in her. Someone told me Hideyoshi sent a message to her at the time of her husband's death, many years ago, expressing his feelings to her; but she refused to listen to him. Indeed, she grieved for her husband so much that she took holy orders. It seems that it was Hideyoshi's displeasure at this that led him to confiscate the immense Gamo territories in Aizu.

Anyway, Ochacha was old enough to know what was best for her, and the fact that she yielded so readily to the power of Lord Hideyoshi, inevitable as it may have been, shows that she did. How happy I felt to hear that the person called the Lady of Yodo was the eldest daughter of Asai Nagamasa! The springtime of prosperity has finally come to this child, I thought, after all her mother's pain and suffering. Even though I was dragging out my own worthless life far away, I remained as faithful to her as if I were constantly at her side; and I prayed that she would be spared the ordeals of her mother. Soon I heard the rumor that she had given birth to a son, and I was relieved to think that good fortune would now surely smile on her for the rest of her life. But, as you know, Lord Hideyoshi died in the autumn of 1598, and a few years later came the Battle of Sekigahara. Once again the world was changing, and every day brought fresh troubles to her. Maybe she was being punished for having betrayed the memory of her parents by becoming the mistress of their enemy! I can't help thinking it was a strange fate that brought two generations, mother and daughter, to death by suicide in a doomed castle.

Ah, if only I had remained in her service until the end, I could at least have cheered her up—just as I had consoled her mother at Odani—and then accompanied her to the other world and begged her mother's forgiveness. But instead I spent the time lamenting my misfortune, fretting and worrying as I listened day after day to the roar of gunfire.

I'll never forget how shamefully some of Hideyoshi's former retainers behaved: joining Ieyasu's forces in the siege of Osaka Castle, and firing cannon balls into the very quarters of Ochacha and her son Lord Hideyori! Everyone was eager to curry favor with the powerful Lord Ieyasu. Think of Kyogoku Takatsugu, who turned traitor at the time of Sekigahara. Years ago, in spite of his betrothal to Ohatsu, he ran away from Kitanosho before its fall and took refuge with Lord Takeda; after Takeda was defeated he wandered hither and yon, afraid of his own shadow. But finally he was pardoned and even given a large domain—and at whose request? Wasn't it Ochacha—because of his tie with her sister—who helped him? Long ago he had come fleeing through the snow to throw himself on the mercy of Lady Oichi, and later he relied on the sympathy of her daughter: to think that he owed his life twice over to them and yet betrayed Ochacha and Lord Hideyori at the critical moment, demoralizing their forces!

Oh, but there's no use talking about such things any more! I don't know how many sorrowful or bitter memories I have; but today, when Takatsugu and even the Shogun Ieyasu himself have gone to the next world, the past seems like an empty dream. Now that all the noble ladies and gentlemen I knew are dead, how much longer, I ask myself, will I drag out my own frail life? I have lived a very long time, and all I can do now is pray for happiness in the next world. Still, I wanted the chance to tell this story to someone. . . .

I beg your pardon, sir? You wonder if I remember Lady Oichi's voice? Indeed I do! I remember the lilt of it when she spoke to me, and how beautifully she sang as she played the koto: she had an exquisite voice, clear, but with an underlying warmth and richness, a voice that combined the vibrant tone of the nightingale and the soft melodiousness of the dove. And Ochacha's voice sounded just the same—the servants were always mistaking the two. I could easily understand why Hideyoshi adored her. Everyone knows what a great man he was, but only I could see from the very first what was in his heart. To think that it was I who knew his deepest secret, I who had the honor of rescuing the Lady of Yodo, the mother of his heir Lord Hideyori—when I remember all this I feel that I have nothing more to live for.

No, thank you, sir, no more. I've drunk too much already, and I've kept you too long with the tiresome memories of an old man. I have a wife at home, but I've never told her all the things I've told you tonight. I only wish you would be kind enough to put something down in writing about me, so that later generations will know my story.

Well then, please lie down again for a moment, sir. Let me massage your back just a little more, before the night gets any later.

# A Note about the Author

JUNICHIRO TANIZAKI was born in 1886 in the heart of downtown Tokyo, where his family owned a printing establishment, and studied Japanese literature at Tokyo Imperial University. His first published work, a one-act play, appeared in 1909 in a literary magazine he helped to found. His early novels suggest that his student days were ostentatiously bohemian, in the fashion of the day. At that time he was strongly influenced by Poe, Baudelaire, and Oscar Wilde.

He lived in the cosmopolitan Tokyo area until the earthquake of 1923, when he moved to the gentler and more cultured Kyoto-Osaka region, the scene of *The Makioka Sisters*. There he became absorbed in the Japanese past, and abandoned his superficial Westernization. Japanese critics agree that this intellectual and emotional crisis changed him from merely a very good writer to a great one.

Tanizaki's most important novels were written after 1923; among them are *A Fool's Love* (1924), *Some Prefer Nettles* (1928), *Maelstrom* (1930), *Ashikari* (1932), a modern version of *The Tale of Genji* (1939–41), *The Makioka Sisters* (1943–8) (English translation in 1957), *Captain Shigemoto's Mother* (1949), and *The Key* (1956) (English translation in 1961). By 1930 he had gained such fame that his "Complete Works" was published. He received the Imperial Prize in Literature in 1949.

Tanizaki now lives on the Izu Coast, which is known as "the Japanese Riviera."

A NOTE ABOUT THE TRANSLATOR

HOWARD SCOTT HIBBETT took his doctorate in Japanese literature at Harvard. He lived in Japan for three years. He has taught at the University of California and is now professor of Japanese literature at Harvard.

## A Note on the Type

THE TEXT of this book was set on the Linotype in
JANSON, a recutting made direct from type cast
from matrices long thought to have been made by
the Dutchman Anton Janson, who was a practicing type founder in Leipzig during the years 1668–
87. However, it has been conclusively demonstrated
that these types are actually the work of Nicholas
Kis (1650–1702), a Hungarian, who most probably
learned his trade from the master Dutch type
founder Dirk Voskens. The type is an excellent
example of the influential and sturdy Dutch types
that prevailed in England up to the time William
Caslon developed his own incomparable designs
from these Dutch faces.

The Perigee Japanese Library brings you the best in Japanese literature. These beautifully designed books by award-winning authors will give you hours of reading pleasure.

---

*Junichiro Tanizaki* was born in 1886 in Tokyo. After the earthquake of 1923, he moved to the Kyoto-Osaka region and abandoned his superficial Westernization. He won the Imperial Award for Cultural Merit in 1949 for *The Makioka Sisters*.

### The Makioka Sisters
Translated by Edward G. Seidensticker

A saga of four sisters and their confrontation with the "new" Japan. "A magistral fresco of cultural change, warmly and perceptively articulated in terms of human beings" (*The Atlantic*).

### Some Prefer Nettles
Translated by Edward G. Seidensticker

The profile of a loveless marriage and a husband's search for peace through the rediscovery of tradition. "[Tanizaki] has an unusual ability to create beautiful images and to give pleasure" (*The New Yorker*).

### Seven Japanese Tales
Translated by Howard Hibbett

A collection of stories about sexual and psychological obsessions. "It is an art comparable to that of Flaubert's short stories, and there can be no higher praise" (*Saturday Review*).

---

*Yukio Mishima*, born in Tokyo in 1925, was considered a Renaissance man. Acclaimed by *The New York Times Book Review* as "an established international genius," he wrote thirty-three plays, countless short stories and articles, and thirteen novels. A passionate Japanese patriot, he committed *seppuku* (ritual suicide) in 1970 at the height of his career.

### The Sailor Who Fell from Grace with the Sea
Translated by John Nathan

This masterpiece of hysteria and violence revolves around a widow's love affair with a naval officer and its effect on the woman's son and his band of thirteen-year-olds. "Profoundly, even beautifully macabre... recalls Henry James and William Golding" (*Saturday Review*).

## The Sound of Waves
Translated by Meredith Weatherby

Set in a Japanese fishing village, this lyrical story of first love and courage traces the idyllic affair of Shinji and Hatsue, who are threatened by the ugly gossip of unfeeling villagers. "An altogether joyous and lovely thing" (*The New York Times*).

## Thirst for Love
Translated by Alfred H. Marks

Forced to submit to the advances of her father-in-law, a young widow develops an insatiable desire for a young farm boy. Evoking conflicting class attitudes toward sexuality, *Thirst for Love* is renowned for its dramatic power.

## The Temple of the Golden Pavilion
Translated by Ivan Morris
Illustrated with line drawings

A probing novel about a young Buddhist priest obsessed with the beauty of a famous Kyoto temple, yet compelled by such intense feelings of alienation from the world that he destroys himself and all he loves. "An amazing literary feat" (*Chicago Tribune*).

## Forbidden Colors
Translated by Alfred H. Marks

A brilliant novel about a man whose loveless marriage fuels his homosexuality and drives him first into the powerful grasp of an aging writer and then into the streets of postwar Japan, gay bars, and parties. A story of love and sexual anguish.

## After the Banquet
Translated by Donald Keene

A masterful portrait of the battle between idealism and opportunism, focusing on the love of the proprietress of a luxurious Tokyo restaurant for an aristocratic politician. "Always fascinating and frequently brilliant" (*The Christian Science Monitor*).

Yasunari Kawabata, winner of the 1968 Nobel Prize for Literature, was born in Osaka in 1899. In addition to being a novelist, he was an eminent literary critic and discovered, among others, Yukio Mishima. He died by his own hand at age seventy-three, leaving no note of explanation.

### Snow Country
Translated by Edward G. Seidensticker

The moving story of a doomed love affair between a rich Tokyo dilettante and a young geisha. "The writing throughout is subtle, delicately moving, and full of striking imagery" (*The Atlantic*).

### Thousand Cranes
Translated by Edward G. Seidensticker

A young man's involvement with the mistresses of his dead father provides a case study of possessiveness and self-loathing. "Bold in way that humbles the dredgings of our Freudian novelizers" (*Commonweal*).

### The Sound of the Mountain
Translated by Edward G. Seidensticker

An elderly man tries to cope with his children's failing marriages, the death of close friends, and his love for his daughter-in-law. "A story of infinite simplicity and infinite complication" (*Newsweek*).

### The Master of Go
Translated by Edward G. Seidensticker

A contest for supremacy between a heretofore invincible master of go and his younger, more modern challenger—and thus between old and new Japan. "Any reader who can respond to Chekhov's plays will rise to the austere, autumnal nobility in Kawabata's tale" (*Time*).

### Beauty and Sadness
Translated by Howard Hibbett

A terrifying yet lyrical tale of revenge prompted by jealous love. "This last novel is distinguished by purity ... and a sustained elegiac tone. It is cold ... and all the more disquieting for that, since it is a tale of passionate love" (*The New York Times Book Review*).

Here's your opportunity to have the Perigee Japanese Library delivered right to you! Just call toll-free **1-800-631-8571** or fill out the coupon below and send your order to:

**The Putnam Publishing Group**
**390 Murray Hill Parkway, Dept. B**
**East Rutherford, NJ 07073**

The books in the Perigee Japanese Library are also available at your local bookstore or wherever paperbacks are sold.

| | | | PRICE U.S. | CAN |
|---|---|---|---|---|
| _____ | The Makioka Sisters | 399-50520-2 | $12.95 | $16.95 |
| _____ | Some Prefer Nettles | 399-50521-0 | 8.95 | 11.75 |
| _____ | Seven Japanese Tales | 399-50523-7 | 10.95 | 14.50 |
| _____ | The Sailor Who Fell from Grace with the Sea | 399-50489-3 | 8.95 | 11.75 |
| _____ | The Sound of Waves | 399-50487-7 | 7.95 | 10.50 |
| _____ | Thirst for Love | 399-50494-X | 8.95 | 11.75 |
| _____ | The Temple of the Golden Pavilion | 399-50488-5 | 8.95 | 11.75 |
| _____ | Forbidden Colors | 399-50490-7 | 10.95 | 14.50 |
| _____ | After the Banquet | 399-50486-9 | 9.95 | 12.95 |
| _____ | Snow Country | 399-50525-3 | 8.95 | 11.75 |
| _____ | Thousand Cranes | 399-50526-1 | 7.95 | 10.50 |
| _____ | The Sound of the Mountain | 399-50527-X | 8.95 | 11.75 |
| _____ | The Master of Go | 399-50528-8 | 8.95 | 11.75 |
| _____ | Beauty and Sadness | 399-50529-6 | 9.95 | 12.95 |

|  |  |
|---|---|
| Subtotal | $ _____ |
| *Postage & handling | $ _____ |
| Sales Tax (CA, NJ, NY, PA) | $ _____ |
| Total Amount Due Payable in U.S. Funds (No cash orders accepted) | $ _____ |

*Postage & handling:
$2.00 for 1 book, 50¢
for each additional
book up to a maximum
of $4.50